DONATED
MATERIAL

Matt Jensen:
The Last Mountain Man
Purgatory

MATT JENSEN:
THE LAST MOUNTAIN MAN
PURGATORY

William W. Johnstone
with J. A. Johnstone

PINNACLE BOOKS
Kensington Publishing Corp.
www.kensingtonbooks.com

PINNACLE BOOKS are published by

Kensington Publishing Corp.
850 Third Avenue
New York, NY 10022

PUBLISHER'S NOTE
Following the death of William W. Johnstone, the Johnstone family is
working with a carefully selected writer to organize and complete Mr.
Johnstone's outlines and many unfinished manuscripts to create additional novels in all of his series like The Last Gunfighter, Mountain
Man, and Eagles, among others. This novel was inspired by Mr. Johnstone's superb storytelling.

All Kensington titles, imprints, and distributed lines are available at
special quantity discounts for bulk purchases for sales promotions, pre-
miums, fund-raising, educational, or institutional use. Special book ex-
cerpts or customized printings can also be created to fit specific needs.
For details, write or phone the office of the Kensington special sales
manager: Kensington Publishing Corp., 850 Third Avenue, New York,
NY 10022, attn: Special Sales Department; phone: 1-800-221-2647.

PINNACLE BOOKS and the Pinnacle logo are Reg. U.S. Pat. & TM
Off.

ISBN-13: 978-0-7860-1868-0
ISBN-10: 0-7860-1868-2

First printing: August 2008

10 9 8 7 6 5 4 3 2 1

Printed in the United States of America

Chapter One

The rain that had been threatening for the day started shortly after nightfall. In the distance, lightning flashed and thunder roared and the rain beat down heavily upon the small Arizona town, cascading off the eaves before drumming onto the roof of the porch just below the second-story window of the Morning Star Hotel.

Matt Jensen was standing at the window of his hotel room, looking down on the street of the town. There were few people outside, and when someone did go outside, they would dart quickly through the rain until they found a welcome door to slip through. The town was dark, the rain having extinguished all outside lamps, and the lanterns that were inside provided only the dullest gleam through rain-shrouded windows. The meager illumination did little or nothing to push away the gloom of the night.

The room behind Matt glowed with a soft, golden light, for he had lit the lantern and it was burning very low. Though Matt was used to the outdoors, and had spent many a night sleeping on the prairie in such conditions, this was one of those nights where he appreciated being under a roof.

Matt Jensen was just a bit over six feet tall with broad shoulders and a narrow waist. He was a young man in years, but his pale blue eyes bespoke of experiences that most would not see in three lifetimes. He was a lone wolf who had worn a deputy's badge in Abilene, ridden shotgun for a stagecoach out of Lordsburg, scouted for the army in the McDowell Mountains of Arizona, and panned for gold in Idaho. A banker's daughter in Cheyenne once thought she could make him settle down—a soiled dove in The Territories knew that she couldn't, but took what he offered.

Matt was a wanderer, always wondering what was beyond the next line of hills, just over the horizon. He traveled light, with a bowie knife, a .44 double-action Colt, a Winchester .44-40 rifle, a rain slicker, an overcoat, two blankets, and a spare shirt and spare socks, trousers, and underwear.

He called Colorado his home, though he had actually started life in Kansas. Colorado was home only because it was where he had reached his maturity, and Smoke Jensen, the closest thing Matt had to a family, lived there. In truth, though, he spent no more time in Colorado than he did in Wyoming, Utah, New Mexico, or Arizona. He was in Wickenburg, Arizona, now, having arrived just ahead of the rain and just before dark.

He had no reason to be in Wickenburg—but then, as he liked to remind himself, he had no reason not to be in Wickenburg. He had arrived here in a restless drift that neither proposed a particular destination nor had a sense of purpose.

He was about to turn away from the window when, in a flash of lightning, he saw two men holding one man while a third was hitting him. When the lightning went away, he could see nothing except the darkness of the alley, and for a moment, Matt wasn't sure that he had seen anything. It might have been a trick of shadows and light.

Another lightning flash, this one prolonged for a full second, revealed the scene again. It was no trick of lighting—three men were attacking a fourth. Matt had no idea who the man being held was, nor did he know who was beating him. He didn't know why the man being held was being beaten, but he didn't like the odds.

His common sense dictated that he do nothing, but instinct overcame common sense.

"Damn," he said aloud. Lifting the window, he crawled out onto the edge of the hotel's porch roof, moved through the rain to the edge, then dropped down to the ground. By now he was so close that, even through the staccato rhythm of the falling rain, he could hear the sound of fists on flesh and the grunts of pain.

Matt moved quickly through the rain, unseen and unheard by either the assailants or the hapless man being beaten. Reaching out, he grabbed the shoulder of the man doing the actual beating, spun him around, then knocked him down with a hard blow to the man's chin.

"What the hell?" one of the two who were holding the man shouted.

Matt started toward him, but he and his partner released the beating victim, then ran quickly up the alley. The beating victim collapsed, and Matt decided that attention to his condition was more important than chasing down the two villains.

"Look out!" the victim suddenly shouted, and turning, Matt saw the man he had knocked down reaching for his gun. Because he was still lying on the ground, it was an awkward draw, which gave Matt time to step through the mud and kick the pistol out of the man's hand.

Unarmed now, the man turned over onto his hands and knees and crawled far enough away to regain his feet. Then he, like the other two men, ran away.

"Are you hurt?" Matt asked, turning back to the victim.

"A few bruises and cuts," the man said, rubbing a finger against his cut lip. "No broken bones, thanks to you."

"Come on, let's get in out of the rain," Matt suggested.

"That's a good idea. Oh, have you had your supper yet? If not, I'd like to treat you. I owe you."

"You don't owe me anything," Matt said. "I think anyone would have come to your aid if they had seen what was going on."

"I'm not so sure of that. But I'd like to buy you dinner anyway. The name is Garvey. Stan Garvey."

"Matt Jensen."

"I'm glad to meet you, Mr. Jensen." Garvey chuckled. "That's an understatement. I'm damn glad to meet you." He pointed. "Little Man's Café is just down the street here. Little Man makes a damn good pot roast."

Matt followed Garvey into the restaurant, and the

two men stood just inside the door for a moment, dripping water. Because it was quite late for dinner, the restaurant was nearly empty.

"Hello, Stan, wet enough for you?" someone asked. The man who greeted them was wearing the white apron and cap of a cook. He was very short, standing just over five feet tall.

"Hello, Little Man. Two pot roast dinners," Garvey said.

"Two pot roast dinners coming right—uh—damn, Stan, what the hell happened to you?"

"I fell down," Garvey said.

"You fell down?"

"Yes."

"Well, all I can say is, it must've been one hell of a fall."

"You have any apple pie left?" Garvey asked pointedly, making it obvious that he didn't want to talk about it.

"Yes. You want it now?"

"No, for dessert."

Leading Matt to a quiet corner of the dining room, Garvey took out a handkerchief to dab at his bloody lip. The handkerchief was as wet as his clothes.

"Who were those men?" Matt asked.

"I don't know the two who were holding me," Garvey said. "But the one doing the hitting was a man named Odom. Cletus Odom."

"What did you do to make Odom so angry?"

Garvey held up his finger as if suggesting that Matt wait for a moment. Then he got up from the table and walked over to the counter. Picking up a newspaper, he returned to the table and handed the paper to Matt.

"This might have done it," he said. He pointed to a story on the front page.

A VILLAIN WALKS AMONG US

Story by Stan Garvey

If there were no other reasons why Arizona should strive for early statehood, then the lack of any sense of justice would be reason enough. On the fifth, instant, three masked men entered the Bank of Wickenburg with the express purpose of robbing it. Their attempt was foiled by the fast and heroic action of Adam Thomas, who slammed shut the safe.

When the leader of the robbers demanded that Thomas reopen the safe or forfeit his life, Thomas maintained his resolve. As a result, the leader of the robbers shot and killed this brave husband and father of two.

There are credible eyewitnesses who say that, despite the fact that he was wearing a mask, they recognized Cletus Odom as the robber and murderer. They are not shy in making these claims, but, thus far, no arrests have been made. That means that Cletus Odom is free to roam about, unafraid of any possibility of apprehension.

Perhaps if Arizona enjoyed statehood, its citizens would have sufficient voice in the state capital to force more effort into bringing the murderer Odom to justice.

As editor of this newspaper, I will do all within my power to see to it that Odom is brought to justice. I call upon all of you, who are citizens of the territory of Arizona, as well as citizens of our fair city of Wickenburg, to write a letter to Governor Fremont asking, no, demanding that justice be done, and that Cletus Odom pay the supreme penalty for his foul deed.

"That's quite a story, Mr. Garvey," Matt said as he folded the paper over and laid it alongside his plate.

"Thanks."

"But with Odom still free, do you not think it was a little risky to write such a story?"

"My good man," Garvey said, "freedom of the press is one of our nation's most precious rights. I will not be intimidated by the mere threat of violence."

Matt smiled. "From my observation, Mr. Garvey, this wasn't a threat, this was an actuality."

At that moment, Little Man arrived carrying two plates.

"Enjoy your dinner, gentlemen," Little Man said. "And, Stan, I'll put the two pieces of pie in a warming oven so they'll be nice and hot for you."

"Thanks," Garvey replied.

The two men began eating. "Oh," Matt said. "I have to say that after several days of eating on the trail, this is very good."

"I thought you might like it. Are you new to Wickenburg, Mr. Jensen?"

"I'm just passing through."

"Passing through, are you? Where are you going?" Garvey laughed. "It's rude of me to be so nosy, I know, and I beg your forgiveness. But this unbridled curiosity is what made me become a journalist, I suppose."

"That's all right," Matt said. "I don't mind answering, because truth to tell, I'm not going anywhere in particular. I've just been wandering from place to place."

"Like a tumbleweed?"

Matt laughed. "You might say that. I have no family encumbrances, nobody to worry about, or to worry about me. This is a big country, Mr. Garvey, and I just thought I would see as much of it as I can."

"Well, I envy you that freedom, Mr. Jensen, I truly do." Garvey touched his eye, which was now swollen. He winced at the touch. "But, from a personal point of view, I'm certainly glad you chose this night of all nights to be in Wickenburg. I'm not sure what condition I would be in now if you had not come to my rescue. How long are you going to stay with us?"

"I'll be leaving at first light in the morning."

"To continue your adventure," Garvey said.

"You might say that."

"Are you a writer, Mr. Jensen?"

"I'm not sure what you mean by that question. If you are asking if I can read and write, the answer is yes."

"No, my question is more specific than that. I mean do you keep a journal of sorts, an account of your wanderings and adventures?"

Matt chuckled. "No, I don't, nor could I imagine anyone would ever want to read about me."

"Oh, don't be so sure about that," Garvey said. "You see, I have a very strong theory that the American West will be the source of lore and legend for many generations to come. And it is people like you—wanderers and heroes—"

"Heroes?" Matt said, interrupting Garvey in mid-sentence.

"Yes, heroes," Garvey insisted. "Did you or did you not come to my assistance tonight? And, I might add, at no small danger to yourself."

"I saw that you were in trouble, and I did what anyone else would have done under the circumstances."

"No, Mr. Jensen, don't be so self-deprecating. Very few would have done what you did tonight. That's why I believe that someday someone will write stories about you. If not about you, personally, certainly about the kind of person you represent. And I don't just mean the penny dreadful," he said.

"I must say, that is an interesting observation, Mr. Garvey, but I would turn that around. If you want my opinion, if any of this West is to be preserved, it will be because of men like you, newspapermen who are not afraid to write the truth. You are the true heroes of the West."

Garvey raised his cup of coffee. "A toast, Mr. Jensen," he said, a big smile spreading across his face. "A toast between heroes."

Laughing, Matt touched his own coffee cup to Garvey's.

"A toast," he said.

Chapter Two

Purgatory

McKinely Peterson had named his saloon the Pair O Dice, because he thought the idea of "paradise" in a town called Purgatory made an interesting contrast. The saloon was a great success, but Peterson didn't live long enough to enjoy it. He was killed within six months of opening the saloon, and, because he died intestate, the saloon was put up for sale at a city marshal's auction.

Announcement of the auction appeared as a two-line entry in the *Purgatory Purge,* the town's only newspaper.

Pair O Dice Saloon to be sold at city marshal's auction, 2 a.m. Saturday.

Andrew Cummins was the city marshal of Purgatory. It was not by coincidence that Andrew Cummins was also the only one who showed up for the auction. And because the city marshal owned Pair O Dice, the saloon soon became the de facto city marshal's office as Cummins spent all his time there.

Although there was a mayor and a city council, the real power in town belonged to Marshal Cummins. He backed up his power by having a personal cadre of eight deputies, all chosen for their skill with a gun and their willingness to use physical force when necessary. In fact, they often used physical force when it wasn't necessary, but complaints to the city council fell upon deaf ears. One reason the city council was not responsive to citizens' complaints was because four of the seven council members were Cummins's deputies.

Marshal Cummins was able to maintain a large force of deputies because the town had imposed a draconian tax, which was extracted, not only from every business, but from every household, every week.

"Hey!" Cummins shouted to the others in the saloon.

Cummins was standing at the front of the saloon, looking over the batwing doors out onto the street. The westbound train was sitting down at the depot, waiting to continue its journey. Half-a-dozen passengers had detrained, and one, who had separated himself from the others, was standing in the street, looking around as if trying to get his bearings. From the way the man was dressed, it was obvious that he was from the East.

"Hey!" Cummins shouted again. He laughed, then pointed. "If you boys want a laugh, come over here and take a look at this."

"Take a look at what?" Emil Jackson asked. Jackson was one of Marshal Cummins's deputies.

"Take a look at the hat on that little feller out there," Cummins said, pointing.

The object of Cummins's derision was a bowler hat with a small brim and a low round crown.

"What is that thing he's wearin' on his head? Is that a piss pot?" Moe Gillis asked. Like Jackson, Gillis was a deputy.

"What are you three laughing at?" one of the other deputies asked.

"This here fella and the piss pot he's wearin' on his head," Moe said.

Soon, all the other deputies were standing at the batwing doors, looking out into the street at the small-ish man who was wearing, not only a bowler hat, but a three-piece suit.

"Hey, Marshal, I'll bet you can't shoot that hat off his head," Jackson said.

"Sure I can."

"A beer says you can't."

"You mean you'll buy me a beer if I shoot the hat off his head?" Cummins asked.

"Yes. But you buy me one if you miss."

"All right," Cummins said. "I guess it's about time I showed you boys why I'm the marshal and you are the deputies." He drew his pistol and aimed, then lowered it.

"What's wrong? You can't do it?"

"Stand here in front of me and let me use your shoulder as a brace," Cummins said.

"Hell, no, you have to do it yourself. Or admit you can't do it."

"You don't worry about me, I can do it," Cummins said. He aimed again, then, sighing, leaned against the wall and braced the pistol against the door frame.

Cummins pulled the trigger and the pistol roared and jumped up in his hand.

"Oh, shit!" Jackson shouted.

The little man wearing the bowler hat fell back in the street. Several of the deputies ran out to him.

There was a small, dark hole in the man's temple, and a trickle of blood ran down across his ear.

"Son of a bitch, Marshal, you kilt him!" Jackson said.

"It was an accident," Cummins said. "You all seen it. It was an accident. I didn't mean to shoot him."

By now several others from the town had been drawn to the scene and they stood around, looking on in horror and morbid curiosity.

"What happened?" someone asked.

"Who is this fella?"

"Anybody know him?"

"He just got off the train," another said. "I saw him get off, but I don't know who he is."

"Who shot him?"

"I did," Cummins said.

"Good heavens, Marshal, why?"

"I didn't shoot him on purpose," Cummins said. "I was—uh—"

"He was showing me his gun," Jackson said. "And it went off."

"Damn, Marshal, you need to be more careful with that thing."

"Yeah, I know," Cummins said.

An hour later Marshal Cummins stepped into the undertaker's parlor. The man he shot was lying naked on a lead-covered slab. Beneath the slab was a bucket filled with blood. Hanging from a hook over the slab was a bottle of formaldehyde, and a little tube ran from the bottle through a needle in the arm and into the dead man's veins.

"Hello, Prufrock. How are you doing with him?" Cummins asked the undertaker.

"I'm about finished," Prufrock replied. "Who's going to pay me for this? The town?"

"No," Cummins said. "I'm the one who killed him, I'll pay the charges. I didn't mean to kill him, but I feel like I should pay the charges anyway. Have you found out who he is?"

"His name is Cornelius Jerome," Prufrock said. "He's from New York City."

"How do you know?"

"There's a letter in his pocket to Governor John C. Fremont," Prufrock said.

"He wrote a letter to the governor?"

"He didn't write it, his pa did," Prufrock said. "Turns out his pa is some bigwig back in New York. You want to read the letter?"

"Yes," Cummins answered.

"It's over there, on that table."

Walking over to the table, Cummins saw, in addition to the letter, the other personal effects belonging to the man: a pipe and a pouch of tobacco, a pair of glasses, and a billfold. Looking in the billfold, Cummin's saw over three hundred dollars in cash. He read the letter.

To The Honorable
John C. Frémont, Governor of Arizona Territory.

*Governor, I am sure you remember me as one of your
most active supporters in your run for the Presidency in
1856. I also served as your adjutant in St. Louis
during the Civil War. Although our paths have not
crossed since that time, I have followed your fortunes
with great interest.*

*By this letter, I want to introduce my son, Cornelius
Jerome. Actually, this will not be the first time you have
met him, for indeed, you often held him on your lap
during the exciting days of your election campaign. It
is my intention that my son make his fortune, if not in
money, then by life experiences, as he sojourns through
our great American West. I call upon you as an old
friend to make him welcome, and to provide him with
the advice you would deem necessary.*

> *Sincerely, your friend,*
> *Ronald J. Jerome*
> *New York, N.Y.*

"He sounds rich, doesn't he?" Cummins asked.

"I'd say so."

"Who would have thought that about this odd-
looking little man?"

"What do you want me to do with the body?"

"What do you mean? You're doing it, aren't you?"

"I mean after I'm finished here. What should I do
next?"

"Bury him," Cummins said.

"Shouldn't we send him back home?"

"How can we do that? We don't know where he came from," Cummins said.

"Sure we do," Prufrock said. "It's right there in the letter."

Pointedly, Cummins tore up the letter. Then he took the three hundred dollars from the Jerome's billfold and pressed it into Prufrock's hands.

"What letter?" he asked.

"I don't know," Prufrock replied, stuffing the wad of money down into his pocket. "I didn't see any letter."

By any definition of the term, Cletus Odom was an ugly man. A scar, like a purple flash of lightning, ran from his forehead, through his left eye, and down his cheek to hook in under his nose. As a result of the scar, the eyelid was now a discolored and misshapen puff of flesh. For a while, the eye had been black and swollen as a result of an encounter he'd had three weeks ago in an alley in Wickenburg. Angry over an article that had appeared in the Wickenburg newspaper, Odom had found a couple of men in the saloon there who, for the price of a drink, agreed to help him "teach the newspaper editor a lesson."

Odom had not expected anyone to come to Garvey's aid and was surprised when someone appeared, out of nowhere, to interrupt him.

"Instead of beating him up, I should have just killed the son of a bitch," Odom said aloud.

But enough thinking about that. It was time to move on, and he had a plan in mind that would net him a lot of money. All he needed to implement the

plan were a few men who would work with him. And
he had already set about recruiting them.

Odom reached the tiny town of Quigotoa, Arizona,
just after nightfall. Quigotoa was a scattering of flyblown and crumbling adobe buildings that were laid
out in no particular pattern around a dusty plaza. What
made the town attractive to people like Odom was its
reputation as a "Robbers' Roost," or "Outlaw Haven."

The town had no constable or marshal, and visita-
tions by law officers from elsewhere in the territory
were strongly discouraged. There was a place in the
town cemetery prominently marked as "Lawmen's
Plot." Here, a deputy, an Arizona Ranger, and a
deputy U.S. marshal, all uninvited visitors to the town,
lay buried.

Odom had come to Quigotoa as a first step to set
his plan into operation, and stepping into the Casa
del Sol Cantina, he spotted someone sitting at a table
in the back. He was a big man, with a broken nose
that lay flat and misshapen on a round face.

"Hello, Bates," Odom said when he stepped up to
the table.

"I thought you was goin' to get here today," Bates
replied.

"It is today."

"Yeah, I meant earlier."

"I'm here now," Odom said. "Did you get someone?"

"Yeah. You want to meet him?"

"Tomorrow," Odom said. "I had a long ride today."

"All right," Bates said.

Leaving Bates, Odom bought a bottle of tequila,
then picked up a Mexican whore and went with her to

her little crib out back, as much for her bed as for her services.

"Do you think Rosita is pretty, Señor?" the whore asked as she smiled at him.

"Pretty?" Odom replied. He took a swallow of tequila, drinking straight from the bottle. "What the hell do I care whether you are pretty or not? You are a *puta*—a whore. And all whores look just alike to me. All I want you to do is shut up, get naked, and get in bed. I'm not in the mood for any of your prattle."

The smile left Rosita's face. "*Sí, señor,*" she said flatly. Mechanically, she took off her clothes, then crawled in bed beside him. She turned off all feeling as he climbed on top of her.

Chapter Three

Even as Odom was settling down for the night in Quigotoa, Matt Jensen had just found a likely place to camp for the night. Dismounting, he took off the saddle and blanket, which caused his horse, Spirit, to whicker and shake his head in appreciation over being relieved of the burden.

This was Matt's second horse to be named Spirit; the first was killed by an outlaw who was trying to kill Matt. Spirit One was a bay, given to Matt by Smoke Jensen, Matt's mentor and friend. Spirit Two was a sorrel. Matt had named him Spirit as well, in part to honor his first horse, but also because he considered Spirit Two to be worthy of the name.

Matt spread the saddle blanket out on the ground to provide a base for his bedroll, then, using the saddle for a pillow, prepared to spend the night on the range. To the casual observer, the saddle, which was ordinary in every detail, was no different from any other saddle. There was, however, one very extraordinary thing about it. The saddle had a double bottom, which allowed him to secret away more than a thousand dollars in cash, which Matt used as his emergency reserve.

Nobody who happened to see Matt would ever suspect that he was carrying so much money. In fact, Matt had a lot more money than that in a bank account back in Colorado. He had come by the money honestly, as his part of a gold-panning operation he had entered into with Smoke Jensen, back when he was but an eighteen-year-old boy.

Smoke and Matt Jensen panned the streams for gold as long as they continued to be productive. For the entire time Matt had been with Smoke, they had buried the gold, each year taking just enough into town to buy goods and supplies for another year. But in the spring of Matt's nineteenth year, they took everything they had panned over the last six years into town, having to enlist four pack animals to do so. When they cashed it out, it was worth a little over thirty thousand dollars, which was more money than the local bank had on deposit.

"We can have the money shipped from Denver," the assayer said.

"Can you write us a draft that will allow us to go to Denver to get the money ourselves?" Smoke asked.

"Yes," the assayer said. "Yes, of course, I can do that. But you don't have to go to all that trouble. As I say, I can have the money shipped here."

"It's no trouble," Smoke said. "Denver's a big city, I think I'd like to have a look around. How about you, Matt?"

"I've never seen a big city. I'd love to go to Denver," Matt replied enthusiastically.

"Write out the draft," Smoke said.

"Very good, sir. And who shall I make this payable to?"

"Make it out to both of us. Kirby Jensen and Matt . . . ,"
Smoke looked over at Matt. "I've never heard you say your
last name."

"Smoke, just make the draft payable to you," Matt said.

"No, what are you talking about? This is your money, too.
You helped pan every nugget."

"You can pay me my share after you cash the draft."

"It might be easier if it is made to just one man," the assayer
said.

Smoke sighed. "All right," he said. "Make it payable to
Kirby Jensen."

The assayer wrote out the draft, blew on it to dry the ink,
then handed it to Smoke.

"Here you are, Mr. Jensen," he said. "Just present this to
the Denver Bank and Trust, and they will pay you the
amount so specified."

Smoke held the bank draft for a moment and looked at it.
"Hard to believe this little piece of paper is worth all that
money," he said.

In Denver, Matt and Smoke went to the bank, where the
teller proudly counted out the money. Smoke divided the
money while they were still in the bank, giving Matt fifteen
thousand and fifty dollars.

"That's a lot of money," Matt said.

"Yes, it is," Smoke agreed. "Most folks don't make that
much money in twenty years of work, and here you are, only
eighteen, with fifteen thousand dollars in your pocket. What
are you going to do with it?"

Matt thought for a moment before he answered. "I'll figure
something out," he said.

* * *

It was getting late in the evening and Smoke and Matt were on their way back, a good ten miles down the road from Denver, when they decided they would start looking for a place to camp for the night. Often, during the ride, Matt had leaned forward to touch the saddlebags that were thrown across his horse. It made him almost dizzy to think that he had so much money. It also made him feel guilty, because he knew this was more money than his father had made in his entire life.

If Matt's father had been able to come up with this much money, they would have never left the farm in Missouri, and Matt would just now be beginning to think of his own future.

Matt had been thinking about his future ever since they left Denver. It wasn't the first time he had considered such a thing. He knew he would not be able to stay with Smoke forever.

But now, with this money, the future was no longer frightening, nor even mysterious to him. He knew exactly what he was going to do.

Matt's thoughts were interrupted when four men, who had been hiding in the bushes, suddenly stepped out into the road in front of them. All four were holding pistols, and the pistols were pointed at Smoke and Matt. The leader of the group was Kelly Smith, a man with whom Smoke had been playing cards the night before.

"You boys want to get down from them horses?" Smith asked.

Slowly, Matt and Smoke dismounted.

"Well, now," Smith said. "You didn't think I was really going to let you get out of town with all that money, did you?"

"What money?" Smoke asked.

"Why, the thirty thousand dollars you got at the bank today," Smith said. "The whole town is talkin' about it."

"Is that a fact?" Smoke asked.

"Oh, yes, it's a fact," Smith said. "You've got that money, plus the money you took from me in the card game last night."

"Well, now, Mr. Smith, if I had known you were going to be that bad of a loser, I'll be damned if I would have played poker with you," Smoke said. "And here you told me you were a professional gambler and all. I guess it just goes to prove that you can't always believe what people say."

Smith laughed, a dry, cackling laugh. "You're a funny man, Jensen," he said. "I'll still be laughin' when I'm in San Francisco spending your money."

"What makes you think you're going to get my money?"

"Are you blind?" Smith asked. "There's four of us here, and we've got the drop on you."

"Oh, yeah, there is that, isn't there? I mean, you do have the drop on us," Smoke said almost nonchalantly. "By the way, Matt, do you remember that little trick I showed you?"

"I remember," Matt answered.

"Now would be a good time to try it out."

"Now?"

"Now," Smoke replied.

Even before the word was out of his mouth, Smoke and Matt both drew and each fired two quick shots. Kelly Smith and the three men who were with him were dead before they even realized they were in danger.*

The mournful wail of a distant coyote calling to his mate brought Matt back to the present, and looking up, he saw a falling star streak across the black velvet sky. He closed his eyes and drifted off to sleep.

---

*The Last Mountain Man—MATT JENSEN NUMBER 1

* * *

At dawn the next day, the notches of the eastern hills were touched with the dove gray of early morning. Shortly thereafter, a golden fire spread over the mountaintops, then filled the sky with light and color, waking all the creatures below.

Matt rolled out of his blanket and started a fire, then began digging through his saddlebags for coffee and tobacco. He would have enjoyed a biscuit with his coffee, but he had no flour. He had no beans either, and was nearly out of salt. He did have a couple of pieces of bacon, and they now lay twitching and snapping in his skillet, alongside his coffeepot.

After his breakfast of coffee and bacon, he rolled himself a cigarette, lighting it with a burning stick from the fire. Finding a rock to lean against, Matt sat down for a smoke as he contemplated his next move. It was clear that he was going to have to replenish his supplies.

"Spirit, I think it's about time we went into town again," he said.

Sometimes on the long, lonely trail, Matt felt the need to hear a human voice, even if it was his own. Talking to Spirit satisfied that need, and because he was talking to his horse, it didn't seem quite as ridiculous as talking to himself.

Quigotoa

In the Casa del Sol Cantina the next morning, Odom rolled a tortilla in his fingers and, using it like a spoon, scooped up the last of his breakfast beans. He washed it down with a drink of coffee, then lit a cigar and looked up as Emerson Bates came over to his table.

"Here's the man I was tellin' you about," Bates said, indicating the man who was with him. "His name is Paco Bustamante."

The man with Bates was short, but looked even shorter by comparison with Bates. He had obsidian eyes, a dark, brooding face, and a black mustache that curved down around either side of his mouth. He was wearing an oversized sombrero.

Odom frowned. "He's a Mex," he said. "I don't work with Mexicans."

"Paco's a good man," Bates insisted.

"How do you know?"

"Me an' him have done a couple of jobs together," Bates said. He chuckled. "Besides, you slept with his sister last night."

Odom took a puff of his cigar, then squinted through the smoke. "Well, if you come along—Paco—you only get half a share," he said, setting the Mexican's name apart from the rest of the sentence.

Without a word, Paco turned and started to walk away.

"Wait a minute," Odom called to him. "Where you goin'?"

"For half a share, Señor, I don't do shit," Paco said. It sounded like "sheet."

Odom laughed. "I reckon if you got that much gumption, you might do after all."

Paco came back to the table.

"What will you do for a full share?" Odom asked.

"Anything you say, Señor," Paco replied.

"There might be some killin'," Odom suggested.

"I do not want to be the one who is killed," the Mexican said. "But I do not mind if I am the one doing the killing."

"You're in," Odom said.

If Odom had expected some expression of gratitude from Paco, he was disappointed, for neither by word nor gesture did he respond. Instead, he looked at Odom with his unblinking, black eyes.

"What about Schuler?" Odom said. "Did you get him?"

"Odom, are you sure you want Schuler?"

"Yeah, I'm sure," Odom said.

"He's a drunk."

"I know he's a drunk. But he's also a good powder man. The last job I pulled, the son of a bitch slammed the safe shut on me. I don't intend to let that happen again. If I have to, I'll blow the damn safe this time, but I want someone who can do it without killing us all. Now, go get him."

"I already got 'im," Bates said. "He's out front."

"Bring 'im in."

With a sigh, Bates walked to the front door, pushed the beaded strings to one side, and called out.

"Schuler, get in here."

The man who answered Bates's call was of medium height and very thin. His face was red, though whether from a natural complexion, or from skin long unwashed and subjected to alcohol, no one knew. His eyes were so pale a gray that, at first glance they looked to be without color of any kind. He shuffled up to the table.

"You know why I asked for you?" Odom asked.

"Bates said you had a job for me."

"I might. If you can do it."

"I can do it."

"How do you know you can do it?"

"You have something you want blown," Schuler said.

"What makes you think I want something blown?"

"I'm a drunk," Schuler replied. "You wouldn't want me for anything unless it was for something that I was the only one who could do it. I'm a powder man. That means you want something blown."

"Let me see your hands."

"Why do you need to see my hands?"

"Hold them out here, let me see them," Odom ordered.

Schuler held his hands out for Odom's inspection. They were shaking badly.

"Damn," Odom said. "Look at that. Hell, shaking like that, you couldn't even light the fuse, let alone plant the charge."

"Give me a drink," Schuler said.

"You've had too much to drink already."

"Give me a drink," Schuler said again.

Odom poured a drink from his bottle and handed it to Schuler. Schuler tossed it down, then held his hands out again. They were as steady as a rock.

"I'll be damn," Odom said. "All right, you're in."

"I'm in what?"

"Does it really matter as long as there's money in it?"

"How much money, Señor?" Paco asked.

Odom studied them through his half-drooped left eye. "A lot of money," he finally answered. "If you was to take all the money the four of us have ever had in our whole lives and put it in one pile, it wouldn't make as much as one share of the money I'm talking about now. Are you boys interested?"

Bates smiled. "Hell, yes, I'm interested. I told you that from the beginnin', you know that."

"What about you, Paco?"

"*Sí, señor.* I am interested."

"What do you want me to blow?"

"A safe."

"Where is the safe?"

"In a train."

"A train. You are planning to hold up a train?" Schuler asked.

"Yeah. You have a problem with that?"

Without asking, Schuler poured himself another drink, then wiped his mouth with the back of his hand.

"No," he said. "I don't have a problem with that."

"When do we do it?" Bates asked.

"Couple more days," Odom replied. "I'll let you know when it's time."

Chapter Four

When Matt Jensen first encountered the town of Purgatory, Arizona, it rose from the prairie in front of him so indistinct in form and substance that it resembled nothing more than a rise of hillocks and rocks. But as he drew closer, the hillocks and rocks began to take on shape and character until it was obviously a town.

It had been a long ride since the last water hole, and Matt's canteen was down to less than a third full. But the sight of a town gave promise of more water, so he stopped, and allowed himself a long drink.

"I wish I had some for you, Spirit," he said, patting the animal on the neck. "But there's water just ahead, and I promise you your fill, as well as a good rubdown and a supper of oats."

Matt hooked the empty canteen onto his saddle, then slapped his legs against Spirit's side to urge him on down into the town. A rabbit jumped up alongside the road and ran in front of him for a little while before darting off to one side. A hand-painted sign greeted him at the edge of town.

PURGATORY

Pop. 263

OBEY OUR LAWS

Just beyond the sign was a house, and in the yard of the house was a water pump. An old woman was pumping water into a bucket, though it was obvious that the pumping action was difficult for her. Smelling the water, Spirit whickered again, and tossed his head. Matt headed toward the pump.

"Good afternoon, ma'am," Matt said. He swung down from the horse. "May I pump for you?"

The woman, who could have been anywhere between fifty and eighty, looked at him with eyes that were too tired to be frightened. Without saying a word, she relinquished the pump handle.

Matt filled the bucket, then handed it to the woman. "I wonder if I might have a little of your water for my canteen and my horse," Matt asked.

"You are welcome to the water," the old woman answered.

"Thank you," Matt said. He took his hat off, put it under the pump, and filled it with water. Holding the hat in front of his horse, he watched as the animal drank thirstily. It took three more hats to slake the horse's thirst. Not until then did Matt fill his own canteen.

"You are a kind man, sir, to see to the thirst of your horse before yourself," the old woman said.

"I've managed to drink a little from time to time,"

Matt said. "He hasn't. His thirst was much greater than mine."

Matt put the canteen back onto his saddle, then handed the woman two dollars.

The woman took the money without comment. Never once, during Matt's entire time here, had the expression on her face changed. The old woman looked as if just staying alive had become a tiring effort.

Matt rode on into town, looking it over as he entered. The town consisted of the usual stores and businesses: a general store, an apothecary, a leather-goods store, a gun shop, a dress shop. All the buildings were of ripsawed, sun-dried lumber, most with false fronts, thus aspiring to more substance than they actually possessed.

Matt rode slowly on up the street, the fall of Spirit's well-shod hooves making enough noise to generate an echo that rolled back from the false fronts of the various stores and establishments. Except for Matt, the street was empty. Several of the townspeople inside the buildings heard the sound of a solitary rider, but few ventured to look outside and see who it might be.

Matt stopped in front of the Pair O Dice saloon, the name illustrated by a pair of dice showing the number seven.

Millie's Dress Emporium was directly across the street from the Pair O Dice, and Mrs. Emma Dawkins was there being fitted for a new dress. Her son, Timmy, was sitting on the floor by the front window.

"Mama, there's a man riding into town," Timmy said. "A stranger."

"Don't stare at him, dear," Mrs. Dawkins said.

"Strangers are none of our concern." Then, to Millie, Emma continued with her ongoing conversation. "My sister is getting married back in St. Louis and I simply must look my best."

"My dear, you will be the envy of everyone at the wedding," Millie promised as she pinned up the hem of the skirt.

Young Timmy Dawkins continued to stare at the rider who had just come into town, and saw him dismount in front of the saloon. He had never seen the man before, and wondered where he came from and why he was in Purgatory.

"He's going into the saloon," Timmy said.

"Who is going into the saloon, dear?" Emma asked.

"The stranger."

"I told you not to stare at strangers."

Matt hung his wet hat on the saddle horn so that the sun would dry it. He then patted himself down, raising a cloud of dust as he did so. Just as he started toward the front porch and the promise of a late morning breakfast, a man stepped out of the saloon. He was a tall man, dressed in black. He had a star on his chest, and he wore his pistol hanging low to his right side.

"That'll be five dollars," the lawman said.

"I beg your pardon?"

"Five dollars," the lawman repeated.

"I don't understand. Five dollars for what?"

"For a visitors tax," the lawman explained. "We charge everyone who visits our town five dollars."

"Oh, well, I can take care of that," Matt said.

He turned to go back to his horse. "I just won't visit your town."

"You already have."

"Mister, I just rode into town," Matt said. "I didn't know anything about your five-dollar tax."

"You don't have five dollars? Maybe I should lock you up for vagrancy."

"It's not the money, it's the principle of the thing," Matt said. "Whoever heard of a town charging five dollars just to visit? Why, if you were going to do such a thing, the least you could do is post a sign just outside of town so people could be warned."

"Tell that to the city council. But first, give me the five dollars."

"I told you, I'm not going to visit your town. I'll just ride on."

"And I told you, you've already visited the town. Now you'll either give me the five dollars, or I'll shoot you down in the street and take it off your dead body."

"What?" Matt said, his voice rising in surprise over the lawman's statement.

"You heard me."

"Mister, you need to let this drop. I told you, I'm going to—"

Suddenly, Matt saw the lawman's hand going for his pistol.

"No!" Matt shouted, going for his own pistol at the same time.

Matt was fast, very fast. He not only had his gun out, but he fired it, just as the lawman was clearing leather.

The bullet hit the lawman in the chest and, with a surprised expression on his face, the lawman dropped his gun, then slapped his hand over the wound. Ironically, when he dropped his gun, it slipped back into his holster. He turned around and walked back into the saloon through the batwing doors.

"What was it, Moe?" Marshal Cummins asked. "What was that shot about?"

Moe looked at Cummins with a peculiar expression on his face, then fell to the floor. At that moment, Matt stepped inside as well, still holding the smoking gun.

"Moe!" someone shouted.

"My God! He's dead!"

"Drop that gun, mister!"

Looking up, Matt saw a man, wearing a star, pointing a pistol at him. One man pointing a pistol might not have been so bad, but there were four other pistols being pointed toward him, as well as a double-barrel shotgun, all being wielded by men who were wearing stars.

"How many marshals does this town have?" Matt asked.

"I'm Marshal Cummins," the first man said. "These men, and the man you just murdered, are my deputies."

"I didn't murder him. He drew on me first," Matt said.

"He drew on you, huh?" Marshal Cummins said. "Mister, you are a liar, and a poor one at that. Moe's gun is still in his holster."

"Yes, it fell back in the holster when I shot him," Matt said. His explanation sounded weak, even to his own ears.

"Mister, I didn't fall off the turnip wagon yesterday," Cummins said. "Now drop that gun."

Matt took in the situation around him, then, realizing that resistance would be futile, he dropped his gun and raised his hands.

"Put some cuffs on him, Jackson," Marshal Cummins said.

"My goodness, what was that?" Emma Dawkins asked at the sound of the gunshot.

"It's probably some fool drunk over in the saloon," Millie answered. She was on her knees with a mouth full of pins. "My apartment is just upstairs, you know, and sometimes at night, there is so much yelling and shooting going on over there that you would think they are having a battle. All they are really doing is just getting drunk and raising Cain. Turn to the left just a bit, would you, dear?"

"I seen it, Mama," Timmy said.

"It's 'saw,' not 'seen,'" Timmy's mother corrected. "And what did you see?"

"I saw the stranger shoot Deputy Gillis."

"What? What on earth are you talking about?"

"The man that shot Deputy Gillis," Timmy said.

"You mean he just rode up and shot him?"

"No, ma'am. Deputy Gillis went for his gun first, then the stranger went for his, and he shot first."

"Are you saying the stranger killed Deputy Gillis?"

"I don't know," Timmy said. "He hit the deputy because I saw the blood, but then the deputy turned around and went back into the saloon, and the stranger followed him in."

"Hush," Emma said. "You don't know what you are talking about."

"Uh-huh, yes, I do," Timmy said.

"No, you don't," Emma insisted. "You don't have the slightest idea of what you are talking about. Never mention it again."

"But Mama—"

"Did you hear me?"

"Yes, Mama."

"Then there is no 'but Mama' about it."

"I think you are doing the right thing, Emma," Millie said. "Heaven knows what-all trouble you could get in in this town."

"I know," Emma replied. "I hate doing it, I've always stressed that Timmy tell the truth. But sometimes it's better to be safe than to be right."

"I understand," Millie said. "This will be our secret."

"Get a rope!" someone yelled. "Let's hang the son of a bitch now!"

"I got a new rope! I'll go get it!"

"No!" Cummins said, his voice so loud that it reverberated back from the windows of the establishment.

"Come on, Marshal Cummins, you know damn well he's guilty. Hell, you got a whole saloon full of eyewitnesses." The protester was wearing a deputy's star.

"That's right, Hayes, we do," Marshal Cummins said. "That's why we're goin' to do this legal. We're goin' to try him now, find him guilty, then send him to Yuma and let them hang him."

"When we goin' to try him? The circuit judge ain't due back for near 'bout a month," Hayes said.

"We don't need to wait for a circuit judge," the marshal said. "We'll try him right here, right now. You forget I'm an associate judge."

"What about the jury?" the bartender asked.

"Hell, there's at least thirty men in here," the marshal said. "Pick twelve of them. Oh, and to make it legal, don't pick none of my deputies."

"All right," the bartender said. "I'll be one of the jurors. You, you, you," he said, pointing to others in the saloon until he had assembled a jury of twelve men.

"Put the jury here," Cummins said, pointing to an area of the saloon that was near the cold, iron stove. "Set up twelve chairs. Deputy Pike, you'll be the bailiff. Morgan, you and Gates move a table over there to give me a place to sit. Oh, and set a table there for the defense and there for the prosecution," he added.

There was a scurry of activity as the saloon was turned into a courtroom.

"As of now, the bar is closed," Cummins shouted.

"Come on, Marshal, what's the harm of a drink if all we're goin' to do is watch?" Jackson asked. "You done said there can't none of us deputies be on the jury."

"I intend this to be a proper court," Cummins said. "The bar is closed. Hayes, you're going to be the prosecutor."

"I ain't no lawyer, Marshal," Hayes said.

"I know you're not," Cummins answered. "But we only got us one real lawyer in town, and that's Bob Dempster. I think it's only fair that the defendant get the real lawyer."

"Dempster?" Hayes said. He laughed. "Yeah, all right, I don't mind goin' up against Dempster."

"He's back there in the corner," Cummins said. "Deputy Posey, go get him."

When Matt looked back into the corner Cummins had indicated, he saw a man sitting at a table. A whiskey bottle was on the table beside him, and his head was down on the table. He was either asleep, or passed out.

"Hey, Dempster," Posey called.

Dempster made no response.

"Dempster!" Posey said again, louder this time. "Are you dead? Or are you just drunk?"

Everyone in the saloon laughed.

"Somebody get a pitcher of water," Cummins ordered, and a moment later, someone showed up with it, handing it to Posey.

"Dempster!" Posey shouted, while at the same time throwing the pitcher of water into his face. "Wake up!"

"What? What's happening?" Dempster sputtered, raising up as water dripped from his hair and face.

Again, everyone in the saloon laughed.

"Whiskey," Dempster said, wiping his hand across his face.

There was more laughter.

"No whiskey, Dempster," Cummins said. "The bar is closed."

"Closed?" Dempster looked around in confusion. "What do you mean, closed? It's still light. Oh, is it Sunday?"

"It's closed because the saloon has been turned into a courtroom," Cummins said. "We are about to have a trial, and I have appointed you to defend the bastard who murdered Moe Gillis."

"You have appointed me?"

"Yes."

Dempster shook his head. "Marshal Cummins—" Dempster began, but he was interrupted by Cummins.

"For the purposes of this trial, I am acting, not as marshal, but as an associate judge," Cummins said. "And you will refer to me as such."

"Your Honor," Dempster corrected. "I can't act as attorney," he said. "I'm—uh—in no condition to act as attorney."

"Yeah? Well, you don't have any choice," Cummins said. "I've appointed you and you will defend this man, or I will throw you in jail for contempt of court. And I don't have to remind you, do I, Counselor, that you won't be getting anything to drink while you are in jail?"

Dempster sat at the table for a long moment, looking around at everyone who was staring at him. It was obvious that he was very uncomfortable with the scrutiny of all the patrons. He ran his hand across his wet face one more time.

"Where is the defendant?" he asked.

"Right there," Cummins said, pointing toward Matt. Matt was still standing, with his hands cuffed behind his back.

"Take his cuffs off," Dempster said.

"He's my prisoner," Jackson replied.

"Right now he is the defendant in a court trial, and he is innocent until proven guilty," Dempster said. "As the court-appointed attorney for the defense, I am ordering you to take off his cuffs."

Jackson made no move to comply.

"Your Honor," Dempster complained.

Cummins looked over toward Jackson and nodded. "Take them off," he said.

Jackson complied with the order, and Matt brought his hands back around front, then rubbed the wrists.

"Your Honor, I will need a few minutes to consult with my client," Dempster said.

"I'll give you fifteen minutes," Cummins said.

"And some coffee. Strong and black."

"Pauley, get the counselor some coffee," Cummins said to the bartender, who had already taken a seat as the foreman of the jury.

"Back here, please," Dempster said, motioning toward Matt.

Matt walked back into the corner of the saloon, then sat at the table with Dempster. Dempster's silver hair was unkempt, and though he didn't have a beard as such, he was badly in need of a shave. He was wearing a jacket and white shirt, but both were badly worn and, from the smell, had not seen a cleaning in some time.

"Hey, Marshal, while we're waitin', could we have another drink?" someone shouted.

"Yeah," another added. "After all, it's your saloon. If you keep us from buyin' drinks, you're just cuttin' off your own nose to spite your face."

That comment brought laughter from everyone, including Cummins.

"All right," he said. "Pauley, go ahead and open the bar. You can keep it open for fifteen minutes, but when the trial starts, you have to close it."

"Right," Pauley said, returning to the bar. The fact

that the opening was temporary was very good for business, because nearly everyone in the saloon, including all the jurors, rushed to the bar to get drinks before time ran out.

One of the deputies brought a pot of coffee and a single cup to Dempster's table.

"Bring a cup for the defendant," Dempster said.

"He ain't here to enjoy no coffee," the deputy growled.

"Give him a cup, Foster," Cummins ordered.

Begrudgingly, Deputy Foster went into the kitchen, then returned with another coffee cup. By the time he returned, Dempster was already on his second cup of coffee.

"What is your name?" Dempster asked.

"Jensen. Matt Jensen."

"Did you kill—uh—who is it you killed?"

"I believe they said his name was Gillis. Moe Gillis."

"Gillis," Dempster said. "Well, if you were goin' to kill someone, that son of a bitch needed it more than just about anyone else I can think of. Let me ask you this. Did you kill him in cold blood?"

"No, I—"

Dempster held up his hand. "That's enough. I'd rather hear you tell your side during the trial. It will give it more spontaneity."

"All right."

"Dempster, your fifteen minutes are up," Cummins called.

"Your Honor, can I request a twenty-four-hour delay so that I can—uh—that is so that I could be in better condition to present my case to the court?"

"Dempster, you know and I know that if I give you twenty-four hours, you'll do nothing but drink for the entire time. You won't be in any better condition tomorrow than you are right now."

Dempster ran his hand across his face, then looked over at Matt. "He's right," he said. "A twenty-four-hour delay isn't going to do me one ounce of good. So, what do you say?"

Matt chuckled. "Mr. Dempster, it doesn't look to me like I have much say in this at all."

"You don't," Dempster replied. "And I'm glad you can keep your sense of humor."

"Bailiff," Cummins said. "Call the court."

"Oyez, oyez, oyez!" Jackson called. "Ever'body stand up! This here court is now in session!"

Cummins sat, then banged the handle of his pistol on the table. "Be seated," he said. "Mr. Prosecutor, make your case."

When nobody responded, Cummins said, "Hayes, that's you."

"Oh, yeah," Hayes said. He stood up and looked toward the jury.

"Here's what happened," he said. "We was all in here when Deputy Gillis went out front. Next thing you know, we heard a shot, then Gillis, he come walkin' back into the room just like nothin' a'tall had happened. Then all of a sudden he fell on the floor dead. Before anyone could even say a how-do-you-do, this here fella come in behind him. He had a gun in his hand, and the gun was still smokin'. And get this. Moe's pistol was still in his holster! Now, there ain't one man in here who didn't hear the gunshot, and there ain't one man in here who didn't see what I just told you. So, there ain't no doubt a'tall but that the defendant is guilty."

Hayes sat down to a round of applause. Then, in a bit of showmanship, he stood up and bowed to the others in the saloon.

"That'll be enough, Hayes," Cummins said.

"Sorry, Marshal," Hayes said.

"You will address me as Your Honor."

"Your Honor," Hayes corrected.

"Defense?"

Dempster stood. "Your Honor, I call Matt Jensen to testify in his own behalf."

Matt was sworn in, then took a chair.

Matt testified for himself, explaining how Gillis had confronted him with a demand for five dollars for a visitors tax.

"I didn't know anything about the tax. I'd never heard of a visitors tax, not in this town or any town I've ever visited. So, it was my intention to just ride on out of town," Matt said. "But the deputy wouldn't let me. He said that just by being here, I was already a visitor."

"What he said was correct," Cummins said, interrupting Matt's testimony. "And, as the deputy, he had every right to collect five dollars from you. The five dollars is to pay for law enforcement."

"There's nothing right about that," Matt said.

"Uh-huh, and so, since you didn't agree with him, you shot him, is that it? You shot him down in cold blood," Hayes said.

"Your Honor, I object," Dempster said. "It is not yet redirect."

"I'm going to allow the question."

"It wasn't even a question, it was an interruption. I haven't turned the witness over to him yet," Dempster complained.

"We're after the truth here, Counselor, no matter what technique we use to get it. I am going to allow the question. Answer it, Jensen."

"No, sir, I did not shoot him down in cold blood. He drew on me first. I was faster, and when I shot him, his gun somehow just slipped back into his holster."

Nearly everyone in the saloon laughed.

"It is the truth, I swear it," Matt said.

"Mister," Hayes replied. "There ain't no one person in all of Arizona who is faster than Moe Gillis was."

"I am," Matt said simply.

"I have no more questions, Your Honor," Dempster said.

"All right. Give your closing arguments."

Dempster held up his finger, then walked back to the table where he had left the coffee. He poured himself another cup, then drank it, before he returned to address the jury.

"You have heard the defendant say that Gillis drew on him first," he said. "And since Mr. Jensen is the only eyewitness to the actual confrontation, his testimony should have some weight. We all knew Gillis, we all knew what a hothead he was, and we all know that it would not be out of character for him to draw first, especially if he thought he was right to defend some law, such as collecting a five dollar visitors tax fee. But you have the perception that Mr. Jensen drew first, because the pistol was still in Gillis's holster.

"Perception," he repeated.

Dempster held up a finger. "I would like to remind you that, according to the law, you can only find my client guilty if you are convinced, beyond the shadow of a doubt, that he is guilty. You cannot find him guilty based upon a *perception* of guilt.

"In addition to this, I would like to point this out to you. If you find him guilty as charged, there is an excellent chance that the sentence will be overturned on appeal, based upon all the irregularities in this trial."

Dempster held up a finger. "One, there could be a real question as to Andrew Cummins' authority to try this case, seeing as he acted as the arresting officer. There is no precedence for the arresting officer to also act as judge.

"Two, the Constitution of the United States guarantees every man a competent lawyer to act as his defense. All of you know me. I am a trained lawyer, that is true, but I am also a drunk and I was only given fifteen minutes to prepare for this case.

"And finally, I was given no opportunity for voir dire. I believe this jury to be incapable of rendering a fair decision, based upon the fact that you were all present at the time of the incident.

"I ask that you find Mr. Jensen not guilty."

"Ha!" one of the jurors said. "There ain't a chance in hell we're goin' to do that."

Everyone in the saloon laughed.

Cummins banged his revolver on the table. "Order," he called. He looked over at Hayes. "Mr. Hayes, your summation."

"What?"

"It's your turn to talk to the jury, to wrap up your case."

"Oh, yeah, right," Hayes said. He cleared his throat and looked over toward the jury. For a long moment, he said nothing, then he pointed to Matt.

"This son of a bitch is guilty," he said. "You know it and I know it, and I say, let's hang the bastard." He sat down, again to the laughter and cheers of those assembled.

"It's time now to poll the jury," Cummins said. He looked at the twelve men who had been selected by the bartender.

"Jury, how do you find the defendant?" Marshal Cummins asked the jury.

"Guilty!" they all yelled as one.

"So say you one, so say you all?" Cummins asked.

"Yeah, that's what we all say," one of the jurors said. He looked at the others. "Anyone say anything different?"

There were no dissensions.

"Mr. Matt Jensen, you have been found guilty of murder, and are sentenced to hang."

"I'll get a rope," Hayes shouted.

"Yeah, let's string the son of a bitch up right here, in front of the saloon for the whole town to see!" Another added.

"No!" Cummins replied. "I told you, we are going to do this legal." The marshal looked at Matt. "You'll be put on tonight's train and taken to the territorial prison in Yuma, where the execution will be carried out."

"Who are you going to send with him?" Hayes asked.

"Why? Are you volunteerin'?" Cummins replied.

"Yeah, I'll see to it that the son of a bitch gets to Yuma."

"Hayes, you was the one wantin' to string him up now. I don't know if I can trust you to get him there safe."

"I'll get him there," Hayes said. "You got my word."

Chapter Five

"I'm not going to let you put a convicted murderer in the same car as paying passengers," the station agent said.

"Come on, Randall, he's been tried, all legal, and we got to get him to Yuma to hang," Hayes said. "I ain't goin' to trust him on a horse, and we can't walk all the way."

Randall drummed his fingers on the counter for a moment, then sighed. "I suppose you two can ride in the express car," he said.

"The express car? Yeah, all right, that'll be fine. We'll ride in the express car." Hayes looked over at Matt, who had said nothing from the moment the marshal had put him in shackles.

"All right, Mr. Killer Man," Hayes said. "Take a seat out there in the waiting room. And don't give me no trouble if you know what's good for you."

Matt's ankles were shackled with just enough chain length to allow him to walk at a slow shuffle. He was also shackled by the wrists.

There were four other people waiting for the train, the assembly consisting of a mother and her two children and a salesman. One of the children, a young girl of about five, smiled at Matt as Hayes led him out into the waiting room.

"We're going back home," the little girl said to Matt. "We came here to see my Aunt Suzie. I'm named after my Aunt Suzie."

"Suzie!" her mother called. "Get back over here and leave that man alone."

"Mama, why is he wearing chains like that?" a boy of about seven asked.

"Jerry, get back over here and sit down," the mother said, without answering his question.

Even before the train arrived, Emma Dawkins and her young son, Timmy, were just down the street from the depot, standing in front of small, brick building, looking at a sign.

ROBERT DEMPSTER.

Attorney-at-Law.

"What are we doing here, Mama?" Timmy asked.

"This man is a lawyer," Emma said. "I want you to tell him what you saw."

Pushing open the door, Emma stepped inside. At first, she thought the office was empty, so she called out.

"Hello? Anybody here?"

Dempster came in from the back room.

"I'm here," he said. He looked at the woman. "You are Mrs. Dawkins, aren't you? The dentist's wife?"

"Yes," Emma said.

"What can I do for you, Mrs. Dawkins?"

"My son and I were in Millie's dress shop," Emma said. "A few minutes ago, we saw Deputy Hayes come out of the saloon, with a man in shackles."

"Yes, the man in shackles would be Matt Jensen."

"Why is he in shackles?"

"Why? Because he has just been found guilty of murder," Dempster said. "He is being sent by train to Yuma prison to be hanged."

"For shooting Deputy Gillis?"

"Yes," Dempster said. He squinted at Emma. "Excuse me, Mrs. Dawkins, but how do you know this? This just happened."

"I seen the whole thing," Timmy said.

"Saw," Emma corrected.

"I saw it," Timmy said.

"What did you see?" Dempster asked.

"I seen—uh, I saw—Deputy Gillis draw his gun first. Then the other man drew his gun faster, and he shot the deputy. I didn't know he killed the deputy 'cause all I saw was Deputy Gillis turn around and walk back into the saloon."

"You say you saw the deputy draw his gun first?"

"Yes, sir, I did."

"That's not possible," Dempster said. "When Gillis came back into the saloon, his pistol was still in his holster."

"He pulled his gun about halfway out. Then, when

he got shot, it fell back in the holster, but he drew first," Timmy said.

"Timmy, have you seen very many gunfights?"

"No, sir, I ain't—uh, I haven't ever seen any except this one."

"Neither have I actually. But I've tried cases that had to do with gunfights, and the one thing all of them have in common is confusion. Two people can see the same thing but tell completely different stories, without either one of them lying."

"How can they tell something different without one of them lying?" Timmy asked.

"Because it isn't a lie if you believe what you are saying is the truth. Take your story, for example. I don't believe you are lying. I think you really believe that you saw Deputy Gillis draw first. But a gunfight can be over in the wink of an eye. It could be that when Gillis saw this fella Jensen starting to draw, that he went for his own gun, but it was too late, the other fella had the drop on him. You might have seen Gillis starting his draw, but didn't notice that the other man had already drawn his own gun."

Timmy didn't answer.

"Don't you think it might have been that way?" he asked.

"No, sir, it wasn't that way," Timmy said. "I know what I saw. I saw the stranger, Mr. Jensen, come riding into town on a sorrel. He was a tall man, with broad shoulders and a wet hat."

"A wet hat?"

"Yes, sir. He must've given his horse some water from a hat, because the hat was wet, and he took it off and hung it on his saddle. Then, Deputy Gillis came outside and they talked for a moment—but I don't know what they were talking about. Then, Deputy Gillis started to draw his gun, but Mr. Jensen drew his gun, too, and he drew it faster than Deputy Gillis. When he shot Deputy Gillis, the deputy's gun fell back into the holster, and he turned around and went back inside the saloon. That's what I saw."

Dempster stroked his chin. "Young man, that—that is a very detailed and descriptive observation. And it coincides almost exactly with the way he told it."

"With the way who told it?" Emma asked.

"Matt Jensen. I defended him in the trial."

"You mean, they've already had the trial?" Emma asked.

"Yes, ma'am, I'm afraid so. I sure wish you had come forward earlier. I could have used Timmy's testimony then."

"Maybe it isn't too late," Emma said. "Maybe you can go see Marshal Cummins and he'll change his mind."

"No. Cummins will not change his mind," Dempster said.

"Come on, Timmy," Emma said. "Mr. Dempster, I'm sorry we bothered you."

"It's not a bother, Mrs. Dawkins," Dempster replied. "The boy was just doin' what he thought was right, that's all. And nobody can fault him for that."

Dempster waited until Emma and Timmy left. Then he closed his office and hurried back down to the saloon. Since the trial, the saloon had returned to normal, and there were scores of people there, drinking and reliving the great drama of the trial so recently played out before them. Cummins was sitting at his usual table in the back of the room, and Dempster went straight to him.

"Well, the counselor is back," Cummins said. He had a bottle of whiskey on the table and he poured some into a glass.

"Go ahead, drink up," he said. "It's your pay for defending an indigent client."

"No, thanks," Dempster said.

Cummins chuckled. "What? Bob Dempster is refusing a drink? Quick, someone, get hold of the publisher of the *Purge*. This should be front-page headlines." Cummins held his hand out—then moved it sideways, as if displaying headlines.

"Robert Dempster, run-down has-been lawyer, refuses the offer of a drink!"

"Marshal, I think you ought not to be so quick about sending Jensen to Yuma," Dempster said.

"Oh? And why is this?"

"Something has come up," Dempster said. "New evidence. Evidence I did not have when I made the case for my client."

"And just what is this evidence?"

"You know Emma-Dawkins, don't you? The dentist's wife?"

"Yes, I know her," Cummins said. "Quite a handsome woman, as I recall."

"Well, she and her son just paid me a visit," Dempster said. "Her son—Timmy is his name—was an actual witness to the shooting. He is a remarkably astute young man, and he tells the same story that Jensen told. He says that Gillis started his draw, but Jensen was faster, shot him, and Gillis's pistol slipped back into the holster. I think you should send someone down to the depot before the train arrives, and bring Jensen back."

"That's what you think, is it?" Cummins asked.

"Yes, sir, it is."

"How old is that boy?"

"I don't know. Ten, eleven, twelve maybe?"

"And you think his word carries some weight?"

"Sure, why not? He has no vested interest in this case. And as I said, he is quite articulate. I see no reason why his word would be challenged."

"Challenged," Cummins said. "Yes, that's a good word for it. Because I have an eyewitness that would challenge him."

"Marshal, when you say eyewitness, you can't use the people who were here in the saloon as eyewitnesses, because none of them actually saw the event. All they saw was the result of the event."

"One of them actually saw the event, and he will challenge the boy," Cummins said.

"You have a real eyewitness?"

"Yes."

"I don't understand. If you have a real eyewitness, why wasn't his testimony used in the trial?"

"We didn't need his testimony during the trial," Cummins replied. "We found Jensen guilty without his testimony."

"Who was the eyewitness?" Dempster asked.

"Jackson?" Cummins called.

"Yes, Marshal."

"You was standin' at the window, watchin' when Jensen drew on Moe, wasn't you?"

"No, sir, Marshal, don't you 'member? I was over at the table with the rest of you."

"No you wasn't, you was standin' by the window, lookin' outside," Cummins said pointedly.

"No, sir, I—"

"Listen to me, you dumb shit!" Cummins said sharply. He spoke very slowly. "You was standin' by the window. You saw it all. You saw Moe talking to Jensen, and you saw Jensen suddenly draw his pistol and shoot Deputy Gillis. Do you remember now?"

It wasn't until that moment that Jackson understood what the marshal was suggesting.

"Uh, yes, sir, I remember. And that's just how I seen it happen, too. Moe asked the stranger—"

"Not stranger—Jensen. You have to be very specific about that. It was Matt Jensen."

"Yes, sir," Jackson continued. "Moe asked Matt Jensen to pay the visitors tax, and Jensen got so mad that he pulled iron and kilt Deputy Gillis in cold blood."

"I want you to write that out and sign it," Cummins said.

"What for? We've done had a trial."

Cummins sighed. "Goddamnit, Jackson, will you just do the hell what I tell you to do without givin' me any argument?"

"Yes, sir," Jackson said. "I'll be glad to write it out on a piece of paper for you."

"And sign it."

"Yes, sir, and sign it."

Cummins watched as Jackson wrote out his statement, then signed it.

"Now, Mr. Lawyer," Cummins said, holding the

piece of paper out in front of him. "You put the word of a young boy against the sworn word of Deputy Jackson and we'll see which one of us gets the furthest."

Dempster reached down to grab the glass of whiskey. He tossed it down in one swallow, without so much as a grimace, then pointed a finger at Cummins.

"You railroaded that man, Marshal," he said. "That man is going to be hung for somethin' he didn't do, and you are responsible for it."

Cummins chuckled. "Well, if I am, I reckon I'm just going to have to live with it, aren't I?" he said.

Down at the depot, Matt Jensen was unaware that a young boy had seen everything and had tried unsuccessfully to tell the truth about the shooting. From his perspective right now, the future looked pretty bleak.

"Train's a'comin'," someone shouted, though as the engineer had blown the whistle at almost the same moment, no announcement was necessary. Those who were waiting for the train got up and started toward the door.

"Don't be gettin' anxious now, Killer," Hayes said even though Matt had made no effort to move. "We'll let the decent folks on first."

The floor began to shake under Matt's feet as the heavy train rolled into the station with its bell ringing and steam spewing from the cylinders.

"All right, Killer, on your feet now. Let's go," Hayes said after the train came to a complete stop and everyone else had left the building.

Stepping outside onto the wide wooden boarding

platform, Matt saw that the sliding door on the side of the express car was open, and that the express man inside the car was squatting down to talk to the station agent. Both the express man and the station agent glanced over toward Matt and Deputy Hayes, so Matt knew they were talking about him. After a moment, the agent made a waving motion to them.

"All right, looks like Randall has it worked out for us," Hayes said. "Come on, let's go."

With Hayes's hand on Matt's elbow, the two men walked over to the express car. As it was the first car after the coal tender, it was close enough to the engine to hear the rhythmic venting of the steam relief valve, sounding as if the engine were some steel beast of burden, breathing hard from its labors.

The engineer was leaning on the windowsill of the engine cab, enjoying a moment of rest. There was no such rest for the fireman, who, even though the train was motionless, was shoveling coal into the furnace to keep the steam pressure up. Glistening coals fell from the firebox to the rock ballast between the tracks. There, they glowed for a moment, then went dark.

The engineer looked at Matt, and Matt met his glance with a steady gaze of his own. The engineer nodded a greeting at him, which, under the circumstances, Matt greatly appreciated.

"All right, Killer, you get on first," Hayes said.

"It's not going to be easy with these chains," Matt said.

"Yeah? Well, I'm not about to pick you up and throw you on, so I suggest you get on the best way you can. Try."

Matt put his hands on the edge of the car, then vaulted up easily.

"Well, now," Hayes said with a little chuckle. "I'm real impressed. You done that just real good. You, express man," Hayes called.

"The name is Kingsley," the express agent replied. "Lon Kingsley."

"All right, Kingsley." Hayes gave the express man his gun. "Keep him covered till I get up there. He's a killer."

"A killer?" Kingsley replied, obviously disturbed by the fact.

"Yeah, so be careful with him."

Nervously holding the gun, Kingsley stepped back away from Matt. "D-don't you try nothin' now," he ordered.

"Easy, mister," Matt said. "I don't intend to try anything."

With some effort, Hayes managed to climb up into the express car. He reached out for his pistol. "I'll take that back now," he said.

Kingsley handed the pistol back to Hayes, who put it in his holster.

"Aren't you going to keep him covered?" Kingsley asked.

"Why?" Hayes replied. "He's in chains. It's for sure he's not goin' anywhere."

"I guess not."

"Don't worry, we won't be that much of an inconvenience to you," Hayes promised.

"I reckon you two can ride with me as long as you stay out of my way. I'll be processin' mail along the way."

"We won't be no bother," Hayes promised. He

pointed to the end of the car where there was one chair.
"Sit there," he said.

When Matt started to sit on the chair, Hayes called
out to him.

"Huh-uh, not on the chair, the chair is mine. You'll be
sitting on the floor, so you may as well sit there now and
make yourself comfortable."

As instructed, Matt sat down on the floor, leaned his
head back against the wall, and closed his eyes. He and
Hayes no sooner got settled than the engineer blew his
whistle, then opened the throttle. The train started forward with a series of jerks, then smoothed out as it gradually began gaining speed.

Chapter Six

Shortly after the train left the depot, Cummins held a meeting of all his deputies.

"All right, boys, it's time to go to work. You fellas know what stores, businesses, and homes you are responsible for. Get started, then bring it all to the saloon."

"Marshal, maybe we had better ease up a bit," one of the deputies suggested.

"Ease up a bit?" Cummins said. "What do you mean by that, Crack?"

"Well, I mean, some of the folks, at least the folks I'm dealin' with, are beginnin' to get contrary about payin' taxes ever' week."

"They are, are they?"

"Yeah."

"Well, that's just too bad," Cummins said.

"So, what do I tell 'em when they start complainin' like that?"

"Tell them it's the law," Cummins said. "If they want to live in my town, they have to pay the piper." Cummins giggled. "And we're the piper," he said. "Are you going to have a problem with that?"

"No, I ain't goin' to have no problem with that," Crack said. "I was just commentin', that's all."

"If I want any comments, I'll ask for them. What about the rest of you? Any of you have any trouble with this?"

None of the deputies responded.

"Boys, when you think about it, we've got us a real sweet deal here," Cummins said. He laughed out loud. "You might say that what we have is a license to steal. Ever since the city council voted to put in the law tax, all we have to do is just control a few drunks, make sure nobody gets beat up, and arrest anyone who spits on the sidewalk. Now, what do you say you get to work?"

At the very moment Cummins was charging his deputies with the task of spreading out to collect the "law tax," a secret meeting was being held in the back room of the Bank of Purgatory.

Joel Montgomery, the president of the bank, was conducting the meeting, and he poured himself a drink before calling the meeting to order. "Goodman?" he called. "Are you keeping a lookout?"

"Yes," Goodman said. "There's nobody out on the street."

"Well, there will be soon. This is the day they spread out to collect their tax. So if you see anyone coming this way, let me know."

"I will," Goodman promised.

"Men," Montgomery said. "There's a bottle here. If any of you want a drink before we get started, get it now. Because once we get started, we've got some serious business to discuss."

"It ain't goin' to work," one of the men said. He was short, with a reddish tint to his skin, and a large, blotchy nose.

"What isn't going to work, Amon?"

Amon Goff owned the leather goods store.

"All of us gettin' together and tellin' Cummins we ain't goin' to pay his taxes no more," Amon said. "It ain't goin' to work."

"And why won't it work?" Montgomery asked.

"Because the tax is a law that's done been passed by the city council. If we don't pay it, why, they've got the right to put us in jail. What we need to do is get the city council to pass a law changin' that."

"And how do you propose that we do that, Amon?" Josh Taylor asked. Taylor ran the feed store. "There's only seven men on the city council, and four of 'em are Cummins' deputies."

"I don't know how we're goin' to get it done," Amon said. "I just know that if one of us refuse to pay the taxes, we're goin' to wind up one of two ways. Either dead, or in jail."

"Yeah," a man named Bascomb said. Drew Bascomb owned the freight line. "Even if we fight back, we could wind up getting hung. You seen what happened to that stranger that rode in here today. Gillis tried to collect the five-dollar visitors tax and the stranger shot him. Now, I say, good for the stranger, 'ceptin' he's on the way to Yuma to get hung."

"I heard about that," Montgomery said. "Did any of you see it? I mean, how is it that it just happened today, and already the stranger has been tried and convicted? The judge isn't even in town."

"Cummins held the trial himself," Goff said. "Within five minutes after it happened, Cummins had a jury picked and he held the trial right there in the Pair O Dice saloon."

"That's not legal, is it?" Bascomb asked. "I mean, can Cummins hold a trial without the judge?"

"You may remember that Cummins got himself appointed associate judge," Montgomery reminded the others. "His authority might be questionable, but he probably was within his right to conduct the trial. Now, as to the trial itself, I'm sure there were all sorts of technical errors that would qualify for an appeal. For example, does anyone know if he had a lawyer?"

"Bob Dempster was his lawyer," Goff said.

"Bob Dempster? Good Lord, was Dempster sober?"

"Ha!" Bascomb said. "When was the last time anyone saw Bob Dempster sober?"

"Damn, the stranger could appeal this case a dozen ways from Sunday," Montgomery said.

"Maybe so," Bascomb said. "But he just left on the train to Yuma. Chances are, he'll be hung by this time tomorrow night."

"Fellas, here comes Crack," Goodman said from the window.

"Well, what are we going to do?" Goff asked. "Are we going to pay the taxes this week, or refuse?"

Montgomery ran his hand through his hair, then let out a long, frustrated sigh. "We'll pay them," he said.

"Right now, we have no other choice. But I don't intend to go on paying them. We're going to put a stop to this. There is no way I'm going to let this go on forever."

"How are we going to stop them?" Bascomb asked.

Montgomery shook his head. "I don't know yet," he answered. "That's what we are going to figure out, as soon as we get organized."

At the same time Joel Montgomery and a few other citizens of the town were holding their meeting, Robert Dempster was sitting in a darkened room in the back of his office. A half-full whiskey bottle was on his desk in front of him, and he reached for it—drew his hand back, reached for it again, and again drew his hand back.

His head hurt, his tongue was thick, his body ached in every joint, and he had the shakes.

He reached for the bottle again, picked it up, and filled his glass, though he was shaking so badly that he got nearly as much whiskey on the desk as he did in the glass. Putting the bottle down, he picked up the glass and tried to take a drink, but the shaking continued, and he couldn't get it to his mouth. He put the glass down, leaned over it, took it in his lips, then tried to lift the glass that way, but it fell from his mouth and all the whiskey spilled out.

In a fit of anger, Dempster grabbed the bottle and threw it. The bottle was smashed against the wall and the room was instantly perfumed with the aroma of alcohol.

"No!" he shouted in anger and regret.

He leaned his head back, then pinched the bridge of his nose.

Robert Dempster had not always been an alcoholic. In fact, he had once been a productive member of society, a husband, father, and vestryman in his church. As he sat in the dark room, his body rebelling against the denial of alcohol, he began to remember, though they were not memories he wanted to revisit. In fact, he drank precisely so he wouldn't have to remember, but despite his best efforts, those memories, unbidden though they might be, came back to fill his brain with pain—a pain that was even worse than the pain of alcoholism.

"No," he said aloud, pressing his hands against his temples, trying to force out the memories. "No! Go away!"

Benton, Missouri, five years earlier

Judge Dempster was studying the transcripts of the third day of a trial that, on the next day, would hear the summations before being remanded to the jury. The sound of a slamming door in a distant part of the Scott County Courthouse echoed loudly through the wide, high-ceilinged halls like the boom of a drum. Dempster paid no attention to it as it was a familiar sound. He should have paid attention to it, because while it was a familiar sound during the day, it was not a normal sound for ten o'clock at night.

"Hello, Judge," someone said, interrupting Dempster's reading.

Looking up, Dempster saw three men. All three had been regulars in the courtroom during the trial, but he only knew the name of the one who spoke. That man's name was Carl Mason, and he was the brother of Jed Mason, the defendant in the trial. Jed Mason was being tried for murder in the first degree.

"Mason," Dempster said.

Mason didn't wear a beard, but neither was he clean-shaven. He had yellow, broken teeth and an unruly mop of brown hair.

"Nobody is supposed to be in here at this hour. How did you get in?" Dempster asked.

"You need to have the lock fixed on the front door," Mason replied with a chuckle. "It didn't cause us any trouble at all."

"You have no business here."

"Well now, Judge, that ain't the way I see it," Mason said. "The way I see it, my brother is goin' to get his-self hung if this here trial don't come out like it's supposed to. So I figure I got the right of a lovin' brother to be here."

"You are welcome in court tomorrow for closing arguments," Dempster said. "I think we will also have a verdict tomorrow."

"What will that verdict be?" Mason asked.

"Well, Mr. Mason, I have no way of knowing what the verdict will be."

"Sure you do. You're the judge, ain't you?"

"Yes, of course, I'm the judge."

"Then see to it that my brother gets off."

"Mr. Mason, I don't think you understand. I am bound by the decision of the jury. If they find your brother guilty of murder, I will have no choice but to pronounce sentence on him."

"Yeah? And what would that sentence be?" Mason asked.

"That he be hanged by the neck until dead," Dempster said.

"That ain't goin' to happen," Mason insisted.

"It very well may," Dempster replied. "As I told you, it is up to the jury."

Mason shook his head. "You better find some way to make it be up to you. If you don't . . ." Ominously, Mason stopped in mid-sentence.

"Are you threatening me, Mr. Mason?"

"You?" Mason said. He shook his head. "No, Judge, you ain't the one I'm threatening. I'm threatening them."

"Them?"

Reaching into his pocket, Mason pulled out something gold and shiny, then lay it on the desk in front of Dempster.

"You recognize this, Judge?" he asked.

"It's Tammy's locket," Dempster said with a gasp. He had given his twelve-year-old daughter the locket last Christmas, and she was never without it.

"And this," he said, putting a wide gold wedding band down. Inside the wedding band were the names "Bob & Lil."

"Lil's wedding band," Dempster said with a sinking feeling. "What have you done with my family?"

"You make the right decision tomorrow, and your wife and daughter will be fine," Mason said.

"Please, don't hurt them."

Mason chuckled. "Like I said, Judge, that's all up to you."

Dempster went home to find his wife and daughter missing. There was a note on the receiving table in the foyer.

IF YOU WANT TO SEE YOU WIFE AND KID

ALIVE AGAIN CUT MY BROTHER FREE

Dempster did not sleep a wink that night, and when he showed up in court the next day, he was exhausted from lack of sleep and sick with worry. As the courtroom filled, he looked out over the gallery and saw Mason and the two men who had come to visit him on the previous night. Mason held up a ribbon that Dempster recognized as having come from his wife's hair, then smiled at Dempster, a sick, evil smile.

Dempster fought back the bile of fear and anger, then cleared his throat and addressed the court.

"Last night, while going over the transcripts, I found clear and compelling evidence of prosecutorial misconduct," he said.

The prosecutor had been examining his notes prior to his summation, but at Dempster's words he looked up in surprise.

"What?" the prosecutor said. "Your Honor, what did you say?"

"Therefore, I am dismissing all charges against the defendant. Mr. Mason, you are free to go."

"What?" the prosecutor said again, shouting the word this time at the top of his lungs. "Prosecutorial misconduct? Judge, have you lost your mind? What are you talking about?"

"Are you crazy, Judge?" someone shouted from the gallery, and several others also shouted in anger and surprise.

"This court is adjourned!" Dempster said, banging his gavel on the bench. Getting up, he left the courtroom amid continued shouts of anger.

"Judge, what happened?" his clerk asked when he returned to his chambers.

"I have to go home," Dempster said.

"Is something wrong?"

"My wife and child," Dempster said without being specific. "I must go home."

Dempster's house was four blocks from the courthouse, and he half-ran, half-walked, calling out as he hurried up the steps to the front porch.

"Lil! Tammy!"

Pushing the door open, Dempster stopped and gasped, grabbing at the pain in his heart when he saw them. His wife and daughter were on the floor of the parlor, lying in a pool of dark, red blood. They were both dead.

"No!" he cried aloud. "No!"

The Missouri Supreme Court offered condolences to Dempster for the loss of his wife and daughter, even as they removed him from the bench and disbarred him. After that, Dempster had no choice but to leave town. He took a train to St. Louis and there boarded a train heading west. He had no particular destination in mind, settling in Purgatory because he felt that the name of the town brought a sense of poetic justice to his own situation. As he explained in a letter he wrote to his brother; "If I could have found a town named Hell, I would have settled there."

Dempster forced the memories away, returning to the present—a run-down office in a flyblown town. He looked at the broken bottle and the whiskey stain—which had become symbolic of his life. In the beginning the drinking seemed to help ease the pain, but as time went by the whiskey, which had once helped him by temporarily blotting out the memory, took over his soul. The man who had once been the odds-on favorite for appointment to the Supreme Court of Missouri was no more. That man would never be back.

Dempster put his head down on his desk and sobbed until his throat was raw and his tears were gone.

"Dear God," he said. "I cannot get any lower than this. I want to die, but I don't have the courage to kill myself. Take me, now. Please, dear God, help me beat this or take me now."

Incredibly, Dempster's "prayer of relinquishment" had an almost immediate effect. A sense of calm came over him, a peace that passed all understanding, and he knew what his first step had to be on the long road to recovery.

Getting paper and pen from his desk, Dempster wrote a letter.

To the Honorable John C. Frémont,
Governor of Arizona Territory

Dear Governor Frémont:

My name is Robert Dempster. I am an attorney at law, practicing in Purgatory. I feel it incumbent upon me to call to your attention the condition of affairs here in Purgatory. We are a town that is literally without law, except for the law as administered by Andrew Cummins, who is acting as both marshal and associate judge.

I could list a catalogue of offences he has perpetrated and is perpetrating against the citizens of our town, such as draconian taxes and heavy-handed application of the laws he chooses to enforce. To help him, he has a force of no fewer than eight deputies, all this for a town of less than three hundred people.

However, it is not to seek relief for our own condition that I write this letter. Rather, it is to point out a specific incident that is so glaring that I believe intervention is in order, either from your own resources or the resources of the federal government. I am talking about the trial, conviction, and sentencing of a man, all within one hour of the alleged violation.

The man in question, Matt Jensen, rode into town innocently enough, and was accosted by Moe Gillis, one of Marshal Cummins's deputies. Gillis ordered Jensen to pay a five-dollar visitors tax, but Jensen refused, saying he would ride on out of town. In the resultant disagreement, Gillis was killed. Jensen was arrested and brought to trial within minutes of the incident, and I was appointed to defend him.

I must in all candidness report to you that I am an

alcoholic, and was debilitated by an excessive use of alcohol. Despite the fact that I was in no condition to mount an adequate defense, I was appointed by Marshal Cummins, who, for purposes of the trial, abandoned his roll of marshal and assumed the mantle of associate judge.

During the course of the trial, Jensen claimed that Gillis drew first, and my personal knowledge of Moe Gillis is such that I do not find that claim unrealistic. I was given only fifteen minutes to prepare for this case, which did not allow me to look for eyewitnesses. Later, an eyewitness came forth to testify that he had seen the incident, and the eyewitness's story confirmed Jensen's claim, thus making the killing an act of self-defense. When I took the report to Marshal Cummins, he dismissed it out of hand, and in front of me, ordered one of his deputies to perjure himself by signing a statement that he had also been a witness.

I call upon you, Governor, to please intervene in this case to stay the man's execution (he is to be taken to Yuma), and if that is not possible, to please appoint someone to look into the conditions in this town.

This town has some decent people, Governor, and could be a vibrant and productive community, if only the tyranny of an evil marshal and his minions could be removed.

Sincerely
Robert Dempster

Chapter Seven

The metal bit jangled against the horse's teeth. The horse's hooves clattered on the hard rock and the leather saddle creaked beneath the weight of its rider. The rider was a big man, with brindled gray-black hair, a square chin, and steel gray eyes that could stare through a man.

United States Marshal Ben Kyle's boots were dusty and well worn; the metal of his spurs had become dull with time. He wore a Colt .44 at his hip, and carried a Winchester .44-40 in his saddle sheath

He dismounted, unhooked his canteen, and took a swallow, then poured some water into his hat and put it back on his head, enjoying the brief cooling effect. He was running low on water, but figured to reach the monastery before nightfall, and he knew there would be water there.

There were no natural sources for water at the monastery, but its water was carried in by barrel from a small, not always dependable, river twelve miles to the east.

Kyle was after Emil Taylor and Bart Simmons. Three days ago, the two men had held up a stage, and because the stage was carrying United States mail, Kyle, as a U.S. marshal, had jurisdiction. The trail had led Kyle here, and he was now convinced that the two were headed for the monastery. That wasn't a hard conclusion to make because anyone coming this way would have to stop at the monastery since there was no other source of food or water within several miles in any direction.

Stagecoach robbery was not the only crime for which the two men were wanted. Kyle believed they were also involved, along with Cletus Odom, in the attempted robbery of the Bank of Wickenburg a few weeks earlier. No money was taken because of the actions of the bank teller, but those same actions also enraged the robbers so that the teller was killed. Kyle was after Taylor and Simmons, but the one he really wanted was Cletus Odom, the outlaw who had planned and led the robbery attempt. The murder in Wickenburg was not the only thing Odom was wanted for. He was a desperate fugitive whose face was plastered on reward dodgers all across the Southwest.

Kyle reached the monastery just before dark. The abbey was surrounded by high stone walls and secured by a heavy oak gate. Kyle pulled on a rope that was attached to a short section of log. The makeshift knocker banged against the large, heavy gates with a booming thunder that resonated through the entire monastery. A moment later, a small window slid open and a brown-hooded face appeared in the opening.

"Who are you?" the face asked.

Kyle was a little surprised by the question. The monk on the other side of the gate was Brother James, and because Kyle had been here many times before, he was absolutely certain that James knew who he was. Why was he pretending that he did not know?

"My name is Ben Kyle. I'm a United States marshal."

"What do you want?"

"I'm looking for a couple of men—outlaws—who might have come this way," Kyle said.

Pointedly, the monk cut his eyes to his left. He did that twice. "I'm sorry. This is a holy place. I can't let you in," he said. He cut his eyes to the left again.

Kyle nodded once, to let the monk know that he understood.

"But, Brother, I am out of water. You cannot turn me away," Kyle said, continuing the charade.

"I am truly sorry," the monk said. "God go with you." The little window slammed shut.

Kyle remounted, and rode away from the gate.

Taylor and Simmons were standing just inside the gate.

"What's he doin' now?" Taylor asked.

"He's ridin' off," the monk answered.

Taylor chuckled, then put his pistol away. He looked at the short, overweight monk. "You done that real good, Padre," he said. "I don't think he suspects a thing."

"I am not a priest," the monk said. "Therefore I am not addressed as Father."

"Really? Well, hell, it don't matter none to me what you're called," Taylor said. "I don't care what I'm

called either, as long as I'm called in time for supper."
Taylor laughed at his own joke. "You get it? As long as
I'm called in time for supper," he repeated, and he
laughed again.

"Yes, that's quite amusing," Brother James said without laughing.

"Yeah, well, speakin' of supper, what do you say we
go see if the cook has our supper finished? I'm
starvin'."

The three men walked back across the little courtyard, which, because of the irrigation system and the
loving care bestowed upon it by the brothers of the
order, was lush with flowers, fruit trees, and a vegetable garden. There were a dozen or more monks in
the yard, each one occupied in some specific task.

The building the three men entered was surprisingly cool, kept that way by the hanging gourds of
water called "ollas," which, while sacrificing some of
the precious water by evaporation, paid off the investment by lowering the temperature by several degrees.

"Brother James, who was at the gate?" Father
Gaston asked.

"A stranger, Father. I do not know who he was,"
Brother James replied.

"And you denied him sanctuary?"

"I had no choice, Father," Brother James said,
rolling his eyes toward Taylor and Simmons.

"You sent him away?" Father Gaston asked Taylor.

Taylor was a small man, with a ferretlike face and
skin that was heavily pocked from the scars of some
childhood disease.

"He was a United States marshal," Taylor replied. "A

United States marshal ain't exactly someone we want around right now."

"I see," Father Gaston said. "Still, to turn someone away is unthinkable. It is a show of Christian kindness to offer water, food, and shelter to those who ask it of us."

"Yeah, well, there's enough of that Christian kindness goin' on now, what with you takin' care of us 'n' all," Taylor said. "Now, what about that food? How long does it take your cook to fix a little supper?"

"Forgive me for not mentioning it the moment you came in," Father Gaston said. "The cook has informed me that your supper is ready."

"Well, now, that's more like it! Why didn't you say somethin'?" Taylor said. "Come on, Simmons, let's me 'n' you get somethin' to eat."

Brother James led the two outlaws into the dining room. The room was bare, except for one long wooden table, flanked on either side by an attached wooden bench. On the mud-plaster-covered wall, there hung a large crucifix with the body of Jesus, clearly depicting the agony of the passion. Simmons stood there looking at it for a moment.

"I tell you the truth, that would be one hell of a way to die," Simmons said.

"What would be?" Taylor asked. Unlike Simmons, Taylor had not noticed the cross.

"That," Simmons said, nodding toward the crucifix.

Taylor looked around, then shrugged. "Yeah? Well, I doubt that hangin' is any better, and more than likely me 'n' you both are goin' to wind up gettin' ourselves hung."

Almost unconsciously, Simmons put his hand to his throat, then shuddered. "Don't talk like that," he said.

Taylor laughed. "I'm just tellin' you the facts of life is all," he said. He looked at Brother James. "What about that supper that's supposed to be ready?" he asked.

"Here it comes now," Brother James said.

Another monk, who, like Brother James, was wearing a simple, brown, homespun cassock held together with a rope around his waist, came into the dining room then, carrying a tray. Their dinner consisted of a bowl of beans and a crust of bread.

"What the hell is this?" Taylor asked.

"This is your supper," Brother James said.

"Is this it? What about that Christian kindness you were talkin' about? You didn't offer us no meat," Taylor said with a disapproving growl.

Brother James shook his head. "I'm sorry, in this order we do not eat meat. We cannot offer you what we do not have."

"Yeah? Are you telling me this is what you people eat?"

"Only one day in three do we get beans," Brother James said. "The other two days we get bread only."

"Hell, it ain't that bad, Taylor," Simmons said, shoveling a spoonful of beans into his mouth. "It ain't bad at all. In fact, it's kind of tasty, and it sure as hell beats jerky."

Kyle waited until after dark before he returned to the monastery. Leaving his horse hobbled, he slipped up to one of the side walls. Then, using chinks and holes in the stone facade to provide footholds and handholds, he climbed up, slipped over the top, and dropped to the ground inside the abbey walls.

Most of the buildings inside the monastery grounds were dark, for candles and oil for lamps were precious commodities to be used sparingly. Here and there, Kyle saw that some light did manage to escape through the windows of those buildings where there was light.

The grounds themselves were not totally dark, though, because the moon was full and bright, and the chapel, dormitory, stable, and grain storage buildings all gleamed in a soft, silver light like white blooms sprouting from desert cactus.

The night was alive with the long, high-pitched trills and low violalike thrums of the frogs. For counterpoint there were crickets, the long, mournful howl of coyotes, and from the stable, a mule braying and a horse whickering.

With his gun in hand, and staying in the shadows alongside the wall, Kyle moved toward the building that he knew to be the dining hall. He was sure they would be inside there, because it was one of the few buildings that had a light. Finding a window, he looked inside. There, he saw Taylor, Simmons, and Brother James. Though he had been certain that Taylor and Simmons were here, this was his first, actual confirmation of the fact.

Taylor and Simmons were eating, and Kyle thought that might give him the opportunity he needed to sneak up on them. Moving toward the front door, he opened it quietly.

Except for a single candle on the table, the room

was dark, and that enabled Kyle to step inside, then slip quickly into the shadows.

"Bring me some more beans and bread," Taylor said.

"Yeah, and some bacon," Simmons added.

"I told you, we do not eat meat in this order."

"Yeah, I know what you told us, but I think you're shittin' us," Simmons said.

"Seeing as you are nothing but a turd anyway, how would you know whether he's shitting you or not?" Kyle asked.

"What the hell?" Taylor shouted, standing up and spinning around toward Kyle.

"Hold it right there!" Kyle shouted menacingly. He cocked his pistol and the sound it made was loud and deadly. "Drop your gun belts."

Glaring at him, their features contorted by the candlelight, the two outlaws unbuckled their gun belts and dropped them.

"What are you plannin' on doin' with us?" Taylor asked.

"I'm taking you back to jail," Kyle said.

"There's two of us and only one of you. Plus, it's a long way back. How do you plan to do that?"

"That's not your problem," Kyle replied.

"You'll never get us back."

"Oh, I'll get you back, all right," Kyle said. "Either sitting in your saddle, or draped over it."

When Kyle and his two prisoners rode into Sentinel two days later, the two riders were handcuffed and connected to each other by a rope. They stopped in front of the marshal's office.

"Get down," he said.

"It ain't goin' to be all that easy, what with us bein' handcuffed and tied together with a rope," Simmons said.

"I'll help," Kyle said, giving Simmons a shove. The outlaw fell from his saddle and rolled on the ground.

"You need help, too?" Kyle asked the other prisoner.

"No, I can get down on my own," Taylor said, dismounting quickly.

Kyle herded them into the office. "Back there," he said, pointing toward the cells at the back of the building.

"Say, Marshal, I'm gettin' a little hungry here," Taylor said. "What time do you serve supper?"

"I'll bring you a biscuit and bacon," Kyle said as put them into the cell, then closed the door and locked it. "Stick your hands through the bars."

"Can't get through, what with these handcuffs."

"Hold one hand on top of the other, you can do it."

The prisoners complied and Kyle removed their handcuffs, then hung them on a hook.

"You boys behave yourselves," he said. "I'm going to get a beer."

"Hey, Marshal, when you bring back them biscuits, you reckon you could bring us a beer?" Simmons asked. He laughed out loud.

"That's real funny, Simmons," Kyle said as he left.

* * *

When Kyle opened the door to the Ox Bow Saloon a couple of minutes later, he saw his deputy, Boomer Foley, sitting at a table with Sally Fontaine, the saloon owner. Boomer was a slender man, almost skinny, but appearances were deceiving. Kyle had seen Boomer in action, and he was more than able to handle himself.

Sally was a very attractive auburn-haired woman in her late thirties. She was a widow who had inherited the saloon when her husband was shot and killed by a drunken patron. Most expected Sally to sell the saloon and go back to Virginia where her father had once been a United States Congressman. They were surprised when she announced her intention of remaining in Sentinel to run the Ox Bow. Few thought she would succeed, but it was now three years since Marty Fontaine was killed, and the Ox Bow had not only survived, it did a thriving business.

"Marshal, welcome back," Boomer said, smiling broadly. "Come over here and join us. We was just talkin' about Doc Presnell, wonderin' what kind of a trip he had."

"Is Doc back?" Kyle asked.

"Not yet. He's coming in on the seven-thirty train tonight," Sally said.

"Where did he go again?" Kyle asked.

"Don't you remember? He was in St. Louis attending some medical conference," Sally said.

"Doc's not the only one on the train tonight," Boomer said.

"What do you mean?"

Boomer pulled a telegram from his pocket. "We got this from the marshal back in Purgatory. I reckon he sent it to every lawman between Purgatory and Yuma." He handed the page to Kyle.

ATTENTION ALL LAW OFFICERS STOP PLEASE BE
ADVISED THAT PRISONER MATT JENSEN WILL BE IN
CUSTODY ON TONIGHT'S TRAIN TO YUMA STOP
JENSEN HAS BEEN TRIED FOR MURDER CONVICTED
AND SENTENCED TO BE HANGED STOP MARSHAL
ANDREW CUMMINS

"You sure that's tonight's train?" Kyle asked after he read the telegram.

"Yes, sir, I'm sure. We got the telegram this afternoon."

"That's funny," Kyle said. "I haven't heard of any murder trial being conducted back in Purgatory."

"Could be that it happened while you was gone," Boomer said. "Don't forget, you been gone for a few days now."

"Still, that seems awfully fast to have a murder, hold a trial, then sentence a man," Kyle said.

"Do you know this here Marshal Cummins?"

"Only by reputation," Kyle replied. "I've heard that he is a pretty domineering sort." Kyle sighed. "But, if he is the man the people of Purgatory want, who am I to question them?" Kyle turned to Sally and smiled. "I heard a rumor that a man could get a beer in this place if he knew the right people."

Sally laughed out loud. "Fred?" she called over to the bartender. "Bring Marshal Kyle a beer."

"Yes, ma'am, Miss Sally," Fred answered.

"I take it that was Taylor and Simmons I seen you ridin' in with a few minutes ago," Boomer said

"Yes," Kyle answered.

"Did you have a hard time trackin' 'em?"

"Wasn't hard at all," he said. "Once I saw that they were going southwest from Sentinel, I knew there was only one place they could go."

"The monastery?" Boomer asked.

Kyle nodded. "The monastery."

Boomer chuckled. "If any of them outlaws ever get a lick of sense about 'em, this law business would be a lot harder," he said. "You think they didn't have any idea you'd know exactly where they would be—where they would have to be?"

"I'm not sure they even thought about it."

"You'll be chargin' 'em with robbin' that stage-coach, right?"

"Yes. But I'm also sure they took part in that bank robbery up in Wickenburg," Kyle said. "So I'm hoping they'll shed some light on where to find Cletus Odom."

"Ben, do you actually think these two men will tell you anything about Odom?" Sally asked.

"I think so," Kyle said. "As far as I know, neither Taylor nor Simmons have ever done murder. That is, until the attempted bank robbery in Wickenburg."

"I thought all the witnesses said it was Odom who shot him," Boomer said.

"That's right," Kyle agreed. "But just by being there, that makes Taylor and Simmons every bit as guilty as Odom. I want them to know that, because then I'll offer them a deal. It could be that if they think they are facing a hanging, they may turn on Odom to save their hides."

"I'd sure love to get Odom," Boomer said. "He's

one evil son of a bitch. Oh, beg pardon, Miss Sally, I'm sorry 'bout that."

Sally laughed. "No need to apologize for telling the truth."

"Yes, ma'am, but I hadn't ought to have used language like that in front of a lady."

"Boomer, I run a saloon," Sally said. "Believe me, there's very little I haven't heard." She turned to Marshal Kyle. "Have you had your supper, Ben?" She asked.

"No, I haven't."

"Would you like to join me for supper down at Del Monte's? My treat."

"Well, now, how could I pass up an offer like that?" Kyle replied. "Boomer, how about getting a couple of biscuit-and-bacon sandwiches to take to our prisoners?"

"All right," Boomer said. "Then I'll make the rounds, but I plan to be down to the depot to meet the train when it gets in. Are you two goin' to be there?"

Sally and Kyle exchanged a smiling glance.

"We may, and we may not," Kyle said.

"Well, you'll want to greet Doc, won't you? I mean, he's been gone for the better part of a month," Boomer said. Then, seeing the way the two were looking at each other, he stopped in mid-sentence. "Uh—'course if you're not there to meet him, it won't really matter none. I'll bring Doc down for a drink if he wants one."

"You do that, Boomer," Sally said. "And tell Fred that anything you and Doc drink tonight will be on me."

"Well, Miss Sally, that's just real nice of you now," Boomer said, beaming at the offer.

* * *

As the train to Yuma hurtled across the desert, Deputy Hayes walked over to the door of the express car and slid it open. When he did so, the wind caused several papers to fly around inside the car.

"Here!" Kingsley shouted angrily as he made a grab for the papers and envelopes. "What are you doing?"

"I'm takin' a piss out the door," Hayes answered, laughing.

"I have to have this mail sorted by the time we reach Sentinel," Kingsley said. "I can't do it with all the wind coming through. Close the door."

"All right, all right, hold your horses," Hayes said. "Soon as I shake the lily a bit, I'll close the door."

Matt watched and listened to the exchange between the two men. Matt could smell the smoke that drifted in from the engine, and one gleaming ember even landed on the table of the mail cabinet that was in front of Kingsley.

Agitatedly, Kingsley stamped out the glowing ember. "You're going to set us on fire," he complained.

Hayes slid the door shut. "Damn, Kingsley, if you ain't like some old woman," he said. "You ain't done nothin' but bitch since we left Purgatory."

"I'm not just a passenger on the train, you know. I have work to do," Kingsley said.

"Well, go on, I ain't stoppin' you," Hayes said.

Hayes moved back up to the front of the car, where Matt was sitting on the floor, with his back against the wall.

"Hey, Jensen," Hayes said. "You ever seen a man get hung?"

"Yes," Matt said.

"Yeah, I have, too," Hayes said. "It sure is fun to watch. It ain't pretty, what with the man getting' hisself hung havin' his face go all purple, and his eyes buggin' out like they do." Hayes laughed, then slapped himself on the knee. "No, sir, it ain't pretty, but, damn, it's fun to watch."

"I don't enjoy them as much as you do," Matt said.

"Yeah, well, maybe you'll enjoy this one more, seein' as you're goin' to be the star," Hayes said. "Just think, you'll be standin' up there on the gallows with ever'one lookin' right at you while the hangman puts his noose around your neck."

Hayes made a motion with his hand, as if putting on a noose.

"Then, next thing you know, why, they'll open that trapdoor under you and you'll fall through. Skkkkktttt!" He made the sound with his throat, then he jerked his head to one side, opened his eyes wide, and stuck out his tongue, as if he had just been executed.

Hayes laughed out loud. "Hey, what do you think? Pretty good, wasn't it?"

At that moment, the train wheels rolled over the junction of two tracks, and the clacking sound was much louder than normal.

"What was that?" Hayes asked, startled by the change in sound.

"It was nothing," Kingsley said. "Haven't you ever been on a train before?"

"Yeah, sure," Hayes said. "But I don't think I ever been on one as loud as this one."

"It's no louder than normal," Kingsley said, not looking up from his task of sorting letters.

The sun was a bright red disc just resting on the western horizon. Bands of red and purple laced across the sky as Cletus Odom stood in the middle of the tracks, looking back toward the east. The twin ribbons of steel glinted in the setting sun . . . shining red until they disappeared into the gathering dusk to the east.

"See anything yet?" one of the men behind him called.

"Not yet."

"Maybe we've already missed it."

"We haven't missed it," Odom said. He turned back toward the three men who were bending over the tracks. "How's it coming?" he asked.

"We've pulled out a couple of the spikes," Bates replied. "But they're damn hard to remove."

"They're supposed to be hard to get out. But all you have to do is pull enough of 'em to be able to push the rail out a few inches."

"You sure that'll stop the train?" Bates asked.

"You ever seen a train run on dirt?"

"No."

"Well, if you push that rail out, the only place the train can go is dirt. Yeah, I'm sure this'll stop it."

"Señor, how much money is on the train?" Paco asked.

"How much you got now?" Odom replied.

"Maybe I have one dollar," Paco answered.

"Then it doesn't really matter how much money the

train is carryin', does it? Whatever it is, it'll be more'n you got. Schuler?" Odom called.

"Yeah?" Schuler answered.

"If we have to blow the safe, are you going to be able to handle it? Or are you drunk?"

"I can do the job," Schuler insisted.

"You damn well better be able to do the job."

They heard a whistle in the distance.

"Hurry it up!" Odom said, and he came over to join them as, working quickly, they pulled up two more spikes.

"Bates, you're the biggest one here," Odom said. "Pick up the sledgehammer and hit the rail here a couple of times—just enough to push it out."

Bates grabbed the hammer and hit it. The rail popped out. He was about to hit it a second time when Odom stopped him.

"That's far enough," he said. "Hurry, get the tools out of the way and get down out of sight."

It was less than two minutes after the men put the tools away when they first saw the train. It was approaching at about twenty miles per hour, a respectable enough speed, though the vastness of the desert made it appear as if the train was going much slower. Against the great panorama of the desert the train seemed puny, and even the smoke that poured from its stack made but a tiny scar against the orange vault of the sky at sunset.

They could hear the train quite easily now, the sound of its puffing engine carrying to them across the wide, flat ground the way sound travels across water. As the engine approached, it gave some perspective as to how large the desert really was, for the train that had appeared so tiny before was now a behemoth, blocking out the sky.

"Get ready, boys," Odom said. "It's nearly here."

"Say, how long before we reach the next town anyways?" Hayes asked. "What I need to do is, I need to get off this train and get me a beer. And maybe a bottle of whiskey, too."

"No alcoholic spirits are allowed in the express car," Kingsley said.

"Yeah? So what are you going to do about it? Go to the law? I'm the law!" Hayes said with a cackling laugh.

"No, I'm not going to the law. If you want to drink I can't stop you," Kingsley said. "But I can report you to the railroad."

"Yeah? And what will the railroad do? Tell me I'm a bad boy?" Hayes laughed out loud.

"Well, for one thing, they will see to it that you can't ride the train anymore."

"And that's supposed to mean something to me?" Hayes asked.

"It means that you'd better not consider going anywhere you can't walk or ride a horse," Kingsley said.

Matt laughed.

"What are you laughing at?" Hayes asked.

"Seems to me like Mr. Kingsley has the upper hand," Matt said.

"Yeah?" Hayes replied. Stepping over to Matt, Hayes suddenly slapped Matt in the face. "There ain't nothin' you can do about that, seein' as you're all chained up like you are." Hayes slapped Matt a second time. "Tell me, Mr. Killer, who has the upper hand now?" he asked, laughing.

Hayes was standing over Matt with his legs spread, looking down at Matt, who was still on the floor.

Matt smiled up at him.

"What are you smiling at, you son of a bitch?" Hayes asked.

"I'm about to show you who has the upper hand," Matt said. He kicked upward, and the toe of his boot caught Hayes in his most sensitive area.

"Ooof," Hayes said with an expulsion of breath and a gasp of surprise. He bent over double from the pain.

It was at that exact point in time that the engine ran across the place where the rail had been compromised. For a moment the train continued on, as if nothing had happened.

"What the hell?" Bates asked in confusion where the outlaws were hiding. "Nothin' happened! The train didn't stop!"

"Just wait," Odom said.

Less than a second later, they saw the engine quiver, then drop down on one side. The engine continued forward, but now one side was producing thrust, while the other had lost its purchase. The driver wheels, in the dirt now, continued to churn full speed, and they began throwing up a huge rooster tail of sand. There was a loud, screeching sound, as first the engine, then the tender, then the express car tumbled over on their sides. The following cars were dragged along the track with a horrendous screech of metal and then the cacophony of breaking glass and collapsing wood as they began breaking apart and falling in upon themselves.

The boiler of the engine suddenly exploded with the roar of a hundred thunderclaps. Huge pieces of heavy metal, set into motion by the explosion, were hurled high into the sky, before tumbling back down to land several feet away, each falling piece of metal adding its own sound to the terrible noise of the wreck.

Finally, the screeching, grinding, banging, crashing sound stopped, to be replaced for a moment by total silence. But the silence was quickly filled with cries of pain, shouts of anguish, and calls for help.

The explosion of the boiler had sent hundreds of burning embers of coal from the engine's firebox. Those coals had landed on the wooden passenger cars, most nearly reduced to kindling wood by the wreck, so that within seconds, the cars, many of which still had people trapped in the wreckage, caught on fire.

"Son of a bitch!" Schuler said. "That wasn't supposed to happen! I thought all that would happen was that the train would stop. I didn't know it was going to wreck."

"Yeah, well, the train did stop, though, didn't it?" Odom said. "Jesus, most of the passenger cars are on fire. Come on, let's get in the express car, get the money, and get out before it catches fire, too."

"This ain't right," Schuler said. "You never said anything about killing all these people. All you said you was goin' to do was rob a train."

"Yeah? Well, how the hell was I supposed to get it to stop? Stand in front of it and hold out my hand?"

* * *

When the train left the track, Matt felt the sudden drop of the left side of the car. He had no idea what caused it, but he knew at once that it was very bad, and he spun himself around to put his feet on the lower wall to brace himself.

The car rolled violently onto its side. It slid along the ground for several feet while, inside the car, fixtures broke loose and cargo began sliding around. The mail cabinet fell over on the express man, crushing him beneath its terrible weight. Hayes was slammed against the wall so hard that he was knocked out. Only Matt, of the three, escaped injury because he had managed to brace himself against the wall.

"Mr. Kingsley! Mr. Kingsley!" Matt called, but the express man didn't answer.

"Hayes? Hayes, are you all right?"

Hayes groaned, showing that he was still alive, though, for now, Matt had no idea as to the seriousness of his condition.

From outside, Matt could hear the wails and cries of the injured, and he wondered what had happened and how bad the wreck was. He pulled himself through the strewn wreckage of the car until he reached Hayes.

"Hayes?" he said.

Hayes was out cold, but his steady breathing told Matt that he wasn't dead.

Matt searched through Hayes's pockets until he found the key to his shackles. He was just about to unlock them when he heard someone jerking open the door.

He wasn't sure who was trying to get in to the car, but because he was in shackles, he thought it might not be a good idea to be seen. Holding on to the key, he moved away quickly, then hid behind an overturned cabinet.

He saw four men, with guns drawn, climb into the car. The fact that they were holding guns told him that they weren't here as rescuers. A closer look at one of the men confirmed that, when he saw that it was the same man he had encountered in the alley back in Wickenburg. This was Cletus Odom.

Odom, this is the second time I've met you, and I haven't liked you either time, Matt thought as he watched the men step inside the overturned car and look around.

"*Señor, hemos hecho un desorden grande,*" one of them said as he looked around the car.

"What's that, Paco? I don't speak Mex," Odom replied.

"I said, we have made a big mess," Paco repeated in English.

"What did you expect? When you wreck a train, you make a mess," Odom replied. "Let's find the safe. Schuler, get ready to blow it."

"There are women and children on this train," Schuler said. "You didn't tell me that we might be killing women and children." Schuler was slender, almost gaunt. "This ain't right. I wouldn't have come along if I'd known this was going to happen. We ought to do something to help these people."

"Are you crazy? You want to get hung? That's what's going to happen if you start trying to help anyone now. All you got to do is blow the safe so we can get the money and get out of here."

"Ain't no need to blow the safe," one of the others said. This man was the biggest of them all.

"Why not? What are you talkin' about, Bates?" Odom asked.

"The money is all in a canvas pouch. I found it." Bates said.

"Is the pouch locked?"

"Nope," Bates replied. He stuck his hand down inside and pulled out a couple of bound stacks of currency notes. "It's full of money."

"Damn, I wonder how much."

"Twenty thousand dollars," Bates answered without hesitation.

"What? How do you know that?" Odom asked.

Bates pulled out a piece of paper, then smiled at the others. "'Cause it's all been counted out for us," he said.

"Twenty thousand dollars! *Caramba*, that is a lot of money, I think," Paco said

"We're rich, boys! We're rich," Bates said happily.

"This ain't right," Schuler said, shaking his head. "There ain't none of this right!"

"Well, if you don't like it, you don't have to take your cut," Odom said. "Come on, boys, let's go."

"What—what happened?" Hayes asked, groaning, and trying to sit up.

"Shit, he's alive!" Bates said.

Drawing his gun, Odom aimed it at Hayes and fired. His bullet hit Hayes in the forehead and Hayes fell back.

"Not no more, he ain't," Odom said. "The dumb son of a bitch. All he had to do was be quiet for one more minute and he wouldn't of got hisself kilt. Come on, let's get out before somebody looks in here."

Matt waited until all four men had left the car before he moved from his hiding place. Using the key he had taken from Hayes, he unlocked his shackles. After that, he strapped on Hayes's pistol, then looked down at him.

"Like the fella said, Hayes. If you had been quiet for one more minute, you'd still be alive."

Armed and free, Matt climbed out of the car.

Chapter Eight

When Matt jumped down from the express car, he was totally unprepared for the carnage he saw. The next car after the express car was the baggage car, and the passenger car following it was telescoped into it. The next three passenger cars, while not overturned, were jackknifed, piled up onto each other, and burning. Scattered luggage and clothing created a patchwork quilt of bright colors alongside the track.

Everyone who could do so had evacuated the train. Some, who were bleeding and badly injured, had collapsed near the track. Others, not as severely wounded, were wandering around in a state of shock, as if not sure what had happened to them. There were also several bodies lying on the ground around the train, some evidently thrown from the train, others who might have staggered this far before they died.

It was even worse inside the wrecked cars. Matt could hear the cries of pain and fear from those who were still trapped.

Outside, a few of the people had begun to function

again, and they started back into the cars to pull out more of the injured.

"Get the ones out of the cars that are already burning first!" Matt yelled, taking charge only because no one else seemed to be doing so.

Leading by example, Matt moved up to the first car, which, because of its position, presented the windows at face level. Stepping up to the window and looking inside, Matt drew in a sharp breath of shock. Through the smoke that was coming out of the car, he could see seats that were wrenched from their mounts, and a floor that was running red with blood. There were bodies, and body parts, strewn about.

"Anyone here?" he called.

"Yes, I'm here," a man's voice answered.

Matt went into the car and and found a man lying on the floor, with his legs badly twisted.

"I can't walk," the man said. "Please, get me out of here."

Turning, Matt saw that a couple others had come in with him.

"Hang on," Matt said. "We're going to get you out."

He passed the passenger back to the one behind him and, making a chain of rescuers, they got the injured man safely off the train.

Leaving that car, Matt went to the next to continue the rescue operation. At the front of the car, he saw the woman and the little boy, Jerry, who had asked about his shackles. Jerry was unhurt and free to move around, but he was sitting on the floor by his mother. Matt saw, then, why Jerry hadn't left the train. The boy's mother was trapped under the seat.

Matt crawled in through the window, then worked his way through the smoke and bloody carnage until he reached the front of the car.

"Hello, Jerry," Matt said, remembering the boy's name. "How are you?"

"I'm all right, but Mama can't get up," Jerry answered.

"Ma'am, can you hear me?" Matt asked.

"Yes, I can hear you," she answered in a weak voice.

"Are you hurt?"

"I think I may have broken my arm," she replied.

"What about Suzie?"

"She's here with me," the woman answered. "We're both jammed in here and can't move. I'm worried about Suzie. She hasn't made a sound."

"Let me see what I can do."

The woman and her young daughter were wedged in between the front seat and the collapsed front wall of the car. In addition, the side wall was crushed in as well and pressing down on the seat.

Matt tried to pull the seat out, but he couldn't make it budge. Then he tried to lift the seat up, and couldn't do that either. He was not going to be able to move the seat without help, or at least without tools.

"I'll be back," he said.

"No, please, don't leave us," the woman pleaded. "The car is on fire, I don't want to burn up."

Matt squatted down, then put his hand gently, reassuringly, on her shoulder. "I have to get something that will allow me to move this seat," he said. "I'll be back, I promise."

"All right," the woman agreed reluctantly.

"I'll stay with you, Mama," Jerry said.

"No, Jerry, you get out while you can."

"I'm going to stay here until he comes back," Jerry said resolutely.

"You're a good boy, Jerry," Matt said, running his hand through the boy's hair. "I promise, I'll be back."

Leaving them, Matt crawled back out through the window, then started walking quickly alongside the wrecked train, looking for something he could use to pry up the seat. He was hoping for a piece of metal small enough for him to handle, but strong enough to do the trick, and he picked up several pieces of wreckage, discarding each one as unusable. Then he saw, lying at the bottom of the track berm, a pickax.

For a moment, he wondered how a pickax happened to be here. Then he realized, with a start, that the train robbers must've used the pickax in order to pull the spikes and spread the track, which resulted in wrecking the train. Grabbing the pickax, he retraced his path along the length of the burning train, then climbed back into the car.

"Hello?" he called.

"Thank God you're back," the woman said.

"Yes, ma'am, I told you I would come back for you," Matt replied. Once more, he moved to the front of the car until he reached the mangled seat. Putting the head of the pickax under the edge of the seat, he began working on it, putting all his strength into it. He heard metal screeching, then felt the seat beginning to give way.

"It's moving!" he said. "Hold on!"

Then, with a loud pop, the seat broke loose from its

mount and, dropping the pickax, Matt grabbed the seat and pulled it completely free. He tossed the seat aside, then reached down for the woman.

"Can you walk?" he asked as he helped her up.

"Yes," she said. She stood there with her arm held against her stomach. "There is nothing wrong with my legs, I can walk. Please, get Suzie."

Matt got down on his hands and knees and looked up under the collapsed wall. Suzie was dead, impaled by a piece of wood that had torn from the side of the car. He looked away quickly and, seeing his reaction, the woman cried out.

"No!" she said. "Oh, God, no! Is she—is she dead?"

"Yes. I'm sorry, ma'am," Matt said.

"Please, get her out for me," the woman said.

"I should get you and Jerry off the train first and see if there is someone who can take care of your arm."

"No!" the woman said. "Please!" she begged. "Get my baby for me! Get her out of there!"

Matt nodded. "All right," he said. "I'll get her for you."

Reaching back under the collapsed wall, Matt pulled out the piece of wood that had speared through her little body. Then, gently, he pulled her out.

"My baby!" the woman cried, reaching for the little girl with her good arm. Matt handed the child to her mother, then led the mother and Jerry out of the car.

One of the passengers was a doctor, and though he was bloodied and bruised, he was not seriously injured. Putting aside his own injuries, he had the impromptu rescuers bring all those who were hurt to one place so he could look after them as best he could under the circumstances.

Matt took the woman to him.

"Mrs. Dobbs," the doctor said. "I didn't know you were on the train."

"Doctor, it's Suzie," Mrs. Dobbs said.

"Let me look at her," Dr. Presnell said, reaching out to take the child from Mrs. Dobbs's arms.

"No!" Mrs. Dobbs said, twisting away from the doctor's reach. As she did, the pain in her arm caused her to wince.

"Suzie?" Dr. Presnell said. He looked at Matt, and Matt shook his head sadly.

"All right, Louise, you can hold on to your little girl," Dr. Presnell said. "But let me look at your arm."

"Mrs. Dobbs, won't you let me hold Suzie for you until Dr. Presnell has examined your arm?" Matt offered.

Mrs. Dobbs hesitated for a moment, then nodded, and gave the little girl to him.

Dr. Presnell looked at her arm, then moved it, and she cried out in pain.

"Jerry," Dr. Presnell said. "I want you to look around and find me two pieces of wood about this long," he said, indicating the length with his hands.

"All right."

"I'm going to make a splint," Dr. Presnell said. "If I can find some way to hold it in place."

"There are some items of clothing strewn about," Matt suggested. "I'll collect some of it. Maybe we can tear some of that into strips."

"Good idea," Dr. Presnell replied.

Matt started to walk away, still carrying the dead baby.

"No!" Mrs. Dobbs called. "Don't take her away from me!"

"I'll bring her right back, Mrs. Dobbs, I promise," Matt said.

"Louise, I need his help if I'm going to fix your arm," Dr. Presnell said.

Mrs. Dobbs nodded. "All right," she said.

Mrs. Dobbs did not take her eyes off Matt as he wandered around through the strewn items of clothing, all the while carrying the dead child. Finally, he found a shirt, which he ripped into strips. Then he took the strips of cloth back to the doctor. By now, Jerry had returned with several pieces of wood, gathered from the wreckage of the train.

"Good work, Jerry," Dr. Presnell said. Selecting two pieces that most suited his purpose, and using the strips of cloth Matt gave him, he made a splint. As soon as he was finished, Mrs. Dobbs reached for Suzie and, gently, Matt returned the child to her.

"People, listen to me!" Dr. Presnell shouted. "I'm a doctor! If any of you are injured, let me know! I'll do the best I can for you."

"Doc, somethin's wrong with my wife," someone said and, almost immediately on top of his comment, several others began calling out as well.

"Would you help me, young man?" Dr. Presnell asked Matt.

Matt shook his head. "I'm not a doctor."

"Maybe not," Dr. Presnell replied. "But you do have

common sense, and in a situation like this, common sense is more important than any medical degree."

Farther up the track, in Sentinel, the people who were waiting to meet the train were beginning to grow nervous. The train was already forty-five minutes late. Boomer, who was waiting to meet Doc Presnell, was listening in to the various conversations of those who were expecting people on the train. They were growing increasingly more concerned.

"Deputy Foley, have you heard anything?" an older woman asked. "My daughter is supposed to be coming in on the train and I'm growing very worried."

"Oh, I wouldn't worry that much about it, Mrs. Anderson," Boomer said, trying to ease her concerns. "The train's been late before."

"Yes, sir, I know it has. But if you go over there and look at the blackboard that has the schedule on it, you'll see that the train left Purgatory on time," Mrs. Anderson said. "It should've been here a long time ago now."

"It does seem a little odd, doesn't it?" Boomer said. "All right, I'll go talk to the station agent and see what I can find out."

"Would you? Good, I appreciate that, and I'm sure a lot of other folks will appreciate it just as much."

As several others, by their comments and nods, indicated their concurrence with Mrs. Anderson's request, Boomer went inside the depot, then walked back to the ticket cage. There, he saw the station agent standing over the telegrapher. The telegraph instrument was clacking away madly.

"Mr. Cooley?" Boomer called.

The station agent held up his hand as a signal for Boomer to be quiet for a moment, so Boomer complied.

The telegraph key stopped clacking; then the telegrapher put his own hand on the key and sent a short message back.

"Now, Deputy, what can I do for you?" Cooley asked.

"Mr. Cooley?" Boomer said again after the instrument was quiet. "All the folks here that are waitin' on the train are beginnin' to get a little worried."

"Are they, now?"

"Yes, sir, they are," Boomer replied. "And I don't mind tellin' you, I'm somewhat worried myself."

"Why are you worried, Deputy, you don't have any people on the train, do you?"

"No, sir," Boomer said. He pointed toward the platform just outside the depot. "But there's lots of folks out there who do have people, even family, and they got a right to know what's happening. And it just so happens that Doc is on that train and, Doc being a friend of mine, that gives me cause to worry as well."

Cooley sighed, then ran his hand through his hair. "I'm sorry, Boomer," he said. "I had no right to act like that. The truth is I'm worried as well."

"Has somethin' happened? I mean, that you know?"

"What I know is that we got a telegram that the train left Purgatory Station one hour and forty-seven minutes ago," Cooley said. "The normal time it takes the train to get here is just over an hour."

"You think somethin' has happened?" Boomer asked. "Or could they have just stopped somewhere?"

"There is no place to stop between here and Purgatory," Cooley said. He shook his head. "No, sir, Deputy, I'm sure something has happened."

"A wreck?"

Cooley shook his head. "I think so."

"Then you're goin' to have to tell these folks," Boomer said, pointing to the crowd out on the depot platform.

"I'm afraid to."

"Afraid to?" Boomer replied. "Why on earth would you be afraid to?"

"If there has been a train wreck, and I suspect there has been, I don't know how they are going to take it."

"Mr. Cooley, it'd be my notion that they'd rather hear the truth than stand around worryin' about it, not knowin' one way or the other."

"Would you tell them?"

"Well, yes, sir, I could, I suppose. But that's more likely somethin' the marshal should tell 'em."

"Where is the marshal?"

"He's . . ." Boomer stopped and sighed. He was sure Marshal Kyle was with Sally Fontaine, and he didn't figure that was anybody's business. "Never mind, I'll tell them."

Boomer walked out of the depot, then held up his hands and started calling for everyone's attention.

"People, people, people!" he shouted. "Can I have your attention, please?"

The several conversations stopped, not all at once, but rather in a wave of silence that moved quickly across the crowd until everyone was quiet, and looking at the man who had issued the call.

Boomer cleared his throat.

"People," he said. "The train left Purgatory on time—"

"Well, then, where is it?" someone shouted.

"Let me finish, please."

"Yes, let the deputy finish," someone else shouted.

"Like I was sayin', the train left Purgatory on time," Boomer said. "But as you can plainly see, it hasn't made it here yet. That leads us to believe that there has been a train wreck somewhere between here and Purgatory."

"A wreck?"

"What! No, my God, no!" some woman shouted.

"How bad is it? How many are hurt? Was anyone killed?"

"Hold on, hold on here," Boomer shouted, holding up his hands. "The truth is, we don't even know for sure that there was one."

"But, you just said there was."

"No, I said we believe there has been one. Given that the train ain't here yet, and it should ought to be, well, it just seems most likely that a wreck is what has happened. And of course, the next thing is, if there has been a wreck, we don't know how bad it might be."

"Is it possible there wasn't any wreck at all—that the train may have just broken down out on the road?" another asked.

Boomer turned to look at Cooley, who was standing beside him.

"What about that, Mr. Cooley?" Boomer asked. "Is

it maybe possible that the train has just broke down out on the track somewhere?"

"Yes, of course that is possible," Cooley answered.

"Well, then, maybe we don't have anything to be worried about at all," one of the men in the crowd suggested.

"It's possible, but it's not very likely," Cooley added.

"What do you mean, it's not very likely? Why not?" another asked.

Cooley sighed, giving pointed evidence that he was very uncomfortable with the situation.

"The reason I say that a simple breakdown is un-likely is because if that is what has happened, why, they have a little gadget on board that will allow them to clamp onto the telegraph wire so as to be able to send a message. Most of the time, when it's no more than a breakdown, they'll be able to get in contact with us, to let us know. But there hasn't been any such message so—I hate to say this, but I'm afraid we have to assume the worst."

"Well, I ain't waitin' around here to find out. I'm goin' out there!" one man shouted. "My wife is on that train!"

"Mr. Zimmer, if there has been a wreck, we'll need to organize a rescue party, so I hope several of us will be going out there," Boomer said. "So if you'll wait a bit, I'll go get the marshal. I expect he'll be puttin' to-gether a rescue party, and I'm sure you'll want to be a part of it."

"Yeah," Zimmer said. "Yeah, I want to go. But hurry back, will you? If there really was a train wreck, those folks out there are goin' to be needin' us to come out as quick as we can."

Marshal Kyle was lying in bed with his hands laced behind his head. Sally was lying on her side, with her head elevated and supported by her left hand. The way she was lying, with her arm crooked at the elbow, caused the bedsheet to slide down and expose both her breasts.

A small smile played across Kyle's lips.

"What?" Sally asked. "What are you laughing at?"

"Nothing."

"You're laughing at something. I can see it in your face."

Kyle turned to look at her. "I was just thinking of what a difference one day can make," he said. "Last night, I had to be satisfied with some Indian girl I saw on the trail. Now, here I am with a beautiful white woman in her own bed."

It took just a second for Kyle's words to sink in. Then, when she realized what he said, she gasped.

"What?"

Kyle started laughing.

"What Indian girl?"

Kyle laughed harder. "I'm joking."

"That's nothing to joke about!" Sally insisted, and getting up, she jerked the cover off the bed so that both were exposed.

They looked at each other for a moment, then Kyle reached for her. "On the other hand," he said, "this is no joke."

"Indian girl my foot," Sally said as she sat down on the edge of the bed, then leaned over to kiss him.

Suddenly, there was a loud knock on the door.

"Marshal? Marshal Kyle, are you in there?"

Boomer's loud words were augmented by more knocking on the door.

"Just a minute, Boomer, just a minute!" Kyle said with a frustrated sigh. He reached for his clothes. "Give me a minute."

"Yes, sir," Boomer said. "I don't mean to disturb you and Miss Sally none, but this is important."

"It damn well better be," Kyle said.

A few moments later, when both were fully dressed, Kyle walked over to sit on a settee. He nodded toward Sally as a signal that she could open the door now.

"Good evening, Boomer," Sally said as sweetly and innocently as she could muster.

"Evenin', ma'am," Boomer replied. "Is the marshal here?"

"I'm here in the parlor, Boomer," Kyle called back. "What is it? What is so all-fired important?"

"It's about the train, Marshal. Doc's train."

"What about Doc's train? Did he miss it?"

"No, sir," Boomer replied. "Well, that is, I don't know."

"No, he didn't miss it, or you don't know? Which is it?" Kyle asked, confused by the answer.

"I mean the train ain't got in yet," Boomer said.

"The train hasn't arrived?" Kyle glanced at the wall clock. The clock read five minutes until nine. "It was supposed to have arrived at seven thirty, wasn't it?"

"Yes, sir. And Mr. Cooley, he got a telegram that said the train left Purgatory Station on time. The thing is,

Marshal, it don't take but a little over an hour to get here—but the train is already an hour and a half late."

"Does Cooley know where it is? What happened to it?"

"No, sir, I don't reckon he does know," Boomer said. "There don't nobody know."

"Saddle our horses," Kyle said. "We'll ride down the track toward Purgatory and see what we can find."

"We could do that," Boomer said. "Or we could . . ." He let the sentence hang.

"We could what?"

"We could take a train. Cooley's puttin' on the switch engine, and he plans to run it back down the track toward Purgatory. If the train left Purgatory when it was supposed to, and when the folks back in Purgatory said it did, then we'll find it quicker by goin' on a train than if we was to go back ridin' horses."

"Yeah, I guess you're right," Kyle said. "Also, if there was a wreck, we'd need the train to bring the people back to Sentinel."

"Yes, sir."

"Well, come along then. No sense in wasting time here."

"No, sir, I figured you'd be wantin' to get on this right away," Boomer said. "Miss Sally, I'm sorry to be bustin' in like this, breakin' up your welcome home to Marshal Kyle 'n' all."

Sally nodded. "Don't you worry about it, Boomer, you did the right thing," she said. "If there was a train wreck, Ben needs to get out there as fast as he can."

"Yes, ma'am, that's sort of what I was thinkin', too," Boomer said.

Chapter Nine

By the time Kyle and Boomer made it back to the railroad station, they saw that a car had been attached to the little switch engine. The car was crammed full with rescuers, in the event their worst fears were realized and there was an actual train wreck. For that reason, Kyle believed there were probably as many sightseers as there were actual rescue workers on the train.

"Cooley! You need to add some more cars!" Kyle said. "At least three, and maybe more."

"What for? Ever'body that's goin' is already aboard," Cooley replied.

"What about the people we find at the train wreck?" Kyle asked. "Don't you plan on bringing them back?"

"Oh, yes," Cooley said. "Damn, I completely forgot that."

It took another five minutes for the engine to back up the switch track to find a couple more cars. Not until then was it ready to go.

As Kyle and Boomer started to board, Kyle walked up toward the engine.

"Where you goin'?" Boomer called.

"I'm going to ride up here," Kyle said.

"All right, I will, too."

"No," Kyle replied. "There won't be room for both of us. And I really think you should be back with the others to sort of keep them calm."

"Yes, sir, I reckon you're right about that."

The fireman, seeing Kyle starting to climb up in the engine, reached down to give him a hand.

"You ever been in the cab of an engine before?" he asked.

"No," Kyle said. "Just tell me where the best place is to stay out your way, and I'll go there."

"If you want to look ahead, you can stand there on the left side of the cab," the fireman said. "I'll be busy keeping the steam up, and the engineer looks out the other side."

Taking in the engine cab, Kyle saw a bar running horizontally across the cab from the left to the right.

Seeing him look at it, the engineer spoke up.

"Maybe I'd better explain some of this to you," he said. "If you know what is what, it'll help you to stay out of the way."

"Good idea," Kyle replied.

The engineer pointed to the bar that had caught Kyle's immediate attention.

"That's the throttle," he said. "You make it go by pulling it back. And this sturdy-looking ratcheted lever with a hand release—this vertical bar on the right is the Johnson bar. It controls which way the steam goes into the cylinders. Helps you to decide whether you want to go frontwards or backwards. And right next to it here, this chunky-looking brass handle sticking out to the left is the air brakes."

"Thanks for the lesson," Kyle said. "It will help me keep out of your way, I'm sure."

"All right, boys, here we go," the engineer said; then, after three long whistles, the engineer positioned the Johnson bar and opened the throttle. The train pulled out of the station. At first it was moving rather slowly, but the speed kept building and building until soon the engine was going so fast that the ground below was whizzing by in a blur.

Looking ahead, Kyle saw the track unfold out of the black void, come into the light of the gas headlamp, then slip behind them as the train hurtled through the darkness.

"How fast are we going?" Kyle shouted above the noise of the engine.

"I'd say we're doing at least forty miles per hour," the engineer replied.

"Don't you think we ought to slow down a little?"

"Why?"

"If there has been a train wreck, we may not see it in time to stop," Kyle suggested.

"Oh, damn, you're right!" the engineer said, easing off on the throttle. The train slowed gradually until they were doing no more than fifteen miles per hour.

Then, ahead in the darkness, Kyle saw the golden glow of several fires.

"There ahead!" Kyle shouted. "The fires! Do you see them?"

"Yes," the engineer said. "They were smart to light some fires."

"I hope they are fires that were lit, and not a burning train," Kyle said.

The engineer reached up to the pull cord, and the whistle let out a long, melodic, wail.

Back at the site of the train wreck, Matt worked with Dr. Presnell and the others pulling out the injured, freeing the trapped, and removing the dead. He wanted, with everything that was in him, to run away now that he had the chance. But when the train caught on fire, he knew there was no way he could leave all the people who had been so badly injured trapped in the burning wreckage.

Working with the others, he managed to get everyone out of the train, including those who had been killed on impact, so that even as the train burned down to the truck and wheel assemblies, there was no smell of burning bodies to add to the horror of the occasion.

In the distance, Matt heard the two-toned sound of a train whistle. He wasn't sure he heard it the first time, but when it sounded again, he knew exactly what it was.

"Listen, do you hear that? That's a train! They are coming for us!" someone shouted, though by now everyone had heard it and several cheered.

"We'd better get up to the track and wave it down!" someone shouted.

"Yes, get one of the lanterns and wave it," another suggested.

"They don't need to wave the train down," Matt said to Dr. Presnell, who even then was doing the best he could do toward cleaning a wound. "I'm sure the train was sent here just for us."

"I am sure as well," Dr. Presnell said. "But right now, they need to feel like they have some input into their own fate. Let them yell all they want."

"Yeah, I see what you mean, Doc," Matt said.

By now, several of the uninjured and those not seriously injured had moved up to the track, where they began waving at the oncoming train. They were shouting as well, though it was obvious that no one on board the oncoming train could hear them.

The train, now with the bell clanging, continued coming, now moving no faster than a slow walk. Finally, it screeched to a stop no more than a few feet from the compromised track.

"God help us, look at this, Marshal," Boomer said, his voice almost reverent as he and Kyle stepped down from the train, even before it had come to a complete halt. "The last three cars of the train has burned completely to the ground. Only the coal tender, the express car, and baggage car ain't burned up. I wonder how many have been killed."

"We'll figure that out later," Kyle said. "For now, we need to get busy helping those who are still alive. I just hope—"

"Marshal! There's Doc Presnell!" Boomer said excitedly, answering Kyle's concern before it was even spoken."

"Hello, Ben, Boomer," Doc Presnell said, greeting his two friends as they came toward him. Doc had a black eye and a cut on his face. Otherwise, he appeared to be all right, though there was blood on his hands and clothes. It didn't take but a moment to see that it wasn't Doc's blood—it was blood from the many injured passengers he had been working with.

"What happened, Doc?" Boomer asked.

"I'll be damned if I know," Doc replied. "One minute I was enjoying my dinner in the dining car. The next thing I know we ran off the track. Since that time, it's been all chaos."

"The prisoner!" Kyle said.

"What prisoner?" Doc asked.

"According to a telegram I received, this train was supposed to be carrying a prisoner," Kyle said. "I'd better check on him."

"Boomer, can you give me a hand here?" Doc asked.

"Sure, Doc, I'll do what I can," Boomer said.

Leaving Doc and Boomer, Kyle started looking through the gathering of shocked, frightened, and injured people until he saw someone wearing the blue jacket and hat of a railroad conductor.

"You the conductor on this train?" Kyle asked.

"Look, mister, I don't know any more about what caused the train wreck than you do," the conductor answered defensively.

"No, no, it's not about the train wreck," Kyle said quickly, holding up his hands to calm the conductor.

"Then, what is it about?"

"I understand you had a prisoner on this train, someone who was being taken to Yuma prison," Kyle said. It was a statement, not a question.

"You're talking about the murderer we picked up in Purgatory?"

"Yes. Where is he?"

"I don't know."

"Have you seen him since the train wreck?"

"I didn't see him before the wreck."

"You didn't see him when they put him on the train?"

"No. I was told he would be in the express car," the conductor said. "But I didn't see them put him on. As far as I know, Lon Kingsley is the only one who saw him."

"Lon Kingsley?"

"The express man," the conductor said.

"Can you point him out to me?"

"I can point him out, all right, but it won't do you any good to talk to him."

"Why not?"

"He's dead. Him and the deputy that was ridin' in the car with him. We found 'em both dead in the express car."

"What about the prisoner? Did you find him dead, too?"

"No, the only two people we pulled from the express car was Kingsley and the deputy," the conductor said. "They're both lyin' over there if you want to see them."

"Like you said, they're both dead, so it won't do me any good to see them, but I am going to take another look inside the express car."

Walking back toward some of the railroad officials who'd arrived with the rescue train, Kyle borrowed a lantern, crawled upon the side of the express car that was facing up, then let himself down through the open door into the car. It had not burned, but it had turned over onto its side so it was badly damaged. He moved around inside the car, having to be very careful to pick his way about, since what had been the left wall was now the floor.

"Hello?" a voice called from the open door. "Anyone in here?"

"Yes, I'm here," Kyle answered.

The person who called started to climb down into the car.

"No need to come in here, the car is empty," Kyle said.

"Who are you?"

"I'm United States Marshal Ben Kyle. And you are?"

"I'm Hodge Deckert with the United Bank Exchange," Deckert said. "We are responsible for transferring large amounts of money between banks, and we had a shipment on this train. I've come to retrieve the money."

"Good luck," Kyle said.

"Good luck? What an odd thing to say," Deckert replied as he started looking. "Oh, oh," he said after a moment. "This isn't good."

"What isn't good?"

Deckert held up a small piece of paper. "Here is the transfer document," he said. "This was in the bag with the money."

"Maybe it just fell out in the wreck," Kyle suggested.

"No," Deckert said, looking around. "I don't see the bag, and if the transfer slip just fell out in the wreck, some of the money would be here as well." Deckert sighed. "The money is gone."

"How much money are we talking about?" Kyle asked.

"Twenty thousand dollars."

"That's a lot of money."

"Yes, sir, it is. And it was on this train, which means one of these passengers had to have come in here and took it."

"Maybe," Kyle answered.

"What do you mean maybe? Who else could have done it?"

"The train was also transporting a deputy and his prisoner," Kyle said. "Both were riding in the express car. Right now, the prisoner seems to be missing."

"A deputy and his prisoner were riding in the express car? There should be only one person in this car—and that would be Mr. Kingsley, the express agent."

"I guess the railroad made an exception in this case," Kyle said.

"This is unconscionable," Deckert said. "My company shall certainly send a strongly worded message to the railroad for this breach of security."

Finding no one in the car, Kyle decided to have a look at all the bodies to see if there might be one in chains. He had the conductor point out Kingsley and Hayes. That was when he saw the small bullet hole in Hayes's forehead.

"I'll be damn," Kyle said.

"What is it?" the conductor asked.

"The deputy," Kyle replied. "He's been shot. I guess that solves the mystery as to who took the money."

* * *

The officials who were running the rescue operation broke the passengers down into three groups. Those who were not injured, or were only slightly injured, were allowed to board the train on their own. Those who were seriously injured were put into a car that was being converted into a hospital, while the last car was serving as a morgue-on-wheels.

Matt walked with Louise Dobbs as she and her son, Jerry, went to board the first car. Then one of the officials saw that the little girl Mrs. Dobbs was carrying was dead. He reached for her.

"I'll take care of her for you, ma'am," he said.

Louise jerked the little girl back and glared angrily at the railroad official. "No, she stays with me."

"She can't stay will you, madam."

"But she must!" Louise insisted. "Suzie would be terrified if she is separated from me!"

"Madam, your little girl is dead," one of the railroad officials said. "It will not matter to her whether she is with you or not."

"It matters to the lady," Matt said. "Let the girl stay with her, it can't hurt anything."

"Who are you?" the official asked.

"It doesn't matter who I am. I'm someone who knows right from wrong," Matt answered. "Let the girl stay with her mother."

"This is not railroad policy," the official said.

"How about train wrecks?" Matt asked. "Are train wrecks railroad policy?"

"No, of course not."

"Maybe not, but you had one, didn't you?"

"Sir, I fail to see how that is relevant."

"Here is what's relevant. The mother wants to keep her little girl with her," Matt said.

"What's going on here?" Kyle asked, coming up on the conversation. Then, seeing the woman holding the little girl, he took off his hat. He knew the woman, knew that she and her husband lived on a small ranch just outside Sentinel.

"Why, Mrs. Dobbs," he said. "I didn't know you were on—" It was not until that moment that he saw that the little girl was dead. He stopped in mid-sentence and paused for a moment before he resumed speaking. "Oh, no, not your little girl," he said solicitously. "Mrs. Dobbs, I'm so sorry."

"I want to keep her with me," Mrs. Dobbs said. "But he says that I can't."

"As I tried to explain to the lady, we have a car reserved for the deceased. The little girl must go in there."

"No!" Louise said, holding her baby even more tightly.

"I think you can make an exception in this case," Kyle said.

"You may be a United States marshal, but I am an agent for the Southern Pacific Railroad," the man said haughtily. "And I will inform you, Marshal, that in terms of railroad policy, I am the one who makes the decisions."

"Really?"

"Yes, really."

"You are under arrest," Kyle said.

"What?" the railroad agent gasped. "Under arrest for what?"

"For manslaughter," Kyle said. "By maintaining an unsafe railroad, you caused the death of this little girl."

"Are you insane? I had nothing to do with that!"

"You said you represent the railroad, didn't you?"

"Yes, I do."

"I hold the railroad responsible for the death of this little girl, as well as the deaths of the others who were killed. And as you are a representative of the railroad, I am putting you under arrest. Boomer, put cuffs on him."

"Wait a minute, wait a minute!" the railroad agent said. "Isn't there some way we can work this out?"

"There may be," Kyle said. "Do you have any suggestions?"

The railroad agent sighed. "Suppose I let the little girl stay with her mother."

"Then I suppose we could work something out so that you wouldn't be under arrest," Kyle said.

"That's not right, Marshal. That is pure coercion."

"Really?" Kyle said. "I don't look at it that way. I look at it as common sense."

"Very well," he said. "The woman can keep the girl."

The railroad agent's acquiescence was met with words of approval from the other passengers nearby.

Noticing that several of the other passengers had gathered around, Kyle took the opportunity to address them.

"Ladies and gentlemen, may I have your attention for a moment? I would like to ask for your assistance. I am United States Marshal Ben Kyle. We had word that this train was transporting a prisoner—a convicted murderer—to Yuma Territorial Prison for hanging. He was riding in the express car."

"Are you sayin' he ain't in there now?" one of the passengers asked.

Marshal Kyle nodded his head. "That's what I'm saying. He's gone, and the deputy who had him in custody is dead. I believe the prisoner killed the deputy who was transporting him."

"What makes you think the prisoner killed the deputy?" the passenger asked. "A lot of folks got killed in this wreck."

"Yes," Kyle said. "But how many of them were shot between the eyes?"

"You say the deputy was shot between the eyes?"

"Yes."

"You're right. That could only mean that he was killed of a pure purpose," the passenger said.

"What does this fella look like?" another passenger asked.

"I don't know," Kyle replied. "We didn't get a description of him, just his name. His name is Matt Jensen and he would've been in chains when he got on the train."

Matt glanced at the passengers. Of those who had boarded at Purgatory, only Jerry and his mother had survived. That meant they were the only ones who could identify him. He saw Jerry staring back at him.

"Marshal?" Jerry said.

Jerry's mother shushed him, then put her arm around him and pulled him to her.

"Yes, son, what is it?" Kyle asked.

Jerry looked up at his mother, and she shook her

head no. It was then obvious to Matt that she was not
going to give him away.

"I didn't see anything like that," Jerry said.

"What about the rest of you?" Kyle said to the
others. "Are you telling me that not one of you saw a
prisoner being put on board when the train was in
Purgatory?"

The uninjured passengers looked at each other and
shrugged, but no one spoke up.

"All right, folks, let's get on the train now," the railroad official said. "We have to get out of here so we
can bring up the wrecker engine to start cleaning this
mess up and getting the track open again."

"Young man," someone said to Matt, and looking
around, he saw that he had been addressed by the
doctor. "I noticed you while we were rounding up all
the injured. You seemed to know what you were
doing. I wonder if you would ride in the car of the injured with me?"

At first Matt was going to refuse, but then he decided that riding in the car with the severely injured
might actually be the best thing for him. The marshal
would, no doubt, be questioning everyone in the
other cars.

"Yes, of course," he said. "I would be glad to."

By the time the train reached Sentinel, three more
of the injured had died, including the first man Matt
had pulled from the wreckage. The three deaths
weren't due to inadequate care, but happened because the victims had been so severely injured that

even had they been in a hospital with the best of treatment, they would not have survived.

Matt found himself in a somewhat unique position now. Although he had a rather substantial bank account back in Colorado, there was absolutely no way he could access it from here. To do so would require him to write a draft, and while an exchange of telegrams between the banks could validate the check, it would also expose him as Matt Jensen, a wanted man.

Once he stepped down from the train in Sentinel, though, he saw what might be a partial solution to his problem. Some officials of the railroad had set up a table inside the depot building and there, they were giving twenty dollars to each of the passengers, explaining that it was a compensation for what they had been through.

Every cent Matt had had been taken from him when he was arrested back in Purgatory. For him the twenty dollars seemed like a godsend, but when he stepped up to the table, he was told that he would have to show his ticket to collect the money.

Matt made a show of patting himself down, then he said, "I must've lost the ticket back at the site of the train wreck."

"I'm sorry, sir, but without the ticket, we have no way of knowing you really were there," the train official said. "I hope you understand. If we didn't do that, then just anyone could come in here and claim they were on the train."

"This man was on the train, and I will vouch for him," Doc said. "Without him, I fear many more would have died than did."

The railroad official ran his hand through his hair, then sighed. "All right, Doc, if you say he was on the train, I'll take your word for it." The man gave Matt a twenty-dollar bill. "On behalf of the railroad, I wish to extend my apologies for the ordeal," he said in what had become a rote statement.

"Thanks," Matt replied. He turned to the doctor. "And thank you," he added.

"No, young man. On behalf of the passengers, I thank you." The doctor extended his hand. "You know, I never got your name. I'm Dr. Presnell."

"The name is Cavanaugh, Martin Cavanaugh," Matt said.

"It's good to meet you, Mr. Cavanaugh. If you are ever in this part of the country again, please look me up. I would love to buy you dinner sometime."

"Thank you," Matt said.

Leaving the depot, Matt started up the street toward the saloon. In a small town like Sentinel, the saloon would not only offer Matt the opportunity for a cool beer—he had worked up quite a thirst today—he might also get a line on the people who had caused the train wreck in the first place. It was not that he expected anyone here to have any additional information on the train wreck, but someone might have heard of the man named Odom. And though Matt wasn't a lawman, he had made himself a vow while holding the little girl's body in his arms. That vow was that he would go after Odom and the others who had caused this.

When Matt told Dr. Presnell that his name was Martin Cavanaugh, it had not been a complete lie.

Martin Cavanaugh was the name of Matt's father. After his parents were murdered by a ruthless gang of outlaws, young Matt Cavanaugh wound up in an orphanage. Conditions in the orphanage were as brutal as any delinquent detention home, and unwilling to take it anymore, Matt ran away. He would have died, had Smoke Jensen not found him shivering in a snowbank in the mountains. Smoke took him to his cabin and nursed him back to health.

It had been Smoke's intention to keep the boy around only until he had recovered, but Matt wound up staying with Smoke until he reached manhood. During the time Matt lived with Smoke, he became Smoke's student, learning everything from Smoke that Smoke had learned from his own mentor, a mountain man known as Preacher, many years earlier. Matt learned how to use a knife or a gun to defend himself; he learned how to survive in the wilderness, and how to track man or beast. But the most important lesson Matt learned was how to be a man of honor.

When Matt reached the age of eighteen, he felt that the time was right to go out on his own. Smoke did not have the slightest hesitancy over sending him out, because Matt had become one of the most capable young men Smoke had ever seen.

But just before Matt left, he surprised Smoke by asking permission to take Smoke's last name as his own. Smoke was not only honored by the request, he was touched, and to this day there was a bond between them that was as close as any familial bond could be.

Matt could take back the Cavanaugh name to provide

himself with some cover until he could clear himself, and that didn't bother him. What did bother him was the fact that he might have brought dishonor to the Jensen name—it mattered not that he was an innocent man, wrongly charged. The unpleasant fact was that not only was he considered an escaped murderer, he was also now being accused of robbing the train and killing Deputy Hayes.

The Ox Bow Saloon was filled with patrons when Matt stepped inside. Nearly all were talking about the train wreck, and not only about the train wreck, but also about Matt.

"Yes, sir, Marshal Kyle said this here Jensen fella not only kilt the deputy, but he stole the money that was being transferred. Twenty thousand dollars it was."

"Twenty thousand dollars? Damn, with that much money, I don't know but what I'd'a been tempted myself."

"Tempted enough to shoot a fella between the eyes in cold blood?"

"No, I don't reckon I could have done that. It would take someone who was particular mean to kill a man what had just been in a train wreck."

"I heard the marshal talkin' to Mr. Blanton over to the newspaper office. They'll have posters out on this Jensen fella soon, and there's a reward of five thousand dollars bein' put up for him."

"Ain't enough, if you ask me. Anyone that would shoot somebody in cold blood after a train wreck? Hell, that fella needs to be caught and needs to be hung."

"Yes, well, I reckon he was about to be hung anyway,

or so I understand. He was bein' took to Yuma for that very purpose. Besides which, the reward says 'Dead or Alive.'"

"Hey, you, mister," one of the customers said to Matt. "You was on the train, wasn't you?"

Was this someone who had seen him being put on the train in chains, someone who could recognize him?

"Yes, you was on the train, I recognize you," the man said.

Matt braced himself for a confrontation.

"You pulled how many out of that burning train? Ten? Fifteen? Mister, as far as I'm concerned, you're a genuine hero."

Matt relaxed.

"Folks," the speaker said to the others. "While most the rest of us was wanderin' around with our thumb up our ass wonderin' what to do, why, this here fella was doin'. Fred, whatever this fella is drinkin', I'm buyin'."

"And I'll buy the next one," another patron said.

"Thank you," Matt said, surprised by the unexpected accolades he was receiving. "But I thought I'd just have maybe one beer, then get something to eat."

"If you don't mind biscuits, bacon, gravy, and fried potatoes, you can eat here," an attractive auburn-haired woman said. "On me," she added.

"On you?"

"I'm Sally Fontaine. I own this place."

"Well, I thank you, ma'am, but it's not necessary for you to buy my supper. I can pay for it."

"I know it isn't necessary," Sally said. "But from what

I've heard about you, it would be my privilege to buy your supper."

Matt smiled. "Thank you."

"What's your name, mister?" the saloon patron who had first pointed him out asked.

"Cavanaugh. Martin Cavanaugh."

The patron lifted his beer mug, then called out loudly to the others in the saloon. "Here's to Martin Cavanaugh!"

"Martin Cavanaugh!" the others answered as one.

"Here you go, sir," Fred said, bringing Matt's supper to his table.

"Thanks," Matt said, digging into the meal, realizing this was the first time he had eaten all day. His plans to have a late breakfast in Purgatory this morning had been thwarted by a gunfight, a mockery of a trial, and then a train wreck. He ate his meal with much enthusiasm.

After his supper, Matt got into a card game. Playing very conservatively, and raising or calling only on sure hands, he doubled his money.

Leaving the saloon, he walked through the dark to the Homestead Hotel, only to learn that, due to the train wreck, there were no rooms available.

"Is there anyplace else in town that rents rooms?" he asked.

"There's Ma Baker's Boardin' House, but it's all full up as well."

"I see," Matt said. He turned to leave.

"Mister, was you on the train that had the wreck?"

"Yes, I was."

"I'll tell you what. The hotel don't rent out stalls in

the stable for sleepin', and I'm not supposed to do this, but if you want, you can bed down in the stable out back. You ought to be able to find enough clean straw to accommodate you."

"Thanks," Matt said. "I reckon I'll just take you up on that."

"It'll cost you a quarter."

"I thought the hotel didn't rent out the stalls for sleeping."

"They don't."

"Then what's the quarter for?"

"The quarter is for me for bein' willin' to take the risk," the clerk said. "I could get fired if my boss found out."

Matt chuckled, then reached down into his pocket and pulled out a quarter. "Sounds reasonable enough to me," he said.

That night, lying in one of the stalls and looking through an open window of the stable at the moon and stars that were shining so brightly above, Matt thought about this day. He had rarely had a day so filled with events. He'd spent the previous night out on the desert, ridden into town for breakfast, killed a man who was bent on killing him, stood trial, been found guilty and sentenced to hang, been put in chains and placed on a train bound for Yuma Prison, then lived through a wreck of that same train. And to make matters worse, that wreck had been purposely caused by men named Odom, Bates, Paco, and Schuler.

Matt had run across Odom before, but he had never

heard of any of the other three men. He knew their names only because he had heard them all call each other by name. He had also gotten a very good look at all of them. And while he had vowed to find them to avenge the death of the little girl he had pulled from the wreckage, he now had a new and even more important reason for finding them. If he could bring them justice, it would clear him of the murder of the deputy, and the theft of the money the train was transporting. That would still leave him wanted for the killing back in Purgatory, but he believed that a legitimate trial would settle that issue for him.

Matt picked up a piece of straw from his bed, smelled it to make certain it was clean, then stuck it in his mouth. As he sucked on the straw, he contemplated the path he had just laid out. It would be difficult at best. But for a man without money, and without a horse, it would be almost impossible.

His first order of business would have to be to get his horse and saddle back. He had money hidden in the saddle, and it was hidden so well that he would bet that, if he could recover the saddle, the money would still be there.

Chapter Ten

Joe Claibie worked as a hostler for the Maricopa Coach Line. But he also dealt in horses, sometimes buying horses from the stage line and reselling them. He was an honest man in his dealings, marking them up only enough to make a decent profit. But like many who worked with horses, there was always that dream that someday he might find a really great horse at a bargain price.

Although it didn't seem likely that he would find such a horse at a marshal's auction, he kept his eye on the horses that Marshal Cummins had confiscated from his prisoners. By law, Cummins was required to hold an auction, selling off each confiscated horse to the highest bidder. The money would then go into the Purgatory city coffers.

At first glance, it might seem unusual to realize that most of the auctioned property was bought by the marshal himself. But then, when one realized that the marshal had a habit of setting the "marshal's auction sales" at odd times and in odd locations, it was easy to understand how that might happen.

The marshal had recently confiscated a particularly good-looking sorrel from the man who killed Deputy Gillis, and would be holding an auction soon. Claibie intended to take a look at the horse and if it looked good to him, he would make it a point to find out when, and where, the auction was to be held.

"I heard that the marshal confiscated the horse from the fella that shot Gillis," Claiborn said to Deputy Jackson.

"It's 'Deputy' Gillis," Jackson said resolutely. "And he wasn't just shot, he was murdered in cold blood."

"Yes, well, I'm not sayin' otherwise," Claibie replied. "I'm just askin' about the horse. Is it true that the marshal confiscated the man's horse and is goin' to hold an auction?"

"Yeah, that's true, but I don't know when the auction will be," Jackson said. "It'll be announced in the paper, same as it always is."

"Where's the horse now?"

"It's where the marshal keeps all his horses, down to the city corral," Jackson said.

"I think I'll walk down there and take a look at him," Claibie said.

"Look out! Look out!"

Claibie heard the warning shout as he was approaching the corral and looking toward the commotion, he saw Kenny Watson, the young stable hand who worked for the city corral, on the ground. The horse rearing over the stable hand was now in the rampant position, and as it came back down, its slashing forelegs barely missed Kenny, who had to roll across the ground to get away from the horse. The horse reared again, but by now Kenny had rolled against a water trough. In this position, there was nowhere he could go to get away from the flailing stallion.

Without a second thought, Claibie grabbed a saddle blanket from the top rail of the fence, then vaulted over and hurried toward the horse, shouting and waving the blanket. Seeing Claibie and the flapping blanket, the horse stopped his attack against Kenny and came toward this new irritant.

"Kenny, get out of here while I keep him busy!" Claibie shouted to the young stable hand.

Kenny crawled and scrambled toward the fence, where he was helped up and over by eager hands.

Using the blanket as a bullfighter would a cape, Claibie managed to entice the horse into one, errant pass. The horse corrected himself and reared again, this time coming right at Claibie. At the last minute, Claibie jumped to one side, tossing his blanket at the horse as he did so. The blanket landed on the horse's head, temporarily blinding him.

Now the creature reared and whinnied, kicking at the air in rage, as Claibie managed to make it back to the fence. The same hands who had helped Kenny out of the corral, now reached down to pull Claibie up and over the fence. He had barely made it when the horse tossed the blanket off. Then, looking around and seeing that his would-be victims were gone, the horse shook his head, blew, and then trotted back toward the other side of the corral as docilely as if nothing had happened.

"Thanks, Claibie," Kenny said as he dusted himself off.

"Boy, what the hell did you do to get that horse so mad at you?" Claibie asked.

"I didn't do nothin' except try to ride him," Kenny replied. "I don't know what got into that crazy horse."

"He's high-spirited all right," Claibie agreed. "Is this the horse Marshal Cummins is goin' to put up for auction?"

"Yeah," Kenny said. "Though why anyone would want this horse is beyond me."

Claibie looked at the sorrel, which was now prancing around the corral, lifting its legs high in an excess of energy and tossing its head.

"I'll say this for him," Claibie said. "He's a good-looking horse."

"Bein' a pretty horse ain't good enough if he tries to take your head off ever' time you ride him."

Claibie chuckled. "You've got a point there," he said.

"I don't understand the problem, though. The man that shot Deputy Gillis must've been ridin' him," Kenny said. "Or else, how would the marshal've got ahold of him?"

"Could be this is a one-man horse," Claibie said.

"A one-man horse?"

"There are such horses, horses that are trained so that only one person can ride them," Claibie said.

"That don't make no sense to me," Kenny said. "No, sir, that don't make no sense a'tall. Why would anyone want to train a horse that way? You make him a one-man horse, that means you can never sell him."

"It also means nobody can steal him," Claibie said. "And when someone gets a horse like this one, well, I reckon the natural tendency is to want to hold on to him. And you can do that by training him so that only you can ride him."

"You've worked with horses all your life, Claibie. You ever seen any other horses like this? I mean, trained so's that only one person could ride 'em?"

"Oh, yes, I've seen them," Claibie said.

"Well, can that ever change? I mean, you take this horse. You think this horse can ever be rode?" Kenny asked.

Claibie looked at the horse. The sorrel was now standing on the opposite side of the corral, looking back toward Claibie and Kenny.

"Yeah, I think it could be rode. By the right person anyway." Claibie laughed.

"What's so funny?"

"The marshal isn't the right person."

"Think he'll be able to sell him?" Kenny asked.

"Well, not at the auction, since if it goes true to form, he'll have the auction in the middle of the night, when no one is there to bid against him. What happens afterward is anybody's guess. Kenny, do me a favor."

"What's that?"

"Don't tell the marshal that this is a one-man horse."

Kenny looked confused for a moment. Then he burst out laughing. "All right," he agreed. "I won't say a word. But I sure plan to sneak me a peek first time Marshal Cummins tries to mount this critter. Yes, sir, that's goin' to be a sight to see."

* * *

The reaction of any ordinary man who had, by circumstances, escaped the sentence of death by hanging would be not to return to the town that had handed down his sentence. But Matt Jensen was no ordinary man. Matt Jensen was a man with a mission. He planned to clear his name, and avenge the killing of an innocent little girl—not necessarily in that order.

To do this, Matt needed a horse, and the horse he wanted was Spirit, but Spirit was back in Purgatory.

"I can sell you a ticket to Purgatory if you don't mind ridin' up on the seat with the driver," the ticket agent told Matt the next morning when he went to the stage depot to inquire about passage to Purgatory. "The thing is, you see, with the railroad between here 'n' Purgatory still out, why, we're runnin' twice as many trips as normal, and ever' one of 'em is full."

"I don't mind riding with the driver," Matt said.

"Truth to tell, Mr. Cavanaugh, the ride is better up there anyhow," the agent said as he handed Matt the ticket.

"Yes, I've ridden there before," Matt said.

Matt took a seat in the waiting room, then watched as two others attempted to buy a ticket on the next stage, only to be turned away because the coach was full.

All the other passengers on the stage had come to Sentinel by the eastbound train. In Sentinel, they learned that they would have to leave the train, and continue by coach for the next thirty-six miles, before they could reboard an eastbound train at Purgatory.

"This is no way to treat customers," one of the waiting passengers said. "I intend to write a strongly worded letter to the president of the Southern Pacific, expressing my displeasure."

"The railroad doesn't care," another said. "To them, we are just tickets. They have no concern over the disruption they are causing."

"They can be that way because they have no competition. If another railroad were to be built, believe me, I would take it."

Matt thought of the injured and dead he had seen lying alongside the wrecked train, and he wanted to suggest to these complaining blowhards that they had no idea what had really caused the disruption. Instead, he just stood up and walked outside to get a breath of fresh air.

Outside, he saw a young man nailing a poster onto the wall of the stagecoach depot.

WANTED

Matt Jensen

for MURDER and TRAIN ROBBERY

$5,000 REWARD
DEAD or ALIVE

Contact U. S. Marshal Ben Kyle, Yuma, A. T.

"Whoowee, wouldn't I like to run across that fella?" someone said from behind Matt. Turning, he saw a short man with a gray beard and hair. The man spit out a stream of tobacco juice, then rubbed his mouth with the back of his hand.

"I don't know," Matt said. "If he's a murderer, I'm not sure he's the kind of person you would want to meet."

"Sonny, for five thousand dollars, I'd take a chance. Would you be Mr. Cavanaugh?"

"Yes," Matt said. Turning, he saw an older man with a head of white hair and a full, white beard.

"I'm Gabby Martin," the bearded man said. "I'll be drivin' the stage today. I'm told you'll be ridin' alongside me."

"Yes, I will, if you don't mind."

"I don't mind at all. It's a six-hour trip to Purgatory, and it gets awful lonely up there by myself with nobody to talk to." Gabby chuckled. "And it ain't for nothin' that they call me Gabby, if you get my meanin'."

"I don't mind a little conversation on a long trip," Matt replied.

"Well, good for you, good for you," Gabby said. "I reckon that'll make this run just real pleasant."

A few minutes later, a stagecoach drew up in front of the depot. The coach was weather-worn and the name on the door, MARICOPA COACH COMPANY, was so dim that it could scarcely be read.

Gabby chuckled. "I'll be damn. I thought they had put this one in the barn forever," he said. "I reckon, what with the railroad out 'n' all, that Mr. Teasedale had to round up everything that rolls."

The driver who had brought the stage around was a young man, and he set the brakes, then tied off the reins before he climbed down.

"Here you go, Mr. Martin," the young man said. "It's all ready for you."

"Tell me, Johnny, do you think this old junk heap will make it all the way to Purgatory?" Gabby asked, only half-teasing.

"Oh, yes, sir, I don't think you'll have any trouble a'tall," Johnny said. "You might remember that the right rear wheel had a flattened axle, but I packed it real good with a lot of grease. It should hold up just fine."

Gabby stepped back to look at the wheel in question. A crown of black grease oozed out from the wheel hub. He grabbed the top of the wheel rim and pulled and pushed it a couple of times to examine the play in the wheel.

"If that wheel comes off on me, Johnny, when I get back here I'm goin' to come down on you like flies on a cow turd."

Johnny laughed. "Trust me, it'll be fine."

"Ha! The last time someone said 'Trust me,' she wound up givin' me a case of the pox," Gabby said. "But, I reckon I got no choice but to trust you." He looked at Matt. "What do you say, sonny? You willin' to take a chance?"

"I'm willing," Matt replied.

"I figured you would be. But I'd appreciate it if you didn't say nothin' to the other passengers about that wheel."

"I won't say a word," Matt promised.

"All right, Johnny, let's get the luggage loaded, then you can tell the folks in there we're ready to go."

The luggage was brought out onto the porch, then loaded into the boot, though there was so much that several pieces had to be put on the roof. Gabby and Johnny spent about five minutes loading and securing the luggage. Then Gabby climbed up into the driver's seat.

"Come on up, sonny," Gabby called down to Matt. "Soon as the others get loaded, we'll get under way."

The road ran parallel with the Southern Pacific Railroad tracks, and about two hours after they left Sentinel, they passed the burnt-out, smashed, and strewn cars from the wreck. A huge, rail-mounted lifting crane was on the scene as a railroad work crew went about the business of repairing the railroad and cleaning up the mess.

"That must've been some wreck," Gabby said.

"It was."

Gabby looked over at Matt. "Was you in it?"

"Yes."

"Well, I'll be. All this time we've been talkin', and you ain't said nothin' about bein' in the wreck."

Matt laughed. "Gabby, if you'll excuse me for saying so, all this time *you've* been talking."

Gabby laughed. "Well, I guess you got me on that one, sonny," he said. "It weren't for nothin' that I come by this moniker Gabby. So you was in that train wreck, was you?"

"Yes."

"I figured it was pretty bad, what with all the bodies

and the injured that was brought into town and all. I guess I just didn't have me any idee of what it actual looked like."

"Maybe, seeing the train wreck, the complainers down inside will understand why they are being inconvenienced," Matt suggested.

"Ha, don't count on it," Gabby said. "Folks like that would complain if you hung 'em with a new rope."

Matt chuckled, though as he had been on his way to being hanged, the joke hit a little closer to home than he would have wanted.

"Gabby, have you ever heard of an outlaw named Cletus Odom?"

"I hope to smile I've heard of him. Why are you asking about him? Don't tell me you are a bounty hunter, lookin' to claim the reward on him."

"No, I just heard the name and I was wondering about him, that's all," Matt said. "Why, is there a reward on him?"

"Oh, yeah, there's a reward on him all right. Five thousand dollars it is, same as what's on this Jensen fella. But whoever goes after it will have to earn it, because I'll tell you this about him. He may be just about the meanest son of a bitch that ever drawed a breath. He robbed a coach once, then shot ever' man, woman, and child so's nobody could identify him. Only one of the women lived long enough to tell the law who did it, which is how come we know who it was."

"That was a brave woman," Matt said.

"Yes, sir, she was that."

"This man, Cletus Odom," Matt continued. "Would

he be the kind of man that would wreck a train just to rob it?"

"Hell, yes," Gabby said. "He'd do that in a heartbeat. And to tell you the truth, if we didn't know for sure that this here Matt Jensen fella wrecked the train, I would'a bet a dollar to a doughnut that Odom did it."

"How do we know that Matt Jensen did it?"

"How do we know? 'Cause Marshal Kyle said he done it."

"And you believe everything Kyle says?"

"Well, Ben Kyle is a good man," Gabby said. "He ain't given much to lies and such. So, if he said Jensen done it, then I reckon I have to go along with that."

"How do you think he did it?"

"There's prob'ly lots of ways he could'a done it. He could'a shot the engineer and fireman, so there was nobody to run the train. And it if was goin' too fast around a curve, well, you could see what would happen."

"But why would he have done such a thing?"

"Well, if he stole the money, then he prob'ly wrecked the train just to cause a lot of confusion so's he could get away."

"You seem to have it all worked out," Matt said.

Gabby chuckled. "Yes, sir. Well, truth to tell, though I ain't never done nothin' like that, from time to time I like to plan things out. Sort of a hobby, you might say."

"I see."

"But now, don't go gettin' me wrong," Gabby said. "They ain't no way on God's green earth I'd ever actual do somethin' like that."

"Getting back to Cletus Odom," Matt said. "Do you know much about him?"

"You sure are askin' a lot of questions," Gabby said.

Matt chuckled. "Well, I tell you, Gabby, you like to talk, so I figured I would just see to it that you talk about something I'm interested in."

Gabby guffawed. "You got me there, sonny," he said. "Yes, sir, you really did. Well, let's see, what do I know about Cletus Odom?"

Gabby spit a wad of tobacco, which hit the top of the wheel, then rolled under with the progress of the stage. He wiped his mouth with the back of his hand.

"Cletus Odom," he said again. "All right, sonny, you just sit there and listen, and I'll tell you about Cletus Odom.

"At one time, Cletus Odom was on the right side of the law. Leastwise, you could say that. He was a bounty hunter, you see, but he was the kind who would rather bring in dead quarry than live prisoners. He always made the claim that he didn't have no choice, that he was only defendin' himself. Even then, there was folks that didn't like him, but then he done somethin' that put him on the wrong side of the law for good."

Gabby pulled out a twist of chewing tobacco, offered it to Matt, who declined, then bit off a big chew. He worked the chew down somewhat before he continued his tale.

"Seems there was a couple of cowboys named Evans and McCoy. They rode for the Rocking J. That's a spread about ten miles south of Sentinel. I know'd 'em both, they was good boys—a little rambunctious at times, if you know what I mean. But all in all they was good boys.

"Well, sir, after a drive one day—wan't that much of a drive, all they done was just bring some cows into town from the ranch in order to ship 'em out on the railroad. Then, after they got the cows loaded and drawed their pay, they went into the Ox Bow and started drinkin'.

"Turns out that Odom was in the saloon, too, and he was causin' trouble for this little ole' gal that Evans liked. I mean, she was a whore, there was no gettin' around that, but Evans was sweet on her. Anyhow, when he seen Odom slap her, he walked over and knocked Odom down."

Gabby spit out a stream of tobacco, then wiped his mouth with the back of his hand before he continued the story.

"Well, sir, Odom, he didn't like that much. No, sir, he didn't like that none at all. So he got to eggin' Evans and McCoy on, callin' 'em cowards and other things that no man could take and still call hisself a man. Then, Evans and McCoy pulled iron agin' Odom. And that was their mistake."

"He killed them?"

"He kilt both of 'em, deader'n a doornail," Gabby said. "There was an inquest, but it was ruled self-defense, bein' as a lot of people seen that Evans and McCoy drawed first. 'Course nobody felt good about it, what with Odom eggin' 'em on like he done. So whatever support Odom might have had for bringin' in outlaws was sort of used up that day."

"If he was found not guilty, why is there a reward out for him?" Matt asked.

"Well, sir, like I said, Odom didn't have many friends left after he kilt them two cowboys. Then, not long after that, he kilt a man and brung him in for the reward. Onliest thing is, they had already pulled the paper on the feller he brought in, when they found out that he wasn't guilty. Besides which, the reward didn't say nothin' about 'dead or alive' in the first place. They tried Odom again, an' this time they found him guilty of murder, but he escaped and went on the outlaw trail."

"What about the men who ride with him?" Matt asked. "A Mexican named Paco. A big man named Bates and someone named Schuler."

"They're all ridin' with Odom?" Gabby asked.

"So I've heard," Matt answered, not wanting to give away how he actually knew.

"I'll be damn. I didn't know that. Well, I can tell you about two of them fellers," Gabby said. "Bates, the big fella, is a mean son of a bitch, all right. Word is, he once beat a miner to death with his bare hands. The Mexican, I don't know nothin' about. I ain't never heard of him. But the other fella would be Moses Schuler. Me 'n' Moses Schuler was friends once. He didn't start out to be an outlaw, but I don't doubt that he's rid down that trail by now."

"What sent him that way?"

"Whiskey, I reckon. Once whiskey gets aholt of a man, it don't let him go."

"You say the two of you were friends?"

"Yes, sir. Moses was a powder monkey with the

Cross Point Mine. He was a good one, too. Why, he could shave off shale as easy as cuttin' butter. But that's a dangerous job and Schuler started drinkin' a bit, just to settle his nerves, you understand. Only, he drank too much once, and he double-loaded a shoot. Instead of carving off a little bit of shale, it caused a mine cave-in. There was nine men kilt in that cave-in.

"Moses was never the same after that. He started drinkin' more and workin' less until he was fired. I heard tell that he blew a safe during a bank robbery down in Tucson, but don't nobody know that for sure. You say he's workin' with Odom now?"

"Yes, or so I've heard," Matt said.

"That's too bad. Moses may not be dependable, and maybe he's even stole a few things. But I don't think he would ever kill anyone, not with how he was so upset over the accident in the mine."

"How long since you've seen him?" Matt asked.

"How long? Lord 'a mercy, I'm not sure how long it's been," Gabby said. "I'd make it three years or more."

"So he could be riding with Cletus Odom now and you would never know it," Matt suggested.

Gabby spit out another stream of tobacco juice, then nodded. "You got me there, sonny, you got me there," he said.

"Sorry I was the one who had to tell you about your friend," Matt said.

"Don't worry about it. I reckon I would have found out soon enough anyway. Ah, there's the relay station just ahead. We'll grab a bite to eat here, change teams, then be on our way. Oh, and while I'm looking after the teams, would you mind givin' this to Rittenhouse over there?" Gabby asked. "The marshal wants these posted everywhere."

Gabby gave Matt one of the wanted posters he had seen tacked up earlier.

"Sure," Matt said. "I'd be glad to."

Chapter Eleven

As the coach rolled into the station, Gabby hauled back on the reins and set the brake. With the stage at a standstill, the little cloud of dust that had been following them now rolled by them, and Matt heard some of the passengers coughing below.

Gabby chuckled. "You're better off up here," he said. "That dust really gets inside down there."

"I know. I've ridden shotgun guard a few times in my life."

"I figured you probably knew your way around a stagecoach," Gabby said. He climbed down and yelled at the passengers in the stage. "Folks, we'll be here for half an hour. Stretch your legs, take care of your needs, maybe grab some lunch. Miz Rittenhouse runs the kitchen here, and she makes some mighty fine chicken 'n' dumplin's."

"Chicken and dumplings?" one of the men said. "My God, the driver actually said that as if we could possibly find such pedestrian fare appealing."

Matt climbed down as well, listening to the continuing

complaints of the two men who, it would appear, were trying to outdo each other. He was glad he wasn't riding down in the box.

While the others went inside, Matt walked over to a couple of men who were standing near the corral.

"Yes, sir, what can I do for you?" the older of the two men asked.

"Are you Rittenhouse? Gabby asked me to give this to you," Matt said, showing him the poster.

The man looked at it for a moment, then whistled. "Five thousand dollars? That's a lot of money."

"Yes, it is," Matt agreed.

"Damn. No picture? No description? How's anyone supposed to find this fella?" the relay manager asked.

"You've got me," Matt replied.

Rittenhouse turned to the young man to continue the conversation they were having when Matt had walked up.

"So, you are telling me that you are not going to take that string of horses for me?"

"I can't, Mr. Rittenhouse," the young man said. "Ma says Cindy is goin' to have the baby just anytime now, and I wouldn't want it to come while I was off pushin' horses."

"Damnit, Jimmy, I've got to get that string to Purgatory," Rittenhouse said. "Now, suppose you just tell me how the hell I'm goin' to do that."

"I'll take them for you," Matt said.

Rittenhouse looked at Matt. "I beg your pardon?"

"You have a string of horses you want to take to Purgatory, I'm going to Purgatory, I'll take them for you.

But you'll have to loan me a horse and saddle, I got here on the stage."

"Mister, I don't know anything about you," Rittenhouse said. "How do you expect me to trust you with a string of horses?"

Matt smiled. "I guess you'll just have trust your instinct," he said.

"What's your name?"

"Cavanaugh," Matt answered. "Martin Cavanaugh."

"Cavanaugh? Martin Cavanaugh?" Rittenhouse shook his head. "I know'd me a Martin Cavanaugh oncet. He was a good man, too. A hell of a good man. Cap'n Martin Cavanaugh it was. I served with him durin' the war."

"My pa was a captain in the army during the war," Matt said.

"Your pa, huh?"

"Yes, sir."

"Well, I don't reckon there's much a chance it'd be the same man or nothin' like that," Rittenhouse said. "But just 'cause I'm curious, what outfit was your pa in?"

"Pa started with the First Regiment of the Kansas Militia," Matt said. "But he was wounded, and after that, he became adjutant to General Cox of the Twenty-third Army of Ohio."

Rittenhouse broke into a big smile. "I'll be damn! Yes, sir, that's him! That's the same Cap'n Cavanaugh I was talkin' about!" he said. He stuck his hand out. "Any son of Cap'n Cavanaugh is all right in my book. Are you sure you'd like to take the string on into Purgatory?"

"I'd be glad to," Matt said.

"All I can pay is ten dollars."

"Ten dollars will be fine," Matt replied. "Like I said, I'm going there anyway."

"Jimmy?"

"Yes, sir, Mr. Rittenhouse?"

"Cap'n Cavanaugh was one of the finest officers I ever run across. And his son just saved your job by agreein' to take the horses. You owe him a word of thanks."

"Yes, sir, I do," Jimmy said. "Thank you, Mr. Cavanaugh. I hope you understand, if it weren't for Cindy about to whelp, I'd'a been glad to go."

"I understand," Matt said. "You give your wife my best."

"Yes, sir, I will."

"You owe him a bit more than thanks," Rittenhouse said. "Saddle up Rhoda for him. And get them horses on a line. But before you do all that, get this posted." He handed Jimmy the dodger on Matt.

"Yes, sir," Jimmy said, taking the flyer in his hand.

"You can come on in and have some lunch while Jimmy's getting ever'thing ready for you," Rittenhouse said.

"Thanks, but if it's all the same to you, I'd just as soon get started right away," Matt said.

"I understand. All right, I'll just go in and get your money."

"I appreciate that."

As Rittenhouse walked toward the relay station, Matt watched Jimmy tack up the poster on the wall of the barn. There were several other posters there as well, so Matt walked over to have a look at them as Jimmy got the horses ready. It didn't take him long to find the one he was looking for.

WANTED
DEAD or ALIVE
for MURDER and ROBBERY
CLETUS ODOM
Reward of $1,500

Unlike the wanted poster for Matt Jensen, this reward poster did have a picture of Odom. It was a woodcut, but evidently taken from an actual photograph, because Matt saw a striking resemblance between the picture and the man he had seen robbing the train.

Looking around to make certain he wasn't being observed, Matt tore the dodger down from the gray, weathered plank siding of the barn, and stuck it in his pocket. He was standing at the fence with his arms folded on the top rail when Rittenhouse came back. He handed Matt a ten-dollar bill and a brown paper bag.

"I know you said you didn't plan to eat, but there's some fresh baked bread and ham in the sack. I thought you could gnaw on it a bit while you were on the trail."

"Thanks, Mr. Rittenhouse. I appreciate that."

"No problem," Rittenhouse said. "Say, whatever happened to your pa anyway? I never heard from him again after we was all mustered out. Course, him bein' an officer and me just a private, I didn't expect to. But I have wondered about him from time to time."

"My father died some years ago," Matt said.

"Oh, that's too bad."

Matt didn't elaborate, though he could have said that his father hadn't just died, he had been killed. He could also have gone on to say that he himself had personally killed, or watched the hanging of, everyone who had been involved in one way or another with the murder of his father, mother, and sister.

"It was a long time ago," Matt said.

"Yes, and as they say, time heals all wounds," Rittenhouse said.

At that moment, Jimmy came out, riding a saddled horse, while holding on to a line which six other horses were attached to. He swung down from the horse, then handed the reins to Matt.

"I'll hold the string until you're good mounted," Jimmy offered.

"Thanks."

Matt hopped up into the saddle, then reached down for the string. Jimmy handed it up to him.

"Don't run 'em too hard because it may be they'll have to take out a coach first thing in the morning."

"I'll take care of 'em."

"You should arrive just before dark. Go right to the relay station. They'll be lookin' for them and they'll no doubt meet you when you get there."

Matt nodded, then reached down into the sack to pull out a sandwich. He took a bite, waved at Rittenhouse and Jimmy, then, slapping his legs against the side of his mount, rode out of the station.

* * *

When Odom, Paco, Bates, and Schuler reached the little town of Quigotoa, they stopped in front of the saloon.

"Ha!" Bates said as he dismounted. "I'm goin' to get me a whole bottle of whiskey and a woman. No, two women. I ain't never in my life been able to do nothin' like that before."

"You ain't goin' to do it now neither," Odom said.

"What do you mean, I ain't?" Bates replied. "I got my share of the money comin' to me, don't I?"

"Yes, and we'll make the split here," Odom said. "But then we are goin' to go on our separate ways before we start spendin' any of it. We won't be spendin' any of it here in this town. "

"That don't make sense," Bates said. " Why not spend money here? It's our money now, ain't it? So what's the problem?"

"Think about it, Bates," Odom said. "If the four of us come into a little place like this, then suddenly start spending money like it was water, don't you think some people might get a little suspicious?"

"Hell, I don't care whether they get suspicious or not," Bates said. "What difference does it make?"

"It makes a difference to me," Odom said. "Like I say, we'll split the money here, but you ain't goin' to start spendin' it till we all go our separate ways. Once we do that, you're on your own, and you can do any damn thing you want."

"*Sí, señor,* I believe that is the smart thing to do," Paco said.

"See, even Paco agrees with me," Odom said.

"Paco's a damn Mexican," Bates replied. "What the hell do I care what a damn Mexican has to say about anything? What about you, Schuler?"

"I need a drink," Schuler replied.

"Ha, I ain't never seen you when you didn't need a drink," Bates teased.

The four men stepped into the saloon and looked around. It was nearly empty.

"What the hell?" Bates said. "Is this here saloon open?"

"*Sí*, we are open," the Mexican bartender replied.

"How come there ain't hardly nobody here?"

"It's nine o'clock in the morning, Señor," the bartender said. "We don't get busy until afternoon."

"Whiskey," Schuler said.

"We have tequila and beer."

"Tequila."

"And breakfast," Odom added. "You serve breakfast in here?"

"*Sí, señor,* bacon, eggs, beans, tortillas," the bartender answered.

"That'll do," Odom said. "We'll be there in the back." He pointed to the table that was the most distant from the bar.

When the four men took their seat at the back of the room, Odom put the canvas bag on the table.

"All right," he said. "If this bag has twenty thousand dollars, that is eight thousand for me, and four thousand for each of you."

"Señor, how is it that you get twice as much as we get?" Paco asked.

"Because I am twice as smart," Odom answered, glaring at Paco. "You should be glad I agreed to let you come with us in the first place."

"Paco, we agreed going into this that Odom would get the most money," Bates said.

"I did not agree," Paco said.

"Then I agreed for you," Bates replied.

Paco glared at Bates for a moment, then looked over at Schuler. "How much money is he getting?"

"He is getting four thousand, same as the rest of us," Bates replied.

Why should he get as much money as we are getting? He did nothing. *Estaba borracho todo el tiempo.*"

"What did you say?" Bates asked.

"I said he was drunk the whole time. We did not need him to plant explosives on the safe. He did not earn his way."

"He gets his cut," Odom said, ending the discussion as he counted out the money, eight thousand dollars for himself, then four thousand each for Bates, Paco, and Schuler.

"Here you go, boys," he said. "Don' t spend it all in the same place." He laughed at his own joke.

Chapter Twelve

The stagecoach depot and corral of horses were on the west end of Purgatory. That was good for Matt, because it meant he could deliver the string of horses without having to ride all the way into town and take a chance on being recognized. However, being seen in town wasn't as risky as it might appear to be, because his trial had been held within an hour of the shooting. The trial had not taken place in a courthouse, nor even a city building. Instead, the trial was held in a saloon—the Pair O Dice Saloon—and the jury was made up entirely of saloon patrons, most of whom were drunk. That meant that there were very few of the town's citizens who had actually had the opportunity to see him. He could probably walk the streets without fear of being recognized.

The depot was small and unpainted, except for a sign that read: MARICOPA COACH COMPANY. At the side of the building was a fenced-in corral, and at the rear of the corral, a large barn that was badly in need of painting.

Matt pulled his horse to a halt, dismounted, then tied his mount off before he started tending to the string of eight horses he had brought with him. A man about Matt's age came out of the barn and started walking across the corral, picking his way carefully between deposits of "horse apples." He had on an apron and was using it to wipe his hands as he came up to the fence.

"The name is Joe Claibie," he said. "And you might be?"

"Cavanaugh," Matt said. "Martin Cavanaugh."

"What can I do for you, Mr. Cavanaugh?"

"Actually, I suppose it's what I can do for you," Matt replied. "I've brought you this string of replacement horses for the stage line."

"I thought that might be it," the affable young man said. "You working for Rittenhouse now, are you?"

"Temporarily," Matt answered.

"Temporarily? What do you mean, temporarily?"

"I mean I'm not working for Mr. Rittenhouse full time. He just hired me to deliver this string for him."

"Well, you must've done a pretty good job at it," Claibie said. "I see you got them all here in one piece." He laughed at his joke. "You've already been paid, right? I mean, we don't owe you anything?"

"Not a thing," Matt said.

"Good." The hostler smiled. "You're a good man, Mr. Cavanaugh. You'd be surprised at the number of people who would try and get paid twice."

"I imagine there are a few like that," Matt said. He ran his hand across the bare back of the horse he had been riding. "This horse belongs to you as well."

"It does?" Claibie replied in surprise.

"Yes, Mr. Rittenhouse loaned it to me so I could bring over the string."

"Just a minute," Claibie said. "Let me get a closer look." He made a thorough examination of the horse, then smiled. "I'll be damn. You say Rittenhouse loaned you this horse himself?"

"Yes. Why, is there something wrong?"

"No, no, nothing wrong," Claibie replied quickly. "I tell you, Mr. Cavanaugh. You must've done somethin' to impress him, because this is Blue, and Ole' Man Rittenhouse don't let just anybody ride him."

"Blue is a good horse," Matt said

"You're needin' a horse, are you?" Claibie asked.

Matt nodded. "Yes. Do you have one for sale?"

"Not exactly," Claibe said. "I thought I was going to get one, I showed up at the marshal's auction last night, but the marshal outbid me."

"Marshal's auction?"

"Yes. You see, by law, whenever the city marshal confiscates a horse, like say from an outlaw that's goin' to prison, he is required to hold an auction to sell it off. But lots of times he'll keep news of the auction so quiet that nobody shows up. Then the marshal can buy 'em real cheap."

"Is that a fact?"

"Yep. The marshal's damn smart, he is," the hostler said. "He has purt' nigh become rich by buyin' horses for a dollar, then sellin' 'em for seventy-five to a hunnert dollars. He's got one for sale now, a fine sorrel with a bright, reddish-brown coat. That's the horse I was biddin' on but, like I say, the marshal outbid me." Claibie stroked his chin. "Truth to tell, with this marshal, I don't know if he actually paid the money he bid anyway. There's no way of checking since he was buyin' the horse from his ownself, so to speak." Claibie laughed. "He may have stepped in it, though."

"What do you mean?"

"Hell, Mr. Cavanaugh, there can't nobody ride that horse 'ceptin' Matt Jensen. That's the fella that owned him, and he ain't likely to ever ride again, seein' as how he come into town, kilt Deputy Gillis, was tried, then took to Yuma to be hung, all in the same day."

"Maybe the fact that nobody can ride him will make the marshal sell the horse cheap," Matt said.

"Maybe, but what good would it do you if you did get the horse? Like I said, there can't nobody ride him."

"I'm pretty good with horses," Matt said. "I've broken a few in my day. I'd like to give it a try. What about the saddle? Did the marshal confiscate the saddle as well?"

"I'm sure he did. Lot's of times he sells the saddle with the horse. Wait a minute, let me step into my office here. Would you like to see the paper the marshal put out?"

"Yes, if you don't mind."

"All right, wait here and I'll go get it. But if you buy it, tell 'im Joe Claibie sent you. He might give me a little somethin' for suggestin' it to you."

Matt waited while Claibie stepped into the office. A moment later, he came back outside with a piece of paper and showed it to Matt.

FOR SALE

Sorrel with red coat and white face

Fine Saddle

$150.00

See City Marshal Andrew Cummins

Matt handed the paper back to Claibie. "Thanks for showing this to me, but I'm afraid a hundred and fifty dollars is a little too expensive for my blood."

"Yeah, well, that is a little steep, especially for a horse you would have to break in order to even ride him. Listen, are you be staying around town long? The reason I ask is, if you're looking for a job, I could maybe put you on. Business is real brisk since the railroad got cut."

"That can't last much longer, though," Matt said. "I came by the wreck today. They're working really hard, and will probably have it cleaned up within a few days. And, I don't think you would want to be taking on extra help now, only to have to cut back when your business slows again."

"Come to think of it, I guess you have a point there. Well, I'd better see to the horses. Thanks again."

"Oh, wait," Matt called.

"Yes, sir?"

"Let's say I wanted to have a look at this horse. Where could I see it?"

"When I seen it, it was down at the city corral, but now that it belongs to Marshal Cummins, I reckon you'd probably find it in the marshal's stable."

"The marshal's stable?"

"Yes, it's just behind his office. Ask one of the deputies, they'll take you back and let you see him."

"Thanks," Matt said.

Matt walked on down toward the town, oblivious of the red and gold sunset behind him. He stayed on the boardwalk, keeping close to the buildings so as not to stand out in plain sight for anyone who might have been in the saloon at the time of his trial.

About half a block before he reached the marshal's office, he ducked in between a boot maker's shop and a meat market, then moved back to the alley. The smell of blood and freshly butchered meat was overpowering, and in the alley, he could hear the loud buzzing of flies as they feasted on the discarded beef entrails and bones.

He saw the marshal's stable about fifty yards up the alley and, glancing around to make certain he wasn't seen, moved quickly to it. The top half of the door was open to allow some cooling air for the horses. Matt stepped up to the half-open door and looked into the shadowed interior.

At first, he didn't see Spirit.

"Spirit," he called. "Spirit, are you in here, boy?"

He heard Spirit whinny, heard his foot paw at the ground.

"Good boy," Matt said. "You just be patient for a little while. Once it gets dark, I'll come get you."

Matt went out behind the alley, which was actually behind the town, and finding a dry arroyo that ran parallel with the alley, he slipped down into it to wait for darkness.

It was interesting to watch the transition of the town as darkness fell. The sounds of commerce—the ringing of the blacksmith's hammer, the rattle of wagons and buckboards, the hoofbeats of horses and footfalls of pedestrians, gave way to the sounds of night. He could hear a baby crying, the yap of a dog, the laughter of children, the carping complaint of an angry wife. But soon, even those sounds gave way to the sounds of those who were seeking pleasure. A piano, high and tinny, spilled out the melody to "Buffalo Gals." A bar girl cackled— a man guffawed loudly. From a whore's crib, he heard the practiced moans of a prostitute with her customer.

About one hour after full darkness, Matt climbed out of the arroyo and walked quietly, cautiously, up to the marshal's stable. Opening the bottom half of the door, he moved into the stable, which was partially lit by a silver bar of moonlight that splashed in through the door.

"Spirit?" he called out.

Again, he heard Spirit respond and, heading toward the sound, reached the stall where Spirit was being kept. Stepping inside, he reached out to pat Spirit on the neck. Spirit lowered his head and nuzzled him.

"Did you think I had abandoned you, boy?" Matt asked.

Spirit pawed at the ground.

"I need to find the saddle," Matt said. Taking a match from his pocket, he lit it by popping it on his fingernail. A little bubble of golden light illuminated the stall sufficiently well for him to see the saddle, which was draped across a sawhorse in the back of the same stall that housed Spirit. Extinguishing the match, Matt got the saddle, and then put it on Spirit, all the time talking quietly and reassuringly to him.

Once Spirit was saddled, Matt led him out of the
stable, back across the arroyo. Not until he was on the
other side of the arroyo did he climb into the saddle.
He rode out into the desert country just to the north
of the town of Purgatory. Once again, he was well
mounted and free. It was a good feeling, and he knew
that the only thing he had to do to put all this behind
him was ride back to Colorado.

The instinct to return to Colorado was strong, but
he couldn't get the scene of the little girl, impaled by
the bloody stake from the smashed railroad car, out of
his mind. As he had passed her broken body to her
mother, he had made the decision to go after the men
who had caused the wreck. And he wasn't going to go
back on that decision now.

He would take care of that first. Then he planned
to come back to Purgatory and clear his name. He
wasn't sure how he would be able to do that, but he
did not plan on spending the rest of his life with
wanted posters dogging him everywhere he went.

Matt reached down and patted Spirit on the neck.
"It's good to have you back, boy," he said. "I was getting lonely without my old friend to talk to."

Spirit whickered, and bobbed his head a couple of
times. Matt laughed out loud. "Yes, I know, I know,
you've heard all my stories. You're just going to have
to hear them again," he said.

It was mid-morning of the next day when Matt happened onto a remote building. At first he thought
it might be a line shack for some ranch, no more

substantial did it appear. But as he came closer, he saw that it was a combination store, saloon, and hotel. The sign out front read:

LONESOME CHARLEY'S

Food – Beer – Beds.

Some might wonder how a business so remotely located could possibly survive, but Matt knew that it survived precisely because it was so remote. Any traveler who happened by and needed supplies would have to shop here, as there was no competition.

The building either had never been painted, or was in such need of new paint that no semblance of the old paint remained. The wood was baked gray by the Arizona sun, and the roof over the porch was sagging on one end. There was a wasps' nest in the joint between the roof and the front of the building. A dog lay sleeping on the porch, so confident in his position that he didn't even wake up as Matt stepped by him, then pushed open the door to go inside.

The inside of the building was lit by washed-out sunlight that stabbed in through windows that were so covered with dirt that they were nearly opaque. In addition, bars of sunlight stabbed through the wide cracks between the boards illuminating thousands of glowing dust motes. The inside of the building smelled of bacon, flour, and various spices. An old woman was sitting on a chair, smoking a pipe and reading a newspaper. Matt could see the headline on one of the stories.

TRAIN WRECK ON SOUTHERN PACIFIC!
MANY DEAD! MANY INJURED!

The woman looked up as Matt entered. "My man will be with you in a moment," the said. "He's back in the outhouse."

"I'm in no hurry," Matt replied.

Almost before Matt got the words out of his mouth, a white-haired man, wearing an apron, came in through the back door. He was still poking his shirttail down into his pants.

"Yes, sir, what can I do for you?" he asked.

"I'll take some jerky and coffee," Matt said.

"Yes, sir, we've got some fine jerky. What about bacon? Freshly smoked, it's mighty tasty with biscuits and a little redeye gravy."

"I'm sure it is," Matt said. "But jerky and coffee are all I need right now."

"Yes, sir, I'll get it together for you. We just got the paper in today. We've been readin' all about the big train wreck on the Southern Pacific. Have you heard anything about it?"

"Not too much," Matt answered.

"They're sayin' a fella by the name of Matt Jensen caused the wreck. Got away with a hunnert thousand dollars, too."

"Don't be silly, George, it wan't no hunnert thousand dollars," the woman said. "It was only fifty thousand."

"How much ever it was, I hope they catch him," George said. He wrapped Matt's purchase up in a piece of oilcloth and slid it across the counter to him. "That'll be five dollars," he said.

"Five dollars?" Matt replied, stunned by the amount.

The purchase should have been little more than fifty cents. "That's pretty high, isn't it?"

"You don't have to buy here," George said.

Matt chuckled, then shook his head. He gave George a five-dollar bill. "You know what? You are what they call a sharp business man."

"I appreciate the compliment," George said.

Taking his purchase, Matt told both George and his wife good-bye, then went outside, swung back into the saddle, and rode away.

"That was a handsome young man," George's wife said after Matt left.

"I suppose so," George said. "I sure wouldn't want that fella mad at me, though."

"Why not?"

"There was somethin' about him, a hint of sulfur or somethin', that tells me he is one dangerous man. And the way he was a'wearin' that gun—he knows how to use it, I'm sure."

"Oh, pooh," George's wife said. "A nice, pretty man like that has probably never even shot a gun."

George was silent for a moment before he responded.

"Yeah," he said. "You might be right."

United States Marshal Ben Kyle sat at the desk in his office in Sentinel, drumming his fingers as he looked at the passenger list from the train wreck. By now, all the dead had been identified, as had all the injured. Some of the uninjured passengers had already continued their westbound journey, but he had managed to talk to each of them before they left. None of them recalled seeing a man brought on board in chains, and none recalled seeing anyone in chains leave the scene of the wreck.

Sentinel had been the final destination for four of the passengers, and he had spoken to them as well, but none of them could recall seeing a man in chains. Or at least, if anyone saw him, they wouldn't admit to it. Why was that? he wondered. Were they frightened? Had Jensen gotten to them, threatened them in any way?

As Kyle continued to study the passenger list, he picked up his pencil and then drew a line under two names.

<u>Louise Dobbs</u>

<u>Jerry Dobbs</u>

Marshal Kyle knew Louise and Jeremiah Dobbs. They owned a small ranch just outside of town. Mrs. Dobbs and her two children, Jerry and Suzie, had gone to Purgatory to visit her sister, and were returning when the train was wrecked. Purgatory was where Matt Jensen had boarded and Mrs. Dobbs had to have seen him.

In fact, as he recalled the incident now, young Jerry had almost said something to him. When questioned, Jerry said that he hadn't seen anything, but that was only after a stern glance from his mother.

Kyle had seen the look Louise Dobbs gave her son then, but because her little girl had been killed, he had not wanted to bother her with questions, hoping that he would get the information he needed from one of the other passengers. Unfortunately, that had not worked out for him, and now it appeared as if Mrs. Dobbs would be his only source.

Sighing, Kyle stood up. "Boomer?" he called to his deputy.

"Yes, sir?"

"I'm going to ride out to the Dobbs ranch."

"You're going to question Mrs. Dobbs, are you?"

"Yes," Kyle said. "But I swear, I'd rather be horse-whipped than bother that poor woman right now."

"I don't blame you. Would you like for me to come with you?"

"No, I appreciate the offer, but there's no need for that. You just hold down the fort while I'm gone," Kyle said as he reached for his hat.

"Yes, sir, I'll do that," Boomer said. "Benjamin, why is it, do you suppose, that nobody wants to tell us anything about this Jensen fella? Do you think he has them all buffaloed?"

"I don't know, Boomer. I've been wondering about that myself," Kyle said. "Maybe I can find out something from Mrs. Dobbs."

The Dobbs ranch was about five miles south of Sentinel, and when Marshal Kyle rode up to the house, he saw that there were at least half-a-dozen wagons and buckboards parked out in the yard, the teams still in harness and standing quietly. At first, he was surprised that there were so many people here. Then suddenly, he realized that he must have arrived around the time of the funeral. These were all friends, neighbors, and relatives, come to pay their respects to the Dobbses over the loss of their little girl. For a moment, he wished he hadn't come to impose on them, and he was considering turning around when Jeremiah Dobbs stepped out onto the porch to greet him.

"Marshal Kyle," he said. "How nice of you to come to Suzie's funeral. My wife and I never expected anything like this. You honor us. Please, get down and come in."

Dobbs thought this was a sympathy visit, and Kyle saw no reason, at this point, to disabuse him of that idea. He swung down from his horse, then wrapped the reins around a hitching post.

"How are you doing, Jeremiah?" Kyle asked in as solicitous a voice as he could muster.

"I'm doing as well as can be expected, I suppose," Jeremiah said, "having lost my little girl. It's Louise I'm worried about. She's takin' this real hard, she keeps blamin' herself."

"That's ridiculous," Kyle said. "Why would she blame herself?"

"That's what I keep tellin' her," Jeremiah said. "But she says if she just hadn't gone to see her sister when she did, or, if she had taken better care of Suzie while they were on the train, maybe Suzie would still be with us."

"None of that has anything to do with the wreck, or with Suzie getting killed," Kyle said. "I know she's upset, but as soon as she realizes that there was nothing she could have done to prevent it, I expect she'll come around."

"I certainly hope so."

Kyle followed Jeremiah into the house. There were

at least two dozen people gathered in the parlor, sitting, standing, talking in low, soothing tones. There were a few people down at the end of the large room who appeared to be looking down at something, and as Kyle studied them more closely he realized, with a start, that they were staring at the body of the little girl.

"Would you like to see her?" Jeremiah asked. "Mr. Albriton fixed her up just real nice. She looks just like she's sleeping."

"I—" Kyle began, and then he stopped. He was about to tell Jeremiah that he would just as soon not look at the little girl, but he knew that the viewing of his daughter's remains was very important to Jeremiah.

"Yes, I would be very honored to look at her," Kyle said.

Jeremiah led Kyle through the room toward the open coffin. Nearly everyone in the room recognized him, and they spoke to him as he passed by. In some cases, Kyle gave single syllable answers; in others, he just nodded.

The coffin was child-sized. The lid was open and Suzie could be seen lying in the coffin, her head slightly elevated by a white pillow. She was wearing a pink dress with white lace, and her hands, crossed in front of her, grasped a single yellow rose. Her blond hair cascaded over her shoulders in ringlets of curls. The pallor of death had been pushed back by the artful application of paint and powder.

"Doesn't she look just like a little angel?" one of the women standing over the coffin asked.

"Yes, ma'am," Kyle said. "She does indeed."

"Folks, if you'll all find a place to sit, we'll commence

the funeral now," a man in black said. Kyle recognized him as the Reverend E. D. Owen, pastor of the Sentinel Holiness Church.

For a moment, Kyle just stood there, but Jeremiah called to him and offered him a chair. Clearing his throat, Kyle took the seat and looked around the room at the others. The men, women, and children who had come to Suzie's funeral were all dressed in their Sunday best. Kyle, who was wearing his normal work clothes of denim trousers and a white, collarless shirt, felt a little embarrassed by his dress, though neither Jeremiah nor anyone else, by word or deed, added to his discomfort.

Reverend Owen stood in front of Suzie's coffin, waiting until everyone was settled before he began to speak.

"My brothers and sisters," he began. "We are gathered here to pay our final respects, and to commit to the Lord's keeping the soul of this wonderful child, Suzie Dobbs.

"It is a sad thing when we lose a loved one, and that sadness is particularly bitter when the loved one is a child. Such a loss might cause many to question their faith, to be angry with God for allowing such a terrible thing to happen.

"But I say to you, my brothers and sisters, do not be angry, nor saddened by the loss of this child, for remember, Suzie, like all of us, belongs to God. He loaned her to us for just a little while, before taking her back into His glory. Our time in this life is measured, the years known but to God. But our time in the hereafter is without measure, for we will all meet again in the eternal glory that awaits us all.

"Into God's gracious mercy and protection we commit this child. The Lord bless you and keep you. The Lord make his face to shine upon you, and be gracious unto you. The Lord lift up his countenance upon you, and give you peace, both now and evermore. Amen."

Suzie was buried in a family plot out behind the house, alongside the graves of Jeremiah's mother and father and that of a stillborn infant. Afterward, all returned to the house, where a meal was served from dishes prepared by the friends, neighbors, and relatives.

Louise Dobbs was sitting on the far side of the room. Jerry was on the floor beside his mother, and Louise's left hand was resting on Jerry's shoulder. In her right hand was a tightly gripped, wadded handkerchief, the handkerchief wet with her tears. Occasionally, someone would stop by the chair to say a word or two to her; then they would go on, leaving her to herself.

Kyle hated to use this time to question her, but he had ridden this far and he was here, so he might as well get it done. He drew a deep breath, squared his shoulders, and then walked over to see her.

"Mrs. Dobbs," Kyle said when he stepped up to the chair. "May I offer you my most sincere sympathy?"

"Thank you," Louise said.

"I—uh, wonder if I could ask you a few questions?"

"What about?"

"About the train wreck," Kyle said.

"I don't know anything about it," Louise answered.

"One minute, we were riding along normally, and the next moment, the car was bumping all over the place. Then it went off the track and turned over. I don't remember much after that."

"Yes, ma'am, well, that's not exactly what I want to talk about."

"What is it, then?"

"I'm trying to find the man who caused all this. He killed the deputy from Purgatory. Then I'm sure that, somehow, he caused the wreck so he could steal the money and get away in all the panic and confusion. I think that man's name is Matt Jensen, and he got on the train in Purgatory, the same time you did. I'm hoping you might have seen him."

"He didn't cause the train wreck," Louise said. "And I don't believe he killed the deputy or stole the money."

Louise's answer surprised Kyle. He had thought, at best, that she might claim to have seen him, but be able to offer little information. But her answer not only indicated that she had seen him, it also meant that she had interacted with him in some way.

"Mrs. Dobbs, excuse me, but what do you mean? I am confused as to why you would say such a thing. Do you know this man?"

"No."

"Then, how can you be so sure that he didn't cause the wreck, kill the deputy, and steal the money?"

"Because he saved my life," Louise replied. "And he also saved the lives of several others on the train. If he had done all those things you said he did, I do not believe he would have stayed around to help the others. Do you believe that he would?"

"I don't know," Kyle said. "There's no telling how some people are going to react to certain things. He may have just done that to throw people off."

"No, that wouldn't be necessary. In fact, Jerry and I are the only ones who could have recognized him, so he had no reason to throw people off. I knew who he was the moment he showed up in the car where I was pinned under the seat. He had been in chains when he got on the train, but somehow he got out of them. And I'll you the truth, Marshal, I was very glad to see him because, as I say, he saved my life."

"Let's say that you are right, let us say that he did save your life—"

"There is no 'let us say' to it," Louise said, interrupting Kyle. "He *did* save my life."

"All right, he did save your life. If that is the case, then don't you think that might cause you to have a loyalty to him? A loyalty that is misplaced? Especially if he was the cause of the accident in the first place?"

"How could he have caused the accident?" Louise asked. "You said yourself that he was in chains."

"But, by your own admission, he wasn't in chains when you saw him, was he?"

"No."

"Could you describe him for me?"

"I don't think I can," Louise said.

"You don't think you can, or you don't think you will?"

Louise didn't answer.

"Mrs. Dobbs, please," Kyle said.

"You can say anything you want, Marshal. You are not going to make me believe that this man, Matt

Jensen, did all the terrible things you said he did. Like I told you, he worked harder than anyone to pull people out of the wreckage. Then he helped Dr. Presnell tend to the injured. As a matter of fact, I doubt that he was even guilty of whatever crime put him in chains in the first place."

"First-degree murder," Kyle said. "He was tried and convicted, and was on his way to Yuma to be hanged, until he got away."

"Well, all I can say is, I'm glad he got away."

"I see," Kyle said. He sighed. "Again, Mrs. Dobbs, my condolences for your loss." He turned and walked away.

Unwittingly, Louise Dobbs had given him more information than she realized. She had told him that the man he had looked for had worked with Dr. Presnell. All he had to do now was talk to the doc.

Chapter Thirteen

When Odom and Bates left Quigotoa, Paco and Schuler stayed behind. Schuler stayed because he had gotten drunk the night before and was still passed out drunk the next morning. Paco stayed to, in his words, "look after Schuler."

"Señor," Paco said, shaking Schuler awake. "Señor, wake up."

"What?" Schuler mumbled. "What is it? What do you want?"

"Wake up, Señor," Paco said.

Sitting up, Schuler rubbed his eyes, pinched the bridge of his nose, then looked around.

"Paco, what are you doing here?"

"I have come to wake you up, Señor Schuler."

"Why?"

"Because you are in the room of my sister," Paco said, only *sister* came out as *seester*. "My sister is a *puta*. She needs the room now."

"What time is it?" Schuler's eyes seemed to be floating in their sockets, and it was obvious he was having a hard time focusing.

"It is seven o'clock, I think."

"Damn. I need a drink."

Paco handed Schuler a bottle of tequila, and Schuler turned the bottle up to his lips, then took several swallows before lowering it. The drink had the effect of waking him up, and the eyes that couldn't focus but a moment earlier now stared pointedly at Paco.

"Paco," he said, as if just seeing him for the first time. "What are you doing here?"

"My sister needs this room now," Paco said.

"Hey!" a voice shouted from the hallway outside the room. "If you ain't got a whore in there with you, get the hell out!"

"All right, all right," Schuler called back. "I'm coming."

There was no need for Schuler to get dressed, because he was wearing the same clothes he'd had on when he went to bed the night before. For that matter, he was wearing the same clothes he'd worn last week, and the week before that.

Schuler got to his feet rather unsteadily, stabilized himself for a moment by holding on to the bedpost, then, summoning as much dignity as he could, took two steps across the little room and opened the door.

There was an Anglo cowboy standing in the hall, with his arm draped around Rosita's neck. His hand was cupped around one of Rosita's breasts.

"What the hell were you doing in there anyway, you goddamn drunk?" the cowboy asked Schuler. "You ain't had a woman in so long, you wouldn't even know what a naked woman looks like."

"I'm sorry," Schuler said.

"Yeah, well, sorry doesn't get it," the angry cowboy said. "Just get the hell out of the way and let a man get his business done."

"Yes, I'm sorry," Schuler repeated.

Schuler followed Paco to the head of the stairs, then stopped for a moment in order to steady himself before he tackled the task of going down the narrow, steep flight of stairs. By holding on to the banister, he managed to negotiate them; then, standing on the main floor, he looked around the saloon for the others.

"Do you want breakfast, Señor?" Paco asked.

"Breakfast? No," Schuler answered, the expression on his face reflecting his nausea over the thought of breakfast. "Where are Odom and Bates?" he asked.

"Odom said we are to meet him and Bates in Puxico."

"We are to meet them in Puxico? Why?"

"We will divide the money there."

"I don't understand. Didn't we divide the money last night?"

"*Sí,* we divided the money last night. But then we gave the money back to Señor Odom."

"We did?" Schuler replied.

"*Sí.*"

"Why did we do that?"

"Señor Odom said it would be better if we went to Puxico before we divided the money. Do you not remember this, amigo? We talked about it, and we all agreed."

"No, I—I don't remember," Schuler said. His confusion was very evident now. "I don't think I would agree to such a thing. I don't want to go to Puxico."

"That's because you were drunk, Señor," Paco said.

Schuler ran his hand through his thinning, white hair. "All right," he said. "Are you coming?"

"You go, Señor, I will come later," Paco said.

"Puxico?"

"*Sí*, Puxico."

Paco watched Schuler leave the saloon, then he walked over to the window. He saw Schuler saddle his horse and ride away before he walked back into the saloon to sit at one of the tables.

"Do you want breakfast, Paco?"

"*Sí*."

"Beans, tortillas?"

"No, Señor. I want steak, eggs, and coffee."

"Ha! Did Rosita give you some money or something? You are ordering like a rich man."

Paco laughed, then thought of the saddlebags he had hidden in his room. In them, he had almost eight thousand dollars, counting the money he had just stolen from Schuler.

Chapter Fourteen

The battlefield was a cacophony of sound, with the tinny calls of bugles, the distant roar of cannon fire, the closer rattle of musketry, and the wailing moans of the wounded. It was also a kaleidoscope of images: flags fluttering atop carried staffs, shells bursting in air, and smoke drifting across the field.

"You'd better get ready," the colonel said. "We have just been committed to battle. I expect there will be casualties."

"I'm ready, Colonel."

Overhead, there was a sound, not unlike that of an unattached rail car rolling quickly down a track. It was an incoming shell from the Yankee artillery, and it burst with an ear-shattering explosion nearby.

"Dr. Presnell?"

Dr. Presnell heard the long roll of drums, as the Tenth Georgia was called into a line of battle.

"Dr. Presnell?"

There were already too many wounded. Why were

they going to attack again? He was just one doctor, he couldn't handle everyone all by himself.

"Dr. Presnell?"

There was another cannon blast, this one so close that it woke him up.

Woke him up?

"Dr. Presnell?" someone was saying.

Outside, there was a thunderstorm in progress, and a flash of lightning turned the dimly lit room into the brightest day, but just for an instant. It was followed almost immediately by another roar of thunder. Rain, like the rattle of musketry and the roll of drums, slashed against the windows of the school building.

Doc rubbed his eyes. He had been dreaming!

"Dr. Presnell?" Harry White was saying. White, who was Sentinel's only pharmacist, was helping tend to those who had been injured in the train wreck.

"Yes, Harry?"

"I'm sorry to wake you," White said. "But you said you wanted to know if Mr. Carter's fever broke."

"Yes, thank you," Doc said. "So, it broke, did it?"

"About five minutes ago," White said. White smiled. "You know what? I think all the rest of them might pull through now."

Doc stood up, stretched, then returned White's smile. "I think you may be right," he said. "I'm sorry I fell asleep on you there."

"Oh, my, don't apologize," White said. "You have been tending to these people night and day for several days now. Many of them would have died, had it not been for you."

"I've had help," Doc said. "You have been invaluable to me."

"Thank you," White answered.

"I guess I'll walk around and have a look at them."

There was another flash of lightning and roar of thunder.

"Some storm we're having," Doc said.

"Yes, it is. A few are disturbed by it, but I think it's just because they are still traumatized by the train wreck."

"Yes, I think you are right," Doc said, as he walked up to look at the first of his many patients.

Dr. Galen Presnell was a veteran of the Civil War. He had participated in many campaigns throughout the war, but none worse than Gettysburg, where he treated battlefield wounds that ranged from mere scratches to traumatic amputations. But not since that time had he been involved with such massive numbers of dead and injured. Thirty-three men, women, and children had been killed in the train wreck. Forty more were injured, twelve of whom were seriously injured.

The number of dead had overwhelmed the town's only undertaker, so two more undertakers had come to help Albriton, one from Stanwix and one from Mohawk Summit. Those were the next two towns west of Sentinel on the Southern Pacific line, thus making it easy for them to come over.

Seth McKenzie, who owned the wagon repair shop, had cleared a place in his warehouse for the bodies to be stored until they could be shipped back home. At the same time, the school building had been turned into a makeshift hospital, there being no hospital in Sentinel, and Dr. Presnell's office not being big enough to handle those who required hospitalization.

Dr. Presnell stopped by the bed of each of his patients, spoke for a moment with the ones who were awake, assuring one and all that the worst had passed.

"Cannon fire," one man said.

"I beg your pardon?" Doc replied.

There was more thunder, but this was distant, a long, low, growling roar.

"The thunder, it sounds like cannon fire," the patient said.

"I take it you have heard cannon fire on the battlefield," Doc said.

"Yes, I was with the Second Wisconsin at Gettysburg. Colonel Fairchild's Regiment."

Doc put his hand on the man's shoulder and squeezed gently. "I was at Gettysburg as well."

"Then you know what I mean when I say it sounds like cannon fire."

"I do indeed."

"Who were you with?"

"I was with the Tenth Georgia, under Colonel John B. Weems, assigned to General James Longstreet's First Army Corps."

For a moment, the two men looked at each other. Once committed to a battle that made them deadly enemies, they were now experiencing a moment of reflection that no one else in the room could share, or even understand.

"Welcome home, brother," Doc said.

"Welcome home, Doc," the patient replied.

By the time Doc finished his rounds, the thunder

had moved off and was now little more than a distant rumble. White was standing by a window looking outside when Doc stepped up alongside him.

"Looks like the rain has stopped," White said.

"Harry, if you don't mind, I'm going to leave these folks with you for a while. I think I'm going to go over to the Ox Bow to have a beer."

"You go right ahead, Doctor," White replied. "Lord knows you have earned it."

The rain had left the streets a muddy quagmire, but fortunately, the school building and the saloon, though at opposite ends of the town, were on the same side of the street. Doc was able to negotiate the distance with a minimum need to walk in the mud. Nevertheless, he did have to spend a moment scraping mud from his shoes before he stepped into the Ox Bow.

The Ox Bow was brightly lit with overhead chandeliers and lantern sconces throughout. After he had spent the entire day in the makeshift hospital, the bright and cheery atmosphere of the saloon was a dramatic and very welcome change.

"Doc," Boomer called from a table at the back of the saloon. "Come on back and join us."

Answering the summons, Doc picked his way through the crowd toward Boomer. As he got closer, he saw that Sally was sitting with him.

"How is it going with all those people from the train, Doc?" Dave Vance asked. Vance owned the leather goods store. "Have we lost any more?"

"No, and I don't think we will lose any more now," Doc answered. "I think we're through the worst of it."

"You're a good man, Doc," one of the other customers said.

"Hey, ever'body, let's hear it for Doc!" still another shouted. "Hip, hip!"

"Hoorah!"

"Hip, hip!"

"Hoorah!"

"Hip, hip!"

"Hoorah!"

"Doc, let me buy you a drink!" Vance called out to him.

"Well, I would appreciate that, Dave," Doc replied. He pointed to the table where Boomer and Sally were sitting. "But would you mind if I took it back there to the table with Sally and Boomer? I need to get a load off my feet."

"Doc, you can have your drink anywhere you want it," Vance said.

"Thanks." Doc worked his way through the crowd to Boomer and Sally's table while shaking hands with the many well-wishers who offered to shake.

"Boomer, Sally," Doc said as he joined the deputy and the pretty saloon owner at their table.

"Well, Doc, you ought to run for mayor or something," Boomer said. "Right now it looks like you're about the most popular man in town."

"I think it's just folks feeling pretty good about the fact that the worst is over," Doc replied.

"And their acknowledgment of the fact that it's

because of you," Sally said. "No, sir, Doc, whatever accolades you get now, you more than deserve."

"Well, I appreciate that, Sally, I really do," Doc said.

"Hey, Doc, Dave Vance is buying you a drink. What'll it be?" the bartender called over to him.

"Hello, Fred," Doc called back. "After this last two days, I'm not drinking for pleasure, I'm drinking for medicinal purposes. How about a whiskey, with a beer chaser?"

"You got it," Fred said. "I'll throw in the beer chaser myself."

"How are things going, Doc?" Sally asked. "Do you really think the worst is over?"

"I think so, yes. I'm almost positive we won't lose any more. Actually, I think nearly all of them can go home within another couple of days. We had the last critically injured man die last night. His name was Walter Casey, and he was from Chicago. Can you imagine, coming all the way down here from Chicago, just to get killed in a train wreck?"

"Yes, and not even an ordinary train wreck," Boomer said. "It's a train wreck that somebody caused, just so they could rob the train."

"You have to wonder what kind of man would cause a train wreck and kill all those people just for a few dollars," Doc said, shaking his head in disgust.

"Hanging is too good for whoever did it," Boomer said.

"Oh, there's Ben," Sally said, her face brightening at the sight of Marshal Kyle coming into the saloon.

"Ben," Doc said. "Join us for a beer."

"I don't mind if I do, Doc," Kyle said.

"Did you talk to Miz Dobbs?" Boomer asked.

"Louise Dobbs?" Doc asked.

"Yes," Kyle said as he joined the others at the table.

"How is Mrs. Dobbs doing? I know she broke her arm. Is it giving her much trouble?"

"She seems to be handling that all right," Kyle said. "She's having a hard time over the death of her daughter, though. I didn't plan it, but I got there just as they were having her funeral."

"That must have been awkward," Sally said.

"It was at first, but they seemed to think I had come out there just for that purpose, and they made me feel very welcome," Kyle said.

"Jeremiah and Louise Dobbs are good people," Doc said.

"Poor thing, my heart goes out to her." Sally said.

"So, how did your talk with her go?" Boomer asked.

"I didn't get too much out of her," Kyle said. "Evidently she believes that Jensen saved not only her life, but the lives of several others who were on the train, so she's not all that disposed toward giving any information that might help find him."

"How does she know that it was Jensen who saved her life?"

"Turns out that she and her son Jerry are the only two who could identify him because they saw him back in Purgatory. Then, when he came into the car to get her out, Mrs. Dobbs recognized him," Kyle said. Kyle looked over at Doc. "She said he helped you, Doc."

"Helped me?"

"Yes. She said he rode in the car with you on the relief train, helping you tend to the injured."

"Oh, well, then she was mistaken. That wasn't Jensen," Doc said.

"That wasn't Jensen who rode with you?"

"No, sir. At least, Jensen isn't the name he gave me. He told me his name was Cavanaugh. Martin Cavanaugh."

"Cavanaugh?"

"Yes."

Kyle pulled a piece of paper from his pocket and studied it for a moment, then he smiled and hit his fist into his hand. "That's him," he said, nodding. "Cavanaugh is Matt Jensen."

"How do you know?"

"Because I have the name of every passenger that was on the train," Kyle said. "And there is no Cavanaugh listed. So, since Jensen is the only one we can't account for, and since Cavanaugh is not even listed, it stands to reason that Cavanaugh and Jensen are one and the same."

"That sounds reasonable to me," Boomer said. "And if you think about it, knowin' he had just escaped, there ain't no way a fella like Jensen would give you his real name anyhow."

"It would sound reasonable to me as well," Doc said. "Except for one thing."

"What's that?"

"Isn't this man Jensen supposed to be a convicted murderer?"

"That's right. He shot and killed a deputy over in Purgatory," Kyle said.

"Yes, well you see, that's the problem. I worked nearly a full day with this man Cavanaugh. I don't know what he is, but I know what he is not. He is not a murderer. I'm a pretty good judge of character, Ben, and there's no way Cavanaugh would kill somebody in cold blood. Self-defense maybe, yes, I could see that. But I could not see him killing anyone in cold blood."

"What is it with this Jensen fella?" Kyle said. "He seems to charm everyone he meets. He's got you charmed, he's got Mrs. Dobbs convinced that he saved her life, even though, by wrecking the train, he's the one who put her life in danger in the first place."

"He didn't wreck the train," Boomer said.

"What? You, too?"

"I've never met the man," Boomer said. "But he was in chains, in the train, being taken to Yuma to hang, right?"

"Right."

"I was talkin' to some of the railroad workers today—you know, the ones who have been cleaning up the mess out there?" Boomer said.

"And?"

"Well, sir, they found that some of the spikes had been pulled out."

"Maybe they had just worked themselves out over a period of time," Kyle suggested.

"No, sir," Boomer said. "They know the spikes were pulled out because they had been tossed to one side. Besides which, they found a pickax there, as well as the place where several horses had waited. And from the amount of horse droppin's, the horses were probably there for over an hour, which means they had to be waitin' for the train. The railroad workers think the train robbers pulled up the spikes, then kicked the track out, just so as to cause the wreck."

"It's hard to believe that anyone could be that cruel," Sally said.

"Yes, ma'am, it is," Boomer agreed. "But one thing it does do is it pretty much proves that this here Jensen fella couldn't of done it. Not what with him bein' in chains in the car 'n' all."

"Maybe he didn't, or maybe he had arranged for someone to wreck the train so he could escape," Kyle suggested.

"Ben, seems to me that would be a pretty foolhardy thing to do," Doc said. "He was in the express car. Mr. Kingsley was also in the express car, and he got killed."

"I don't care how much this Jensen person has charmed all of you. He is still a murderer. At the very least he murdered Deputy Gillis, because he has already been convicted of that murder back in Purgatory. And the evidence is pretty convincing that he killed Deputy Hayes as well. But maybe it was someone else who wrecked the train."

"Did the train robbers actually get anything?" Sally asked.

"I hope to say they did," Kyle replied. "The train was carrying a bank transfer of twenty thousand dollars."

"Instead of going after this man Jensen, what about whoever actually caused the train wreck?" Doc asked. "I've got a vested interest in getting them, seeing as how I was on that train and could've been killed myself."

"Doc, my job isn't either-or, my job is both," Kyle said. "So I'll be going after the train robbers and Matt

Jensen. And until I see some physical evidence to the contrary, I'm still not convinced they aren't one and the same. Oh, by the way, Doc, is Deputy Hayes' body still here?"

"Yes, I believe it is. Except for those who lived here, I think all the bodies are still in Seth McKenzie's warehouse."

"Good. I want the bullet that killed Hayes. And, I want to take Hayes' body back to Purgatory. Oh, and give me a description of Jensen."

"I don't know that it is Jensen," Doc said. "Like I said, he told me his name was Cavanaugh."

"All right, then give me a description of Cavanaugh."

"Mid-to-late twenties, I guess. He was a lot younger in the face than in the eyes. Those eyes have seen a lot," Doc added. "He's about six feet tall, broad shoulders, narrow waist, light blue eyes, and hair that's about halfway between blond and brown."

"Sally, you're a good artist, you've drawn pictures of half the people in this town. Would you draw a picture of Jensen for me? Doc, you can watch her draw it, then tell her when she's close."

"You don't need to describe him to me," Sally said.

"What do you mean? You mean you aren't going to draw his picture?"

"No, I mean he doesn't have to describe him to me. He was in here that first night. I bought supper for him. I know what he looks like."

"Good. You draw the picture, and I'll take it over to Blanton to get a woodcut made."

"Marshal?" someone said, coming up to the table where Kyle, Doc, Boomer, and Sally were sitting.

"Yes, Barney, what can I do for you?" Kyle asked, recognizing the whiskey drummer.

"I heard tell you was looking for whoever robbed the train."

"Yes, I am."

"Well, I was on the train and I think I seen them."

"You think you saw them, or you *did* see them?" Kyle asked.

"I think—that is, I'm sure I did see them."

"If you did see them, Barney, would you tell me why in the hell you are just now getting around to telling me about it?"

"I had to think on it some to be certain in my own mind that that is what I did see," Barney explained.

"All right," Kyle replied. "Tell me about it."

"Yes, sir. Well, like I said, I was on the train, but I wasn't hurt none. Anyhow, I got out of the car, and was just sort of wanderin' around, when I seen these here four men go into the express car. I thought maybe they was part of the train. Then, no more'n a minute later, I seen 'em come out carrying a canvas bag. I didn't think nothin' of it at the time 'cause, to tell the truth, I guess I was still all confused and dizzy 'n' all over havin' just come through the wreck. But when I heard the train was robbed, it got me to thinkin' that maybe they was the ones who done it."

"Can you describe them?"

"Yes, sir, I think I can. One of 'em had a scar, a big, ugly, purple scar that run from his forehead, through his left eye, and down. And the eyelid was all puffed up, like it had a big wart on it or somethin'," Barney said.

He used his finger to outline the position of the scar on his own face.

"Marshal, that sounds just like Cletus Odom," Boomer said.

"Yes, it does," Kyle said. "Barney, you said there were others?"

"Yes, sir, there was three others."

"Tell me about them."

"One of them was a big man, I'd say six feet four or so, over two hundred pounds. I mean, he was a big, strong-lookin' son of a bitch." Then, as if just realizing that Sally was sitting at the table he nodded toward her. "Sorry, Miss Sally," he apologized.

"That's all right, Barney, from what I've heard of Cletus Odom, anyone who would ride with him would have to be a son of a bitch."

Barney smiled. "Yes, ma'am, I reckon you're right."

"You said there were four," Kyle said, urging Barney to get back to his descriptions.

"Uh, yeah, four. Well, there was the scar faced man, and the big one, like I said. Then there was one who was small and dark, I think he was probably a Mexican. The fourth one was a drunk."

"Drunk?"

"No, he wasn't drunk when I seen him. But he is a drunk," Barney clarified.

"What do you mean he is a drunk?" Kyle asked. "How can you tell if a man is a drunk if he isn't drunk? And even then, you can be drunk without being a drunk."

"Yes, sir, you can, and that's how I know," Barney said. "You forget, Marshal, I'm a whiskey salesman. I reckon I have seen more drunks than just about anyone. Not even bartenders see as many drunks as a whiskey drummer does. But even they can tell someone who is a drunk."

Kyle drummed his fingers on the table for a moment, then he called out. "Fred, could you come over here for a moment?"

"Sure, Marshal," Fred replied affably. Throwing the bar towel over his shoulder, he came from behind the bar and walked over to the table where Kyle, Boomer, Doc, and Sally were seated.

"Fred, can you tell if a man is a drunk just by looking at him?" Kyle asked. "I don't mean drunk, I mean a drunk."

"Oh, yes, sir, Marshal, sure you can," Fred replied. "You can tell in a heartbeat."

"How can you tell?"

"I don't know quite how to explain it," Fred replied. "But they all have a certain look about them. You can just tell, that's all."

"All right, thanks," Kyle said.

"Can I get anybody anything else?" he asked.

"I'll have me another beer," Boomer said.

The others indicated they were fine.

"All right," Kyle said after Fred returned to the bar. "So, what do we have here? Cletus Odom, a big man, a small Mexican, and a drunk?"

"Yes, sir, that pretty much sums it up," Barney said. "I hope that helps you find the ones that done this."

"It's a start," Kyle said. "Thanks."

Barney left just as Fred put another beer in front of Boomer.

Boomer took a drink of his beer, then wiped the foam away from his lips before he spoke.

"Well, if it was Cletus Odom, then it's a lead-pipe cinch that he's the one that stole the money. Seems to me that lets this fella Jensen off the hook, don't you think?" Boomer asked.

Kyle sighed. "Yes, you might be right. It could be that Jensen just took advantage of the situation to escape. But that still leaves us with the fact that Jensen is a convicted murderer, so even if he didn't rob the train, I don't think I would go so far as to say that this would let him off the hook."

"What about Odom?" Boomer asked. "Shouldn't we ought to do somethin' about him?"

"Yes, if it was Odom, we should do something about him," Kyle said. "But first, we need to find out if it was him. We've got some pretty good pictures of Odom down at the office. Boomer, how about taking Barney down to the office and showing him some pictures. Don't tell him who they are—let him pick one out on his own."

"I know how to do this, Benjamin. I didn't just start deputyin' yesterday, you know," Boomer said, a little miffed that the marshal felt he had to tell him that.

"I know you know how to do it, Boomer, I didn't mean anything by it," Kyle said. "I was just sort of thinking out loud, is all."

"That's all right, I ain't put out with you none," Boomer said, easing his tone a bit. He looked over at Barney. "Come along, Barney I got some pretty pictures to show you." Boomer chuckled. "Well, now that

I think about it, they ain't all that pretty. But I'm goin' to show 'em to you anyway."

Kyle, Sally, and Doc watched Boomer and Barney leave. Then, Doc picked up his mug of beer and took a drink. "I'm glad Barney came along," he said. "I knew Cavanaugh—or Jensen as you say—didn't have anything to do with robbing that train."

"Maybe not, Doc," Kyle replied. "But like I said, he's not off the hook. He is still an escaped murderer."

"And I'm telling you, there's no way on God's green earth that that man who pulled all those injured folks from the train, and who worked alongside me nursing them, could be a murderer," Doc insisted.

Chapter Fifteen

Before he came in sight of the track, Matt could hear the sound of puffing steam engines, the screech of metal being moved, and the loud banging of heavy loads being lifted and deposited. When he reached the scene, he saw two huge, steam-operated cranes lifting the mangled cars and the twisted and broken wheel trucks from on and around the track, then depositing them onto the long line of flatbed cars that had been brought out to the scene of the wreck. Already, new and temporary tracks had been built around the wreck to allow the work trains access.

Matt was surprised at how much progress had been made in cleaning up the mess. At this rate, they would be finished within one more day, and the passenger and freight trains would be returning to their normal operational schedule.

After getting his horse back, Matt returned to the scene of the wreck, not to watch the clean-up operation, but to get a lead on tracking Cletus Odom and the others who were responsible. He started on the south side of the track where he had found the pickax, thinking this was probably the side on which the outlaws had waited. It didn't take him long to find the signs of four horses, and the direction they took when they left. He knew this had to be them, because the number of horses, four, matched the number of train robbers, four.

As he examined the tracks, a sudden smile spread across his face. One of the horses had a tie-bar shoe.

"Spirit, I don't know which one of these sons of bitches are riding a tie-bar shoe, but it doesn't matter. He'll lead me to the rest of them," Matt said as he started on the trial.

The little town of Saucita was American only because it was on the American side of the border. In fact, three fourths of the people in town were either Mexican nationals, or Americans only by an accident of their birth. In layout, the town could have been any village between here and Mexico City, for it was nothing more than a series of adobe buildings built around a center square. In the center square there was a well, and the well was Matt's first stop. He drew up two buckets of water and added them to the watering trough, which was already more than half full.

With Spirit's thirst satisfied, Matt led, rather than rode, him across the square to the Cantina de las Rosas. He tied him off at the hitching rail, then checked the right rear hooves of the other horses that were tied there. He hit pay dirt with the third horse he checked.

Matt pushed through the hanging strings of clack-

ing red and green beads, and then stepped into the
cantina. There were at least two dozen customers in
the cantina, and all were of the same swarthy complexion. There were a dozen or more conversations
going on as well, all in Spanish.

Matt stepped up to the bar. *"Tequila por favor."*

"Ten cents," the bartender said in English, as he put
the glass in front of Matt.

Suddenly, there was the sound of a slap, then a
woman's cry of pain and fear. That was followed by a
loud, angry sentence, spoken in English and ringing
clear through the cacophonous babble of Spanish.

"You dumb bitch! I ordered whiskey, not this Mexican shit!'

"I'm sorry, Señor."

"Sorry my ass. Now get rid of this shit and bring me
a bottle of whiskey."

"Sí, señor."

Looking toward the commotion, Matt saw a man
who was head and shoulders bigger than anyone else
in the room. He had broad shoulders and big hands
and he was eating a steak, not by using a knife and
fork, but by holding it in his hands. In addition to the
woman he had just slapped, there were two other
women with him, one sitting on either side.

This was not a handsome man by any means, and
the only explanation for his popularity with the
women would be that he had a lot of money and was
a free spender. Kyle knew that the man fit that bill, because he recognized him as soon as he saw him. This
was the one called Bates.

Kyle ordered a meal of beans and tortillas, then ate

slowly, all the while keeping an eye on Bates, though without being obvious about it. When Bates left the saloon, Matt walked over to the window and watched as he mounted the horse with the tie-bar. He stayed at the window until Bates rode out of town, then Matt left the saloon, mounted Spirit, and followed.

Matt remained so far behind Bates that were was no way the outlaw could see him. Of course, that also meant that he couldn't see the outlaw, but that was no problem. Bates was still riding the horse with the tie-bar shoe, which meant he might as well have been leaving a painted trail, so easily could it be followed.

When Bates made camp for the night, Matt did as well, satisfying himself with a strip of jerky and a couple of chewed coffee beans, washed down with a swallow of tepid canteen water.

During the night, Matt sneaked into Bates's camp. The fire Bates had built before he went to bed was burned down now, though a few of the coals were still glowing. Bates was snoring loudly from the blanket he had thrown out on the ground. Bates's hat was over his face as Matt moved quietly toward him.

Slipping his knife from his belt, Matt got down onto his knees beside Bates, then brought his knife up to Bates's throat. He hesitated there for just a second. Then, he cut the top from Bates's hat. The last thing he did before he sneaked back out of camp was leave a note, pinned to the hat.

Bates—
I know that you were one of the ones who wrecked and robbed the train. You, Cletus Odom, a Mexican

*named Paco, and a man named Schuler killed a lot
of people that day—including several women and
children.*

   *I could have cut your throat tonight, the way I cut
up your hat, but I'm going to wait until you lead
me to the others. And I know you will do that, Bates,
because anyone who is cowardly enough to kill
children is too much of a coward to face me alone.*

   *I figure you have no more than ten days left to live.
And to show you that I mean business, I am even
going to sign my name to this note. Prepare to die,
Bates.*

Matt Jensen

The next morning, Matt waited on top of a hill,
looking down on Bates's campsite. Matt wasn't on the
actual crest of the hill, but was just below the crest,
behind a cut that afforded him concealment. He
watched as Bates woke up.

The first thing Bates did when he awoke was relieve
himself. Then he rolled up his blanket, and was tying
it to the back of his saddle when he noticed his hat.
Matt could tell the very moment Bates saw the hat because he stopped what he was doing and stared at it
for a long moment as if he didn't know what he was
seeing. Then he saw the note and moved quickly to it,
jerking the note off and reading it.

Matt could hardly keep from laughing as he saw
Bates stiffen, then, gingerly, reach his hand up to his
throat. Bates looked at the hat, then let out a yell.

"Ahhhhhhhh!"

The yell echoed back.

"Ahhhhhhhh! Ahhhhhhhh! Ahhhhhhhh!"

Bates threw the hat down, then pulled his pistol and looked around.

Matt threw a rock and it hit far down the hill from his position, clattering as it bounced down the rocky hillside.

Bates began firing wildly, the shots echoing back, doubling and redoubling the sound so that Bates had the feeling he was being shot at, even though he was the only one shooting.

Quickly, Bates saddled his horse, then swinging into the saddle, urged the horse into a gallop.

Given Bates's weight and size, Matt knew that the horse would not be able to sustain a gallop for very long. Because of that, he was almost leisurely as he saddled Spirit, then rode at no more than a trot in pursuit.

Matt Jensen stopped on a ridge just above the road leading into Choulic. He took a swallow from his canteen and watched an approaching stage as it started down from the pass into the town. Then, corking the canteen, he slapped his legs against the side of his horse and sloped down the long ridge. Although he was actually farther away from town than the coach, he would beat it there because the stage would have to stay on the road, working its way down a series of switchbacks, whereas Matt rode down the side of the hill, difficult, but a much more direct route.

No railroad served Choulic, so the only way to reach it was by horse or by stagecoach. And after a few hours on a bumping, rattling, jerking, and dusty stagecoach, the passengers' first view of Choulic was often a bitter disappointment. Sometimes visitors from the East had to have the town pointed out to them, for from this perspective, and at this distance, the settlement looked little more inviting than another group of the brown hummocks and hills common to this country.

A small sign just on the edge of town read:

CHOULIC, population 294

A growing Community

The weathered board and faded letters of the sign indicated that it had been there for some time, erected when there might actually have been optimism for the town's future. Choulic was like many towns Matt had encountered over the years, towns that bloomed on the prairies and in the deserts desperately hoping the railroad would come through, staking all on that uncertain future, only to see their futures dashed when the railroad passed them by. Despite the ambitious welcome sign, Matt doubted that there were as many as two hundred residents in the town today, and he was positive that it was no longer a growing community.

The town baked under a sun that was yellow and hot.

Finding the saloon, Matt saw what he was looking for. Tied to the hitching rail out front were nine or ten horses, and one of them he recognized as belonging to Bates.

While Matt was dismounting, the stagecoach he had seen earlier came rolling into town, its driver whistling and shouting at the team. As was often the case, the driver had urged the team into a trot when they approached the edge of town. That way, the coach would roll in rapidly, making a somewhat more dramatic arrival than it would have had the team been walking.

The coach stopped in front of the depot at the far end of the street, and half-a-dozen people crowded around it. Matt turned his attention back to the task at hand, and checking the pistol in his holster, he went into the saloon.

The shadows made the saloon seem cooler inside, but that was illusory. It was nearly as hot inside as out, and without the benefit of a breath of air, it was even more stifling. The customers were sweating in their drinks and wiping their faces with bandannas. Matt looked for Bates, but he didn't see him.

The bartender was wearing an apron that might have been white at one time, but was now soiled and stained. On the bar in front of him were two abandoned glasses in which a little whiskey remained. One of the glasses had been used to extinguish the last dregs of a rolled cigarette. Picking out the little pieces of paper with his fingers, the bartender poured it, tobacco bits and all, into the other glass, then poured that back into a bottle. Corking the bottle, he put it on the shelf behind the bar. He wiped the glasses out with his stained apron, and set them back among the unused glasses. Seeing Matt step up to the bar, the bartender moved down toward him.

"Whiskey," Matt said.

The barman reached for the bottle he had just poured the whiskey back into, but Matt pointed to an unopened bottle.

"That one," he said.

Shrugging, the saloon keeper pulled the cork from the fresh bottle.

"I'm looking for a man named Odom," Matt said. "Cletus Odom."

"Mister, if you want whiskey or beer, I'm your man. If you want anything else, I can't help you," the bartender replied.

"How about a man named Bates? He's a big man. He isn't wearing a hat."

The bartender poured the whiskey into a glass.

"Bates' horse is tied up out front," Matt continued.

"Is he wanted?"

"I know Odom is. Bates might be."

"You the law?"

"No," Matt said.

"You a bounty hunter?"

"No."

"Then why are you lookin' for him?"

"It's personal," Matt said.

"Mister, maybe you don't know it but with the clientele I get in here, it ain't a good idea to go around blabbing everything I know. Hell, I could wind up gettin' myself kilt if I was to do somethin' like that," the bartender said.

Matt took out a ten-dollar bill and, though he wasn't obvious about it, he made certain that the bartender saw it.

"You say Bates is a big man. We have a lot of big men who come in here, so that doesn't tell me much. What about the other one you were talking about? What does he look like?"

"He's uglier than a toad," Matt said. "He has a purple scar on his face and a misshapen eyelid."

Matt did notice a slight reaction to his description.

"He is here, isn't he?" Matt asked.

The bartender said nothing, but looking around to make certain no one saw the transaction, he took the money, raised his eyes, and looked toward the stairs at the back of the room.

"Thanks," Matt said.

At the back of the saloon, a flight of wooden stairs led up to an enclosed loft. Matt guessed that the two doors at the head of the stairs led to the rooms used by the prostitutes who worked in the saloon. Pulling his pistol, he started up the stairs.

The few men in the saloon had been talking and laughing among themselves. When they saw Matt pull his gun, their conversation died, and they watched him walk quietly up the steps.

From the rooms above him, Matt could hear muffled sounds that left little doubt as to what was going on behind the closed doors. He tried to open the first door, but it was locked. He knocked on it.

"Go 'way," a voice called from the other side of the door.

Matt raised his foot and kicked the door hard. It flew open with a crash and the woman inside the room screamed.

"What the hell?" the man shouted. He stood up quickly, and Matt saw that it was the big man, Bates. He heard a crash of glass from the next room and he dashed to the window and looked down. He saw a naked Odom just getting to his feet from the leap to the alley below.

"Who the hell are you?" Bates shouted from behind him in the room.

Matt smiled at him. "Where's your hat, Bates?"

"It's you!" Bates yelled. Bates grabbed his knife from a bedside table. "You son of a bitch, I'm going to gut you like a hog!"

Bates lunged toward Matt, making a long, stomach-opening swipe. Matt barely managed to avoid the point of the knife. One inch closer and he would have been disemboweled.

Bates swung again and Matt jumped deftly to one side, then brought the barrel of his pistol down, sharply, on Bates's knife hand. That caused Bates to drop his knife and when it hit the floor, Matt kicked it so that it slid across the floor and under the bed.

Inexplicably, Bates smiled.

"Well, I'd rather kill you with my bare hands anyway," he said, lunging toward Matt.

Again, Matt stepped to one side, but this time he grabbed Bates and pushed him in the same direction that Bates had lunged, thus using Bates's own momentum against him. Bates slammed headfirst through the window, breaking the glass. With a sharp, gurgling sound, he pulled away from the window, staggered back a few paces, then fell to his knees. A large shard of glass was protruding from his neck. The glass had severed his carotid artery, causing bright red blood to spill from the wound down onto his naked chest.

"Where are the others?" Matt asked, kneeling beside

the wounded man. "The others who robbed the train. Where are they?"

"You—go—to—hell," Bates said. Blood bubbled at his lips when he spoke.

Matt heard a horse galloping away, and hurrying back to the broken and now bloodied window, he saw Odom, still naked, riding hard out of town, lashing the animal on both sides of his neck with the ends of the reins, urging him to greater speed.

Matt stood up angrily. He had lost valuable time trying to get the outlaw to talk. He turned and ran from the room, down the stairs, and out the front, then urged Spirit into a gallop in the direction Odom had gone.

Matt found the horse Odom had been riding about five miles out of town, contentedly cropping grass. He also found the body of a man who had been stripped naked. Odom now had clothes and a different horse.

Chapter Sixteen

As soon as the track was repaired and service restored, Marshal Kyle took the nine p.m. train, which was the first eastbound train from Sentinel. Deputy Hayes was in a pine box in the baggage car ahead. Kyle was taking him back to Purgatory, though he had no idea where to deliver the body, other than to the office of the city marshal.

The train was crowded because several eastbound passengers had waited for rail service to be restored, preferring to wait in the comfort of a Sentinel hotel to the long and uncomfortable ride in a stagecoach. Kyle managed to find a window seat halfway back in the second car, and once the train was under way, he watched the little yellow squares of light slide by on the ground outside the night train as he listened to the rhythmic click of the wheels passing over the rail joints.

In addition to Hayes's body, Kyle was carrying several wanted posters for Matt Jensen. This time, the wanted posters had a woodcut likeness of Jensen that was so accurate that several of the people who had been passengers on that ill-fated train remembered seeing him.

"I sure can't see this fella as a murderer, though," one of the injured passengers told Kyle. "He pulled me and two others from the wreckage. I don't reckon I'd be alive today, if it weren't for him."

That passenger's story was not unique, as it was repeated by at least a dozen others, if not from personal experience, then from observation.

"What kind of man are you, Matt Jensen?" Kyle asked quietly as he studied the picture. "On the one hand, you shoot a man down in cold blood. On the other, you go out of your way to save the lives of perfect strangers when you could have used the confusion of the train wreck as an opportunity to get away."

It was Kyle's intention to leave the packet of wanted posters with Marshal Cummins so they could be distributed, not only around Purgatory, but all over Maricopa County.

The run from Sentinel to Purgatory, which took almost six hours by stagecoach, took just over an hour by train. Even though he was on the train for such a short time, the gentle rocking of the car, the click of wheels over rail joints, and the rush of wind had combined to put Kyle asleep. He was awakened by the conductor's call.

"Purgatory, Purgatory!" he called. "Folks, if you are going on through, don't get off the train because we will only be here long enough to let off some passengers and pick up a few more. We will not be here more than a couple of minutes. This here is Purgatory," he repeated. The conductor stopped beside Kyle.

"Marshal, I believe you said you were going to Purgatory?" he asked.

"Yes," Kyle replied. "Thanks for waking me up."

"Well, you only paid as far as Purgatory," the conductor said. "I couldn't let you go any farther now, could I?" He laughed at his own joke.

"I reckon not," Kyle replied. "Conductor, you understand I have something that has to be unloaded from the baggage car, don't you?"

"Yes, sir, Marshal, don't you worry none," the conductor said. "We won't leave till that's all taken care of."

"Thanks."

Kyle felt the train beginning to lose speed, a gradual slowing at first, then slower, and slower still, until by the time they reached Purgatory, the train was traveling at a virtual crawl. Looking through the window, he saw the dark, or at best dimly lit, houses sliding by outside until, finally, the train came to the much more brightly lit depot. There, the train stopped with the screech of steel on steel, and a final jerk, which left them motionless. The few who were getting off here got up from their seats, reached into the overhead bins for their packages, then began shuffling toward the end of the car in order to detrain. The passengers who were going on remained in their seats, some dozing, some reading, others looking through the window.

Stepping down from the train, Kyle stood on a wooden platform that was adequately, if not brightly, lit by several kerosene lanterns. While the train snapped and popped and hissed alongside him, he watched as Hayes's coffin was taken down.

"What have we got here?" the station agent asked, coming over to look at the coffin.

"Who are you?" Kyle asked.

"I'm Colin Randall. I'm the Southern Pacific agent in charge of this depot. Who are you?"

"I'm U.S. Marshal Ben Kyle. This is Deputy Hayes," he said, pointing to the box. "He is one of yours, I believe."

"Hardly one of mine, Marshal," Randall said disdainfully. He sighed. "However, he does belong to Marshal Cummins."

"Do you know where I can hire a wagon at this hour?"

Randall held up his finger as if asking Kyle to give him a moment. "Bustamante!" he called.

"Sí, señor?" A short, stubby, gray-haired Mexican shuffled out from the freight section of the depot.

"Hitch up the wagon and take the marshal where he wants to go."

"Sí, señor."

Kyle waited for a few minutes; then he heard the creaking sound of a wheel in need of lubrication. A moment later, he saw the wagon appear from the side of the depot. Bustamante drove up to Marshal Kyle, then stopped.

"Grab that end, will you?" Kyle ordered, standing at one end of the coffin.

"Sí, señor."

Because there were only two of them, it was a heavy lift to put the box containing Hayes's body on the back of the wagon, but they were able to do so. Then Kyle climbed up onto the seat.

"Where to, Señor?" Bustamante asked.

"The city marshal's office," Kyle answered.

"*Sí.*"

They were the only traffic on the street as they drove from the railroad depot to the city marshal's office. Behind them the train, after a few blasts on the whistle, got under way with the puffing of steam and the sound of the coupling slack being taken up as, one by one, the cars were jerked into motion. There were a few moments of train noise. Then, as the train noise faded, the only sounds remaining were that of the wagon, the hollow sound of the horse's hoofbeats, and the incessant squeaking of the wheel that Kyle had determined was the left front one.

"You need to do something about that wheel," Kyle said.

"*Sí, señor,*" Bustamante replied, staring straight ahead and with no change of facial expression. It seemed fairly obvious to Kyle that this subject had been broached with Bustamante before, and probably responded to in the same way.

The wagon pulled up to the front of the city marshal's office, then stopped.

"Wait here," Kyle told Busatamante.

"For how long, Señor?"

"For as long as it takes," Kyle said resolutely.

"*Sí, señor.*"

Going inside, he saw someone sitting in a chair behind a desk. The chair was tilted back, so that the man's head was resting against the wall. His eyes were closed, his mouth was open, and Kyle could hear the deep, rhythmic breathing of sleep.

"Excuse me," Kyle said.

The response was a quiet snore.

"Excuse me," Kyle said, louder this time.

The man's eyes popped open.

"Yeah, what do you want?"

"Are you Marshal Cummins?"

"No, I'm his deputy."

"Do you have a name?"

"Yeah, I have a name," the deputy answered with a snarl. "Do you have a name?"

"I'm United States Marshal Ben Kyle," Kyle said pointedly. "What is your name, Deputy?"

The deputy tipped his chair forward, then stood up. "The name is Warren. Deputy Ted Warren, Marshal. What can I do for you?"

"I have Deputy Hayes' body on a wagon out front," Kyle said. "I want you to take care of it."

"What? What the hell am I supposed to do with that?"

"I don't care what you do with it," Kyle said. "I brought the body back, now it's your problem. Get it off the wagon."

"How'm I goin' to do that? I'm all by myself here."

"Like I said, that's your problem," Kyle repeated.

"I've got some men in jail, I'll have them help me," Warren said.

"Fine, you do that. Where can I find the marshal?"

"More'n likely he's down at the Pair O Dice."

"The what?"

"The Pair O Dice. It's the saloon, just down the street. He 'n' all the other deputies hang out down there."

"All the other deputies? How many deputies are there?"

"Eight—well, no, only six now, seein' as both Gillis and Hayes has been kilt."

"Six deputies in a town of less than three hundred?" Kyle said, surprised at the number. "My God, man, that's one deputy for every fifty people."

"Yes, sir, well, Marshal Cummins, he likes to keep order," Warren said.

"You get Hayes' body taken care of," Kyle ordered. "I'm going to find the marshal."

"Yes, sir," Warren said. He took a large key ring off a hook on the wall behind the desk. Walking over to the cell, he opened the door and called out to the two prisoners who were inside.

"Poke, Casper, come help me get somethin' off a wagon."

As the two prisoners struggled with the coffin containing Hayes's body, Kyle left the marshal's office and walked up the street to the saloon.

The Pair O Dice was the most substantial-looking building in the entire town. There was a drunk passed out on the steps in front of the place, and Kyle had to step over him in order to go inside. Because all the chimneys of all the lanterns were soot-covered, what light there was was dingy and filtered through drifting smoke. The place smelled of sour whiskey, stale beer, and strong tobacco. There was a long bar on the left, with dirty towels hanging on hooks about every five feet along its front. A large mirror was behind the bar, but like everything else about the saloon, it was so dirty that Kyle could scarcely see any images in it, and what he could see was distorted by imperfections in the glass.

Over against the back wall, near the foot of the stairs, a cigar-scarred, beer-stained upright piano was being played by a bald-headed musician. The tune was "Buffalo Gals," and one of the girls who was a buffalo gal stood alongside, swaying to the music. Kyle was once told that this song was now very popular back East, and was often sung by the most genteel ladies. The Easterners had no idea that the term buffalo gal referred to doxies who, during the rapid expansion of the railroad, had to ply their trade on buffalo robes thrown out on the ground. This was because there were few beds and fewer buildings.

Kyle couldn't help but make a comparison between this saloon and the Ox Bow back in Sentinel. The Pair O Dice did not come out well in the comparison.

Out on the floor of the saloon, nearly all the tables were filled. A half-dozen or so buffalo gals were flitting about, pushing drinks and promising more than they really intended to deliver. A few card games were in progress, but most of the patrons were just drinking and talking.

An exceptionally loud burst of laughter came from one of the tables and, looking toward it, Kyle saw that all the men were wearing stars on their shirts or vests. There were six men and three girls at the table, which was the largest table in the saloon.

Kyle walked over toward them, then dropped the bundle of wanted posters on the table.

"What the hell is this?" one of the men asked.

"What does it look like?" Kyle replied.

"I'll ask the ques—" the man at the table began, but looking up, he saw Kyle's badge. "You're a U.S. marshal?" he asked.

"I am. The name is Kyle. You're Marshal Cummins, I take it?"

"Yeah," Cummins said. He looked at the bundle, then smiled. "I'll be damned," he said. "How'd you get a picture of him?"

"Does it look like him?"

"Yeah," Cummins said. "It looks just like him. What do you think, boys?" he asked.

All the deputies commented in the affirmative.

"Duke, get the marshal a chair," Cummins ordered. "Crack, you get some of these posters passed out."

The two deputies got up to comply with the marshal's order, Crack taking the dodgers with him, and Duke bringing over a chair for the U.S. marshal. Kyle sat at the table with the others.

"Tell me, Marshal, what brings you to Purgatory?" Marshal Cummins asked. "You could've just sent these posters."

"I brought Deputy Hayes' body back," Kyle said.

"You brought his body back? Why in the hell did you do that?"

"He was your deputy, wasn't he?"

"Yes."

"Then I figured this was the place for him. We have enough bodies over in Sentinel now, what with the train wreck."

"Yeah, I reckon you would at that," Cummins said. "So, you say you brought Hayes back. Where is he?"

"He is in your office," Kyle answered.

"In my office? Damn, why did you take him there? What the hell am I supposed to do with the son of a bitch?"

"Well, this is just a guess, mind you, but it's been my experience that it is generally customary to bury bodies," Kyle replied.

"Well, yeah, sure, but families do that, don't they?"

"Does Hayes have a family here?"

"No," Cummins said. "Fact is, I don't even know where his family is."

"I think Hayes was from somewhere in Texas," one of the deputies said.

"He was from somewhere in Texas? That's not very helpful. Texas is a big state," Kyle said.

"Yeah, I know it is. But that's all he ever told me. He just said that he was from somewhere in Texas."

"I think he got in trouble with the law back there," one of the other deputies said.

"He was in trouble with the law, but you hired him as a lawman?" Kyle asked.

"He was a good deputy," Cummins said. "And when someone comes out here, I believe in givin' them a fresh start."

"Then it seems to me that the least you can do is give him a decent burial," Kyle said.

Cummins stroked his chin for a moment, then he nodded. "Yeah," he said. "Yeah, I reckon I can do that."

"Tell me something about Jensen," Kyle said.

"Tell you about Jensen?"

"Yes, what kind of man is he?"

"He's a cold-blooded murderer, that's what kind of man he is," Cummins said.

"That's funny, because from everything I've been able to find out about him, he just doesn't fit the picture of a cold-blooded murderer. What was he like before the murder?"

"Don't nobody know," Cummins said. "He just come into town and shot Deputy Gillis without so much as a fare-thee-well. Nobody had ever seen him before that."

"You mean the day he arrived is the day he shot Gillis?"

"Not the day he arrived, the moment he arrived."

"Did he know Gillis from before?"

"Not that I know of," Cummins said.

"Did Gillis give him any call to shoot him?"

"No," Cummins said. "All Gillis done was try and collect the tax from him."

Kyle looked confused. "What tax? I thought you said he had just come into town?"

"That's true, he had just come into town. But there's a five-dollar visitors tax for ever'one who comes into town. 'Cept you, of course, you bein' the law and all."

"So, what you are saying is, Gillis tried to collect the visitors tax and Jensen didn't want to pay it, so he shot him down in cold blood."

"Yeah, that's what we're sayin'."

"Were there any witnesses?"

"We all saw it," Cummins said.

"Yeah, ever'one of us, plus a bunch of the folks that was in the saloon that day," one of the other deputies said. "They seen it, too."

"And you are?" Kyle asked.

"Duke. The name is Duke."

"So, it happened here in the saloon?"

"Same as. It was out front."

"No," Kyle said. "Out front is not the same as happening inside. Were any of you out front when it happened?"

"Yeah," Cummins answered. "Jackson was out front. He saw it."

"Who is Jackson?"

"I am," one of the deputies said.

"And you saw it?"

"We all saw it, in a manner of speaking," Cummins said, answering for Jackson. "We heard the shot, then we seen Gillis come in here with a hole in his chest. He took about two or three steps, then he fell dead on the floor. Right after that, Jensen come in behind him, and he was still holdin' the gun in his hand."

"And the gun was still smokin'," one of the other deputies said.

"What about Gillis's gun?"

Cummins smiled broadly. "I was hopin' you'd ask me that," he said. "Gillis's gun was still in his holster. He hadn't even drawn it."

"Jackson, tell me exactly what you saw," Kyle asked.

"It's like they said. We heard the shot, then we seen Gillis come into the saloon with a bullet hole in his chest."

"What do you mean you heard the shot? I thought you said you saw it."

"Yeah, uh—yeah, I did see it."

"You said, and I quote, 'Then we seen Gillis come into the saloon.' How could you see him come into the saloon if you were out front?"

"I didn't say he was out front, Marshal," Cummins

said, speaking quickly. "I said he saw it. Jackson was standing over there in the window, looking outside."

"Yeah," Jackson said. "I was standin' over there by the window, lookin' outside."

Kyle stroked his chin for a moment. "I have to agree that your account does sound pretty damming," Kyle said.

"I thought you'd see it our way, once you knew the whole story," Cummins said.

"Yes, well, like I said, the picture folks painted of Jensen after the train wreck just didn't quite fit with what happened here. But then, the evidence is pretty strong that he did shoot Hayes after the train wreck."

"I don't doubt that he did that," Cummins said. "I mean, we already know he was a killer, but he was in chains, and he didn't have a gun, so the truth is, I'm wonderin' how he did it."

"Hayes had a gun, didn't he?" Kyle asked.

"Yes."

"We didn't find a gun with Hayes," Kyle said. "So I figure that the train wreck must've knocked Hayes out, and that's when Jensen got the keys, unlocked his shackles, then took the deputy's pistol. After that, he needed to keep Hayes from coming to and identifying him, so he shot deputy with his own gun."

"Damn, that was a brand-new gun, too," Duke said. "I was with him when he bought it off the gun salesman that come through here. A Smith and Wesson .44. Yes, sir, Hayes set some store in that gun."

"Did you say it was a .44?"

"Yes."

"That's funny."

"What's funny?"

Kyle reached into his shirt pocket and pulled out a bullet. He showed it to the others. "This is the bullet that killed Hayes," he said. "I had the undertaker extract it for me."

"So?"

"This is a .36 caliber."

"You sure that's a .36 caliber?" Cummins asked. "Sometimes a bullet will get all bent out of shape when it's been fired. I've seen it a lot of times, and I know you have, too."

"Does this bullet look all out of shape to you?" Kyle asked.

Cummins shook his head. "No, it don't. But that don't mean nothin'. Jensen must've had a pistol hid on him somewhere."

"Are you telling me that you arrested him, tried him, found him guilty, and sentenced him, but in all that time you never bothered to search him for a pistol?"

"Well, it might have been one of them derringers," Duke said. "They're little and you can hide them real good."

"The only derringers I know are .41 caliber," Kyle said.

"Yeah, well, it don't make no difference whether Jensen kilt Hayes or not. We know he kilt Gillis, and that's what he was bein' sent to Yuma for."

"That's true," Kyle agreed. "No matter what happened with Hayes, it doesn't let Mr. Jensen off the hook. He still stands convicted for killing Deputy Gillis. But it does make my job of finding out what actually happened to Hayes and the money from the train robbery a little more difficult."

"Money?" Cummins said. "What money from the train robbery?"

"The train was carrying a money shipment of twenty thousand dollars," Kyle said. "That money is gone, Jensen is gone. It stands to reason that he took it."

Cummins whistled. "Twenty thousand dollars. Damn, what I couldn't do with that money."

There was a disapproving expression on Kyle's face as he looked at Cummins.

"What are you lookin' at?" Cummins asked.

"What do you mean, what you couldn't do with that money?" Kyle asked. "That's a strange thing for a law enforcement officer to say."

"Hell, it ain't like I was thinkin' on stealin' it," Cummins defended. "I was just commentin' on how nice it would be to have that much money. Don't you agree?"

"It isn't something I let myself think about," Kyle replied.

Chapter Seventeen

"Marshal? Marshal Cummins?"

The lawmen looked around to see Joe Claibie standing by the bar. He was holding one of the wanted dodgers.

"Yeah, Claibie, what is it?" Cummins asked.

Claibie held up one of the wanted flyers that Kyle had brought with him. "Crack give me this here dodger a couple minutes ago."

"Yes, I told him to hand some of them out."

"Well, the thing is, him givin' me this flyer and all makes me think I know who it was now that stole your horse."

"Stole my horse?" Cummins said in an agitated voice. "What do you mean? When was my horse stole?"

"Not the horse you ride," Claibie said. "I'm talkin' about the sorrel you was goin' to sell. You mind that sorrel?"

"Yes, of course I remember it."

"Well, sir, I'm right sure that I know who stole it. It

was this here same fella that you got on the wanted poster here."

Claibie showed the marshal the woodcut picture on the flyer.

"Matt Jensen? Are you tellin' us that Matt Jensen is the one stole that horse?"

"Yeah, that's what I'm tellin' you."

"You're out of your mind. Jensen is long gone from here."

"He ain't that long gone," Claibie said. "He was here just a couple of days ago."

"Are you talkin' about before Gillis was kilt?" Jackson asked.

Claibie shook his head. "No, sir, I'm talkin' after that. Fact is, I'm talkin' about after the train wreck, too, 'cause what he done was, he brung in a string of horses from Sentinel."

"I don't understand," Cummins said. "Why would he bring in a string of horses?"

"He done that because we had had to put on extra coaches 'cause of the train wreck."

"So what you are saying is, after Matt Jensen escaped, he took a job with the stage line, then came back to the same place where he was convicted for murder?" Cummins asked. "Either you are out of your mind, or he is."

"If this here fella in the picture is Matt Jensen, then yes, sir, that's exactly what I'm sayin'," Claibie said.

"All right, suppose it is. Suppose he did bring a string of horses into town. What does that have to do with my horse? What makes you think he's the one that stole it?" Cummins asked.

"Because after he brung them horses in, we started talking about horses and such. I mean, him not havin' one, you see. He rode in here on one of the horses that belongs to the stage line. He said he was lookin' for a horse, so I told him about the sorrel you had for sale and he seemed real interested. I figured maybe he would buy it, and maybe if he done that, why, you'd give me a little somethin' for steerin' him to you. Of course, after seein' his picture on this poster, I know why he was interested. And of course, that bein' his horse you had, why, he wouldn't have no trouble ridin' it or nothin'."

"It wasn't his horse!" Cummins said angrily. "That horse was contraband. I confiscated it legal and proper after the trial."

"Excuse me, Marshal, but when you do that, aren't you supposed to hold an auction, with all the proceeds to go to the city?" Kyle asked.

"I did hold an auction," Cummins said. "And I bought and paid for it, with my own money. That money did go to the city."

"When did you see Jensen?" Kyle asked.

"Two days ago," Claibie answered.

Kyle looked at Cummins. "And when was your horse stolen?"

"Two days ago," Cummins admitted.

"Then I'd say that Claibie is right. Jensen is the one who took it."

"Claibie, if you saw him, why the hell didn't you report him to someone?" Cummins asked.

"How was I to know who he was, Marshal? He never told me his name or nothin'. And I hadn't never seen him."

"You didn't see him at the trial?" Kyle asked.

"I didn't know nothin' 'bout the trial. By the time I heard about Gillis gettin' hisself kilt and all, why, this here fella had already been tried and was on the train to Yuma to get hisself hung."

Kyle looked at Cummins. "Are you telling me that the killing and the trial happened on the same day?"

"Yes."

"And Judge Craig allowed that?"

"Judge Craig didn't have nothin' to do with it," Cummins said. "I held the trial my ownself."

"You held the trial?"

"In addition to bein' the city marshal, I'm also an associate circuit court judge," Cummins said. "It was all legal and proper."

"It was awfully fast, wasn't it?"

"We had to do it fast, Marshal," Cummins answered. "Deputy Gillis was just a real popular man. He was well liked by everyone, and there were folks around here wantin' to string Jensen up that very day. Only way I could keep order was to have a real fast trial."

"The only way you could keep order?" Kyle questioned. "My God, man, you've got six deputies for a town that has a population of less than three hundred people. Do you expect me to believe that you couldn't keep order?"

"Like I said, Deputy Gillis was a very popular man," Cummins repeated. "And feelin's was runnin' real high then. I done what I thought was right."

"You did what you thought was right? Or you did what you wanted to do?" Kyle asked.

Cummins smiled. "Why, Marshal, wouldn't that be the same thing?" he asked.

"Would you like dessert, Marshal? We have a wonderful cherry pie."

Kyle, who had eaten a late dinner in the City Pig Café, looked up at the waiter. "Cherry pie, you say?"

"Yes, sir, just baked today."

"Well, now, I suppose a piece of cherry pie would be good. And another cup of coffee, if you don't mind."

"I'll bring it right out," the waiter promised.

As the waiter walked away, Kyle saw someone approaching his table. The man had unkempt silver hair and clothes that were disheveled, absolute indications that he was down on his luck. Kyle was sure the man was coming to ask him for enough money to buy a drink, and anxious to get rid of him, he reached into his pocket for a nickel. He held the coin out toward the man as he reached the table.

"Here you go, friend," he said. "Have a drink on me."

"Thank you, but no," the man replied. "I've been six days without a drink, and I hope never to take another."

"You don't say," Kyle said, surprised by the man's pronouncement. "Well, then, what can I do for you?"

"Did the governor send you?" the man asked. "Are you here in response to my letter?"

"No," Kyle said, shaking his head. "I don't know anything about a letter."

"Oh," the man said, obviously disappointed. "You are a U.S. marshal, aren't you?"

"Yes."

"I was sure you had come in response to my letter."

"What letter would that be?"

"You are a U.S. marshal?"

"Yes. I'm Marshal Ben Kyle."

"Marshal Kyle, my name is Robert Dempster. I am an attorney."

"An attorney?" Kyle asked, obviously surprised by the man's announcement. Then, realizing how that must've sounded, he apologized. "I'm sorry, I didn't mean to sound—"

"That's all right," Dempster said quickly. "There is no need to apologize. I realize that I make less than a sterling impression. I wonder, Marshal, if I might have a few words with you?"

At that moment the waiter brought the pie and coffee.

"Won't you join me, Mr. Dempster?" Kyle asked. "Waiter, bring another piece of pie and a cup of coffee."

"There's no need for you to—" Dempster began.

"Please, join me," Kyle said.

"All right," Dempster agreed. "I don't mind if I do."

"Another slice of pie and another cup of coffee," Kyle said again.

"Are you sure it's coffee you want?" the waiter asked, looking at Dempster with obvious disdain.

"I believe I said coffee," Kyle said, his voice showing his irritation with the waiter's rudeness.

"Yes, sir, right away," the waiter responded.

"I'm sorry for that man's insolence," Kyle said.

"Don't blame him," Dempster replied. "I've brought this on myself."

"You say you are a lawyer?"

"Yes."

"What—uh—what brought on this—this present condition? Wait, never mind it's none of my business. You don't have to answer that."

The waiter delivered the pie and coffee, and then withdrew without a word.

"It's all right," Dempster said, holding his response to Kyle until after the waiter left. "I can see why one might be curious."

Dempster added a copious amount of sugar and cream to his coffee, then stirred it with a spoon for a long moment, as if gathering his thoughts.

"Back in Missouri, I was a circuit judge," he said.

"That's quite an honorable position."

"Yes," Dempster said. "Which makes the fact that I dishonored it even more reprehensible."

"You took a bribe?"

"In a manner of speaking, I suppose you could say that," Dempster said. "I was trying a murder case when some friends of the defendant informed me that if I did not find some way to free their friend, they would kill my family and me."

"And did you find some way to free the defendant?"

"Yes, I did just as they asked."

"Well, if your family was in danger, I don't know as too many people can blame you."

Dempster took a drink of his coffee. "Only it didn't help," he said quietly.

"What?"

"They killed my family anyway."

"Oh, damn," Kyle said. "Damn, no wonder you—have problems."

"Problems with no solution," Dempster said. "Drinking is no solution."

"You said that you haven't had a drink in six days," Kyle said. "That's a long time between drinks for an alcoholic, isn't it?"

"Yes. I hope it goes much longer."

"What made you stop drinking?"

"Matt Jensen," Dempster answered.

"Matt Jensen? Are you talking about the convicted murderer?"

"Mr. Jensen is no more of a murderer than I am," Dempster said. "His trial was a charade and the biggest miscarriage of justice I have ever seen."

"Was it a real trial? Did he have a judge, a lawyer, and a jury of his peers?" Kyle asked.

"His defense attorney was an incompetent drunk, the judge was crooked, and the jury was fixed."

"That's quite a charge," Kyle said.

"I suppose it is," Dempster agreed. "But I would gladly make that same charge in an open courtroom. Assuming, of course, that the judge hearing the case would be someone other than Andrew Cummins," he added.

"Yes, I can see how you might be hesitant to make such a charge to the very man you are making the charge about. But let me ask you this. What makes you think this man, Jensen, is innocent? I was told by Marshal Cummins that there were eyewitnesses to the shooting who confirmed that he killed Deputy Gillis."

"There was only one eyewitness to the shooting, a young boy, and the story he told me exactly coincided with what Jensen said. Gillis drew first, but Jensen was much faster. He drew his own pistol and shot Gillis.

Gillis's pistol slipped back down into his holster. But it was not until he went into the saloon that anyone else saw him. That's where he died."

"I believe you said you sent a letter to the governor?"

"I did indeed," Dempster said. "I asked the governor to stay the execution until another trial, a fair trial, could be arranged."

"As it turns out, your letter was unnecessary," Kyle said. "It would seem that Jensen has arranged his own stay of execution. He escaped."

"So I've heard," Dempster said. "I hope he gets clear out of Arizona. But I would also hope he could clear his name so this doesn't hang over him for the rest of his life."

"Mr. Dempster, if what you tell me is true, then I must say that you have not painted a very good picture of your marshal," Kyle said.

"Our marshal is a despot," Dempster said. "He rules this town as if it is his own personal fiefdom."

"Why does the town council allow such a thing?"

"He has enough of his deputies placed on the council that he quite easily controls it. They pass any law he dictates and authorize any funding he requests. As a matter of fact, the council no longer even serves the town. They are here for one purpose, and one purpose only. They exist for the convenience of Marshal Andrew Cummins."

"Do the people of the town support Marshal Cummins?"

"Support him?" Dempster replied. "No, they don't support him, but most are too frightened to do anything about it. There are a few merchants who have been holding secret meetings, I understand, but whether or not they will be able to do anything, I don't know."

"Have you met with them?"

Dempster shook his head. "No," he replied. "I have not earned their trust. But I hope to. Right now, the thing that is keeping me sober is my determination to see Marshal Cummins run out of office and justice done."

"That is an honorable goal," Kyle said.

Dempster ate the last bite of pie, then smacked his lips appreciatively. "You know, coming off a three-year drunk, I had forgotten all the good things about life, such as cherry pie. I thank you."

"It was my pleasure," Kyle replied.

Chapter Eighteen

The Bob Dempster who showed up at the meeting held at Joel Montgomery's bank did not look like the Dempster everyone thought they knew. Dempster had taken a bath, gotten a haircut and shave, and was wearing a very nice suit. He arrived at the meeting with Marshal Kyle, Mrs. Dawkins, and her son, Timmy.

"It's good of you to come, Mr. Dempster," Montgomery said.

"I thank you very much for allowing me to come," Dempster replied. "I am well aware of the fact that I have not conducted myself in any way that would inspire confidence."

"I believe everyone deserves a second chance," Montgomery said. "Marshal, Mrs. Dawkins, Timmy, it's good to have you as well. Please, come into the conference room and have a seat. The meeting is about to get started."

Dempster, Kyle, Mrs. Dawkins, and Timmy followed Montgomery to the back of the bank, where

Montgomery opened a door to show them into the back room.

"Do you think it will be safe here?" Mrs. Dawkins asked.

"We've got the marshal with us," Dempster said. "How much safer do you want it?"

"The marshal isn't always going to be here," Mrs. Dawkins pointed out. "And after he leaves, Marshal Cummins will still be here."

"It's safe," Montgomery said. "We've had several meetings here without any problem. I often have to work late, so people are used to seeing a light in here. Besides, at this time of night, the marshal and his deputies are over at the Pair O Dice, drinking."

"That's not all they do over there," Goff said with a ribald chuckle.

"Amon, we have a woman and a child with us," Montgomery chastised.

"Sorry, ma'am, didn't mean nothin' by it," Goff said.

"I've taken no offense, Mr. Goff," Mrs. Dawkins said. "I want to do what is best for the town, but I'm sure you can understand that my primary concern is for the safety of my son."

"Yes, ma'am, that's our concern as well," Montgomery said. "And on behalf of the Citizens' Betterment Committee, I want to thank you and your son, and tell you that we understand the danger, and appreciate your courage in coming to the meeting."

"Citizens' Betterment Committee," Mrs. Dawkins said. She smiled, and nodded her head. "Yes, I like that."

"All right, if everyone will take their seats, we'll get started now," Montgomery said.

Goff, Goodman, Taylor, and Bascomb, who were, in addition to Montgomery, members of the Citizens' Betterment Committee, took their seats around the table. Dempster, Kyle, Mrs. Dawkins, and Timmy joined them.

"Timmy, my wife made some cookies if you'd like one," Taylor said, offering a plate of cookies to Timmy.

"Gee, thanks," Timmy said, taking three of them.

"Timmy, he said one," Mrs. Dawkins said.

"That's all right, Mrs. Dawkins, he can have as many as he wants," Taylor said. Then, seeing the expression on the woman's face, he amended his comment. "Although you are right. Too many wouldn't be good for him."

Timmy put two of the cookies back.

"Gentlemen," Montgomery said. "I called this meeting after Marshal Kyle and Mr. Dempster came to visit me. As you know, Marshal Cummins recently conducted a court trial, if you can call it that, in which he found a man guilty and sentenced him to hang. In order to give some semblance of legality to it, he had the man sent to Yuma Prison, where the hanging was to be carried out. As you also know, Robert Demptster acted as defense counsel for the accused. He came to me with an interesting account of that trial, and I invited him to share the information with the rest of us. Mr. Dempster, the floor is yours, sir."

"Thank you," Dempster said. He cleared his throat, then stood up to speak to the others.

"Mr. Montgomery is correct when he says I acted as defense counsel for the accused. In this case acted is the operative word, for the truth is, I was far too drunk to provide an adequate defense for anyone.

"Marshal Cummins knew this, and counted upon this when he selected me as attorney for the defense.

"I'm not going to go through a litany of all the errors in this trial that could cause a reversal of the outcome—though they are legion. I will tell you, however, that any fair judge would at the least call this a mistrial, and in all probability completely reverse the decision and declare Matt Jensen innocent."

"Mr. Dempster, may I ask a question?" Goff asked, holding up his hand.

"Certainly, Mr. Goff."

"I know that you, being a lawyer and all, are probably concerned about all the technical things of the trial, whether he got a good defense, whether the trial was held too fast, that sort of thing. But shouldn't the bottom line be whether or not he is guilty? I mean, if he killed Moe Gillis in cold blood, then that's murder and it seems to me like it shouldn't make all that difference how the trial was conducted. The man committed murder, and he should pay for it."

"That's just it," Dempster said. "I don't think the man did commit murder."

"How can you say that?" Goff asked. "My brother-in-law was in the saloon that day, and he tells me that he saw Gillis come staggering in through the door, already gut-shot, with his pistol in his holster. Then, a second or two later, this fella Jensen come in behind him, holding a gun in his hand. And that gun, my brother-in-law says, was still smoking."

"There was only one eyewitness to the actual event," Dempster said. "And he tells a different story."

"What about Jackson?" Goodman asked. "I hear Jackson was standin' in front of the saloon, and he seen the whole thing."

Dempster shook his head. "Jackson did not see it."

"He claims that he did."

"Gentlemen, I was present when I heard Marshal Cummins order Jackson to make that claim."

"Wait a minute, hold it. Are you saying that the marshal told Jackson to lie?" Taylor asked.

Goff laughed. "My oh my, who could possibly believe that our marshal would ask someone to lie for him."

The others laughed as well.

"You said there was an eyewitness," Goff said.

"Yes."

"Who was it?"

"It was young Timmy Dawkins," Dempster said.

"A kid? You're saying the only eyewitness was a kid?"

"That's what I'm saying."

"Come on, who's going to believe a kid? And how did he happen to see it in the first place?"

"Timmy, you want to answer that?" Dempster asked.

"I was in the dress shop with Mama," Timmy said. "It's right across the street from where it happened. I was looking through the window and saw it all."

"All right," Goodman said. "Maybe the kid did see it. But like Goff said, who is going to believe a kid? Even if Timmy thinks he is telling the truth, kids don't always see things the way they actually are."

"Timmy happens to be a remarkably observant young man," Dempster said.

"Observant? What do you mean, remarkably observant?"

"Test him."

"What do you mean, test him?"

"Ask him something to test his observation skills."

"All right," Goodman said. "Timmy, there is a calendar in this room. Without looking at it, tell me about the picture."

"It is a picture of a train at night," Timmy said. "The train's headlight is on, and some of the car windows are lit, but not all of them. And there is a coyote on a cliff, looking down at the train."

Goodman smiled. "Yes. That's very good."

"Timmy, am I wearing a ring?" Goff asked.

"No, sir, you aren't. But Mr. Montgomery is," Timmy answered. "It has a red stone."

Montgomery's hands were under the table, and with a smile, he raised them to show a ring with a red stone.

"All right," Goodman said. "I think we can all agree that Timmy is a very observant and very bright young man."

"Good," Dempster said. He looked over at Timmy. "Tell us exactly what you saw on the day of the shooting," he said.

"I saw Mr. Jensen come riding into town," Timmy said. "Of course, I didn't know who he was then. But I saw that he was riding a very pretty sorrel horse. He got off the horse, hung a wet hat onto the saddle—"

"Wait a minute, a wet hat? How could his hat be wet? It wasn't raining that day," Goff said.

"I wondered about that as well," Dempster said. "But it turns out that as Jensen rode into town, he stopped at Mrs. Poindexter's place. She was pumping water into a bucket. He finished filling the bucket for her. Then he pumped water into his hat and gave it to his horse."

"I'll be damn. Then it checks out," Goff said. "Oh, beg pardon for the cuss word, Mrs. Dawkins."

"That's quite all right," Mrs. Dawkins said.

"Go on with your account, Timmy," Dempster said.

"Yes, sir," Timmy said. "Well, after he hung the wet hat on the saddle, he tied his horse to the hitching rail in front of the saloon. Then Deputy Gillis stepped out onto the front porch. They talked for a moment, but I couldn't hear what they were talking about. Then, Deputy Gillis reached for his gun. Mr. Jensen went for his gun, too, and he drew his faster than Deputy Gillis. He shot Deputy Gillis—and the deputy dropped his pistol back into his holster, then turned and walked back into the saloon. Mr. Jensen followed him into the saloon, and that was all I saw."

"Thank you, Timmy," Dempster said. He looked at the others. "You may be interested to know that this is the very same story Jensen told during that debacle of a trial."

Montgomery drummed his hands on the table. "All right, suppose this is true," he said. "At this point, what can we do about it?"

"We can remove the marshal," Dempster said.

"How?"

"If you will back me up with a bill of particulars, I will go to the governor's office," Kyle said.

"Will the governor listen to us?" Taylor asked.

"I think he will," Kyle said. He glanced over at Dempster. "Mr. Dempster has started the ball rolling with a letter he sent to the governor. I'll follow up on it."

"You can count on us, Marshal," Montgomery said.

Chapter Nineteen

Kyle was sitting in the governor's outer office. He was holding his white hat in his lap, and he glanced down toward his boots, which gleamed in a high gloss, polished just for this occasion.

At the back of the room was a door, and in the transom window over the door were the words GOVERNOR'S OFFICE. The door opened, and an aide to the governor came out.

"Governor Frémont will see you now, Marshal Kyle," the aide said.

"Thank you," Kyle said.

The door to the governor's office was open and, looking in, Kyle saw John C. Frémont standing with his back to the door, studying a map that was hung on the wall. The map was very large, and included all the states and territories west of the Mississippi River. It appeared that Frémont had not seen Kyle, so the marshal cleared his throat and tapped lightly on the door frame.

"Why does everyone clear their throat to announce

their presence?" the governor asked without turning around. "Why not just call out, 'Hey, you?'"

"Hey, you," Kyle said, and the governor's resultant laughter was genuine. The tension was eased as the governor turned to face Kyle.

"So, Marshal, you are here to talk about the town of Purgatory?" Governor Frémont asked.

"Yes, sir," Kyle replied.

"Do you know the town?"

"I just came from Purgatory," Kyle said.

"That's not what I asked. I asked if you know the town."

Kyle nodded. "I think I do," he said. "It was more than just a casual visit. I met with some of the town's most influential people."

"Robert Dempster?"

"Yes, sir, I met with Dempster."

"He's a drunk, isn't he?"

"Do you know Mr. Dempster?"

"I know him by reputation only," Governor Frémont said. "From what I understand, he was once a very fine jurist."

"Yes, sir, that is my understanding as well," Kyle said.

"And now he is a drunk."

"I think it might be better to say that now he is a reformed drunk," Kyle said. "When I met him he was sober, and he stayed sober for the entire time I was there."

"I see," Frémont said. "Well, I'm glad to hear that." He stroked his chin, then picked something up from his desk. "He wrote me a letter, you know."

"Yes, sir, so he said."

"It was about the trial of Matt Jensen," the governor continued.

"Yes, sir."

"What do you know about the trial?" Governor Frémont asked.

"Only what I learned while I was there," Kyle replied. "And from what I have learned, the trial was a gross miscarriage of justice. In fact, the word justice can hardly be applied. Cummins was both the arresting officer and, in the case of the trial, the judge. And the shooting, trial, and conviction all happened within less than an hour. I don't see how a trial like that could possibly be fair. The only thing that kept it from being a lynching was the fact that they were sending Jensen to Yuma to be hanged."

"Do you think Jensen killed Deputy Gillis?"

"Oh, there is no question that he did. But I also heard from an eyewitness who testified that he saw the deputy draw first."

"Do you believe the witness?"

"Yes, Governor, I believe him. On top of that, from everything I have been able to find out about Matt Jensen, there is nothing that would make me think he could kill a man in cold blood."

"Do you know Matt Jensen?" Governor Frémont asked.

Kyle shook his head. "Not exactly. I met him at the train wreck, though I didn't know at the time who he was. He was working to pull people from the wreckage, and he helped Doc Presnell attend to the injured. And also it seems anyone who ran into him has nothing but praise for the man."

"Let me tell you what I know about Matt Jensen," Governor Frémont said.

"You know him?" Kyle asked, surprised by the comment.

"No, but Governor John Routt of Colorado does. I checked with neighboring states and this is what I got back from Governor Routt."

Frémont began reading from a sheet of paper:

"Last winter during an attempted train robbery, some bandits killed both the engineer and the fireman of the Midnight Flyer. Now, the deadman's throttle is supposed to stop the train anytime the engineer is incapacitated, but it failed, and rather than stopping the train as the bandits planned, their actions caused a runaway train. Matt Jensen was a passenger on that train. And while he knew nothing about the attempted holdup, he did realize rather quickly that the train was in great danger. He knew also that somehow he would have to get to the engine.

"The only way for him to get to the engine was to crawl along the top of the swaying, ice-covered cars on a train that was speeding through the dark at sixty miles per hour. Matt finally managed to reach the engine and stop the train, just before it rounded a sharp turn. Had he not succeeded, the speed they were traveling would have sent the train, and all 131 passengers over the side of a mountain to a sure and certain death.

"As governor of the State of Colorado, I issued a proclamation declaring a day to be officially entered into the State historical records, as Matthew Jensen Day."

Frémont put the paper down. "Does that sound like someone who would kill in cold blood?"

"No, sir, it doesn't," Kyle said. "That's more like the person I saw at the site of the train wreck."

"But Marshal Cummins believes him to be a murderer," Frémont said.

"He either believes it, or has reason to want others to believe it," Kyle said.

"Does Marshal Cummins have everything under control?"

"Yes," Kyle said. "If you call having the entire town under his thumb as being 'under control.'"

"Under his thumb?"

"Governor, Marshal Cummins has six deputies to help him keep control."

"Isn't that a little excessive?" Governor Frémont asked.

"Excessive? Yes, and much more than a little excessive," Kyle said. "If I had my way, that town would be cleaned up and Cummins would be gone."

"You do have your way," Governor Frémont replied.

"I beg your pardon?"

"I am overturning the results of the trial," Frémont said. "I am granting Matt Jensen a full and complete pardon. It would probably be better to have a new trial so he could be completely absolved—but in the meantime, the pardon will have to do. I also have something else I want you to look into."

"What is that?"

Governor Frémont picked up a letter from his desk.

"This is a letter from a man named Ronald Jerome," the governor said, handing it to Kyle. "He was my adjutant during the war, and he is a longtime friend. It seems his son disappeared in Purgatory."

"Disappeared?"

"Yes. Apparently Jerome bought some property near Purgatory and his son, Cornelius, came out here to take possession of it. And while Cornelius posted a letter to his father every day of the trip, he did not do so on the day he was to have arrived in Purgatory. Would you look into that for me?"

"Yes, sir, I will."

Frémont stroked his chin. "Based upon what you have just told me, and based upon the letter I received from Robert Dempster, I am now convinced that this man Cummins has no right to occupy the office of city marshal. Unfortunately, I have no authority to relieve him unless we can find him guilty of a felony. I'm going to give you that responsibility."

"That is quite a responsibility," Kyle said.

"I know that you can handle it. But first, I want you to find this man Matt Jensen, and inform him that he is no longer wanted for the murder of this man"—the governor checked a piece of paper—"Moe Gillis. I don't want that hanging over his head much longer. When someone is wanted for murder, they are sometimes pressed into doing things they would not otherwise do. I think it is important that we notify him as quickly as we can."

"I agree," Kyle said. "I'm not exactly sure how we are going to do that, but I agree with you that it does need to be done."

* * *

When Paco Bustamante rode into Choulic, he saw a small group of people standing in front of the hardware store. At first, he didn't know what they were looking at, but then he saw a coffin, standing upright. Riding over toward it, he was startled to see that the coffin was occupied by a body.

The body was that of Emerson Bates.

There was a sign above the coffin.

&This corpse was prepared by:

Ebeneezer Cartwright

SEE ME
for all your undertaking needs.

"I think it is disgusting to put a body on display like that just to advertise your work," a woman in the crowd said.

"Well, from what I heard, his throat was cut and he looked pretty bad. I reckon ole Cartwright is some pleased with his work," a man answered.

"Besides which, didn't nobody know where Bates came from, so it ain't like he's goin' to have kin to complain," another said.

One of the other men laughed. "And the only friend he had rode out of town butt-naked."

Paco hung back as the men in the group told and retold, with great relish, the story of Cletus Odom leaping through a window on the second floor, then, without a stitch of clothes, riding out of town.

"I never thought of Odom as bein' someone who would run from anyone," another said. "Who was he runnin' from?"

"He was runnin' from the same person who killed Bates. His name was Cavanaugh."

"Oh, yeah, I know who you are talkin' about. Fact of it is, Cavanaugh is still in town, stayin' over to the Homestead Hotel. He's been askin' a lot of questions. He's trying to find the ones who wrecked that train a couple of weeks ago. I think he's a lawman or somethin'."

"He says he ain't no lawman. He says he just wants revenge against the ones who wrecked the train and killed all those people."

"Revenge, huh?"

"Yeah, revenge. Leastwise, that's what he says."

"Revenge. Damn, I tell you the truth then. I don't think I'd want to be one of the people he's after then. When it is the law that's after you, you can figure that most likely what will happen to you is you'll get a trial and maybe go to jail. Even if you get hung, it'll take a while for them to appeal and all that. But when someone is after revenge, then they don't stop until they find you. And most likely when they find you, the only thing on their mind is killin' you. If you ask me, Odom is makin' a big mistake by runnin'."

"What do you mean, he's makin' a big mistake? Didn't you just say that the only thing a man out for revenge wants to do is kill you?"

"Yes, and the only way you are going to stop him is to kill him first."

"Damn. Remind me never to piss someone off so much that he wants revenge."

A few others laughed nervously.

"How does this fella—Cavanaugh is it? How does he know who he is lookin' for?"

"Turns out he was on the train that was robbed and he saw the outlaws. Not only that, he even knows every one of them by name. According to him, Bates was one of the train robbers, Cletus Odom was another, along with a fella named Schuler. He also says there was a Mexican by the name of Paco."

"Paco?" another said, and he laughed. "The fourth train robber was a Mexican by the name of Paco? Well, that should narrow it down to about a thousand Mexicans."

The others laughed as well.

Paco remounted, then rode back out of town. He had planned to meet Odom and Bates here, but with Bates dead and Odom running, there was no reason for him to remain. Paco's first thought was to just keep riding, but he stopped and thought about what the man back in town had said about revenge. They never give up until they find the ones they are looking for. And in this case, Cavanaugh knew them by name.

Paco had no choice. He had to kill Cavanaugh before Cavanaugh killed him. He dismounted, found a spot of shade, and waited for nightfall.

Matt had no idea what awakened him. It may have been a type of kinesthetic reflex born from years of living on the edge. He rolled off the bed just as a gun boomed in the doorway of his room. The bullet slammed into the headboard of the bed where, but a second earlier, Matt had been sleeping.

At the same time Matt rolled off the bed, he grabbed the pistol from under his pillow. Now the advantage was his. The man who had attempted to kill him was temporarily blinded by the muzzle flash of his own shot, and he could see nothing in the darkness of Matt's room. That same muzzle flash, however, had illuminated the assailant for Matt, and he quickly aimed his pistol at the dark hulk in the doorway, closed his eyes against his own muzzle flash, and squeezed the trigger. The gun bucked in his hand as the roar filled the room. Matt heard a groaning sound, then the heavy thump of a falling body.

"What is it? What's happening?" a voice called. All up and down the hallway of the hotel, doors opened as patrons, dressed in nightgowns and pajamas, peered out of their rooms in curiosity. Slipping on his trousers, but naked from the waist up, Matt stepped out into the hallway, then looked down at the the man he had just killed. The body was illuminated by the soft glow of a wall-mounted kerosene lantern. It was the same Mexican he had seen on the train during the robbery.

"You again?" someone said. "You've already killed one man in this town. How many are you plannin' on killin'?"

Matt glared at the questioner, but he didn't answer him.

"Who is this man?" another asked, pointing to the body on the floor. "He's not a guest of the hotel, is he?"

"You think any Mexicans would stay here?"

"Has anyone ever seen him before?"

"His name is Paco," Matt said.

"Why did you kill him?"

"Because he was trying to kill me," Matt answered. "And that seemed like the practical thing to do."

"Why was he trying to kill you?"

"Because he knew I was going to kill him, if I found him," Matt said easily.

"Mister, that don't make any sense a'tall."

"It does to me."

"What are you going to do about him now?" one of the others asked.

"Nothing," Matt said. "I don't need to do anything about him now. He's dead."

"Well, good Lord, man, you don't plan to just leave him layin' out here in the hall, do you?"

"If you want him out of here, take him out of here," Matt said.

"The hell you say. I didn't kill him."

"He's got a point there, mister," one of the others said. "You killed him. The least you can do is get rid of him."

"All right," Matt said. Leaning down, he picked Paco up and threw his body over his shoulder.

"Now you are being sensible," the complainer said.

Without another word, Matt walked to the rear end of the hall where he raised the window that opened out onto the alley.

"Hey! What are you . . . ?"

That was as far as the questioning hotel patron got, because without any further hesitation, Matt pushed Paco's body through the window. It fell with a crash to the alley below. That done, he lowered the window, then, brushing his hands as if having just completed an onerous task, returned to his own room.

"That should take care of it," Matt said. "Sleep well, everyone."

Chapter Twenty

Matt was eating breakfast at the Choulic Café when a woman came in. Looking around for a moment, she saw Matt and came directly to his table.

"Mr. Cavanaugh?"

This was the same soiled dove that had been in bed with Bates when Matt and Bates had had their encounter. By now, Matt had been in town long enough, and had spent enough time in the saloon, to know her by name.

Matt stood up. "Hello, Jennie," he said.

"Oh, my," Jennie said, flustered by that gentlemanly act. "You don't have to stand for me."

"You are a woman," Matt replied. "I treat all women with courtesy."

"Oh, I, uh—I appreciate it," Jennie said.

"Have you had your breakfast?"

"I'm not much of a breakfast person," Jennie replied.

"You could join me for coffee, couldn't you?"

"I don't know," Jennie said, looking around. "Mr.

Appleby doesn't like for people like me—uh, you know, women who are on the line—to come in here."

"Nonsense, you are my guest," Matt said. He held a chair out for Jennie, then moved around the table to retake his own seat. He was fully aware of some of the glances he was receiving from many of the other diners, but he paid no attention to them.

"What brings you to my table, Jennie?" Matt asked. "Although I'm enjoying the company, I have the feeling that you didn't stop by just to be sociable."

"I hear that you are looking for Moses Schuler," Jennie said.

"Yes," Matt said. "Do you know him? You must know him if you know his full name. I don't believe I've mentioned his first name since I arrived in Choulic."

"Yes, I know him," Jennie said. "I know him very well." She paused for a moment. "Moses killed my husband," she added.

"Your husband?"

Jennie nodded, and Matt saw that her eyes had welled with tears.

"Yes, Mr. Cavanaugh, my husband," Jennie said. "I wasn't born a whore."

"I'm sorry—I didn't mean to imply that you were."

"I know, I know. I guess, when I think about it, I'm just a little sensitive," Jennie said. "Carl and I had been married for a little over a year. His parents didn't approve of the marriage. After all, Carl was an educated man, a mining engineer, and he met me when I was working as a maid for his family. But Carl didn't care what they thought—he loved me and I loved him, so we were married, and we left Louisville to come out West. Carl had taken a position with the Cross Point Mine."

"Oh, I see," Matt said. "Earlier, when you said Schuler killed your husband, you were talking about the cave-in at the Cross Point Mine, weren't you? The one Schuler caused."

"Yes," Jennie said. She looked surprised. "You know about that?"

"I've heard about it."

"It was an accident," Jennie said. "I don't really blame Moses, but he blames himself. That's why he turned into an alcoholic."

"Did you know Schuler before the accident?"

"I knew him very well. I told you that Carl's family was opposed to our getting married. But that's only true about his mother and father. His brother was very supportive—something that Carl and I both appreciated."

"His brother?

"Yes, Mr. Cavanaugh. Moses Schuler was Carl Schuler's brother. My brother-in-law," Jennie said simply.

"I see."

"No, I'm not sure you do see," Jennie said. "I do want to help you find him because I believe he is on the path to self-destruction and needs to be stopped. But before I tell you where to look, I need to ask what you are going to do with him when you do find him?"

"If you are worried about that, don't tell me where he is," Matt said, his reply surprising Jennie. "Because whatever I do will be between him and me. I don't want you saddled with any kind of a guilty conscience."

"I have to know, Mr. Cavanaugh, was he one of the people who robbed the train?"

"Yes."

"You aren't the law, and you aren't a bounty hunter. Why are you after these men?"

"Because of Suzie Dobbs."

"Suzie Dobbs?" Jennie asked. Then, in a sudden insight, she took in a quick, audible breath. "Was she killed in the train wreck?"

"Yes."

"Who was she? Your wife? Your fiancée. Your girlfriend?"

"No, she was a little four-year-old girl," Matt answered. He described how he had pulled her from the wreck, dead with a stake driven through her heart.

"Oh," Jennie said. "Oh, that's awful."

"I then made a vow to myself to find justice for her."

"I'll tell you the truth, Mr. Cavanaugh. I know that Moses has done some things he shouldn't have done since he started drinking. And I'm sure some of it is against the law. Moses is no angel, that's for sure. But I cannot believe that he would have anything to do with killing that little girl."

Matt remembered Schuler's reaction when the train robbers were in the express car. He alone had expressed some remorse and concern over what they had done.

"Of course, I haven't seen Moses in quite a while. It could be that, him being a drunk and all, that he might—well, I suppose if he needed a drink bad enough, you could talk him into about anything."

"Do you know where he is?" Matt asked.

Jennie was quiet for a long moment, as if struggling with her soul.

"Jennie, he alone expressed surprise and remorse at the outcome of the train wreck. I won't kill him unless he tries to kill me," Matt said. "Right now, the one I am really after is Cletus Odom. I'm just hoping that Schuler can help me find him."

"You might try Quigotoa," Jennie said.

"Quigotoa?"

"It's a small town just a little north of here. That's where Moses hangs out most of the time."

"Does he live there?" Matt asked.

"Does he live there?" Jennie nodded her head. "I suppose you could say that he lives there. But a more accurate answer would be to say that the only reason he is there is because the folks in Quigotoa are willin' to put up with him."

It was now two weeks since Dempster had had a drink, and though it was still hard to abstain, it seemed to him to be getting a little easier. The cravings still occurred, but they were more isolated and did not occupy every waking moment as they once had. He was also taking more pride in his personal appearance, and had just taken a bath, shaved, and put on another clean suit, shirt, and tie. Now it was time for another haircut, so he walked down the street to Tony's Tonsorial Treatments.

Nobody recognized him when he stepped into the barbershop.

"Yes, sir, friend, are you needing a haircut?" Tony asked. The barber had one customer in his chair, and there were two more waiting. "There are two more ahead of you, if you don't mind."

"I don't mind at all, Tony," Dempster answered.

Although nobody had recognized Dempster on sight, they all recognized his voice.

"Dempster? Is that you?" one of the waiting customers asked.

"In the flesh," Dempster replied.

"It is you. Who would've thought it?"

"I hope you don't mind if I join you."

"No, not at all, not at all. Have a seat," one of the men said in invitation.

Dempster took off his hat and hung it on the rack. As he did so, he happened to glance through the window, and that was when he saw Cletus Odom riding into town.

"I'll be damn," Dempster said. "What is he doing here?"

"Who? What are you talking about?"

"Cletus Odom," Dempster said. "I just saw him ride by, as big and bold as you please."

"Cletus Odom? Are you sure?" Tony asked.

"Oh, I'm sure."

"How do you know it's him?"

"I know it is him because I once had the dubious distinction of defending him against a charge of murder, back in the days when he was still a bounty hunter. Tony, if you'll excuse me, I'm going to put off getting that haircut until later."

"Anytime, Mr. Dempster," Tony replied. "Anytime."

Leaving the barbershop, Dempster hurried down the street to the bank. When he went into the bank, he caused the same initial reaction he had in the barbershop. People were startled when they recognized him. He walked quickly to the desk of Joel Montgomery, the owner of the bank.

"Mr. Dempster," Montgomery said, rising to greet him. "What a pleasant surprise."

"Mr. Montgomery, may I speak to you alone for a moment?"

"Well, yes, I suppose so," Montgomery said. "What is it about?"

"Possible trouble," Dempster replied without being more specific.

"Bernard," Montgomery called to his teller. "I'm going to be busy in the back for a while."

"Yes, sir, Mr. Montgomery," Bernard answered.

Montgomery led the way to the conference room, then closed the door behind them. "What is it?" he asked.

"I just saw Cletus Odom ride into town," Dempster said.

"The outlaw? Are you sure?"

"I'm sure."

"Oh, my," Montgomery said. He ran his hand through his hair. "Oh, my. If he is in town, it can only be for one reason. He's planning to rob the bank."

"I think you might be right," Dempster said. "Only, we know he is here so that gives us a little advantage."

"So, what do we do now?"

"We are paying a heavy tax to the marshal and his deputies, aren't we?" Dempster asked.

"Yes."

"Then it is time that Cummins started earning his money."

"I—yes, you are right." Montgomery was quiet for a moment. "I never thought I would hear myself say this, but I'm glad that Cummins has all those deputies. Surely they can handle Cletus Odom."

"One would certainly think so, wouldn't one?" Dempster replied.

"So, what do we do now?"

"Now? Now we go to Marshal Cummins, inform him of the presence of a wanted outlaw, and demand that he do his duty."

"Who?" Montgomery asked.

"Who what?"

"Who is going to see Cummins and demand action?"

"I'll do it," Dempster said.

Cummins and two of his deputies were in the marshal's office when Dempster stepped inside. Evidently someone had just told a joke, because all three were laughing loudly.

"Excuse me," Dempster said.

The three men looked over toward him and Jackson laughed out loud. "Well, now, look what the cat drug in," he said.

"Dempster," Cummins said. "It's good of you to drop by." He opened the top drawer of his desk and pulled out a bottle of whiskey, filled a glass, then slid the glass across his desk toward Dempster. "Have a drink."

"Thank you, no," Dempster said.

"No?" Cummins looked at his two deputies. "Boys, did you just hear Mr. Dempster say no?"

"I never thought that old drunk would turn down a drink," Crack said.

"Maybe he thinks he's too good to drink with us," Jackson suggested.

"No, it isn't that," Dempster said. "I'm sure you understand. I'm an alcoholic. I'm trying to quit drinking."

"Hah! You're trying to quit drinking?" Cummins replied. He looked at the others. "Boys, have either of you ever known a drunk who gave it up?"

"I ain't never known one," Jackson said.

"Me neither," Crack added.

"No, and you ain't never goin' to know one 'cause it can't be done." He looked at Dempster again. "So why are you tryin' to fight it? You know you want a drink, and here it is, just waitin' for you. And it is being offered in friendship."

"Maybe he don't want to be our friend," Crack said. "He's been meetin' with Montgomery and them other troublemakers."

Dempster gasped, and Cummins laughed again.

"Well now, Mr. Dempster, you act a little surprised," Cummins said.

Dempster didn't answer.

"You don't think folks can hold meetin's in this town without me knowin' about it, do you?" Cummins asked. "This is Purgatory, Mr. Dempster." Cummins made a fist of his right hand, then used his thumb to point to himself. "And I own Purgatory. Nothing happens in Purgatory without my knowledge, or permission."

"You are the marshal, not the king," Dempster said.

"The marshal, not the king? Hmm, that sounds like a political slogan. Are you considering running for some office, Mr. Dempster?"

In fact, though he had told no one, Dempster had considered running for circuit judge.

"If I run for anything, you'll know it, Marshal Cummins," Dempster said. "Believe me, you'll know it."

"Well now, that sounds like a threat," Cummins replied. "Are you threatening me, Counselor?"

A quick spasm of fear overtook Dempster, and the hackles rose on the back of his neck. The conversation had gone beyond mere banter and he needed to change the tone.

"No!" he said quickly. "No, I'm not making any threat. I just meant that, uh, if I ever did run for office, why, everyone would know about it." He forced a laugh. "They'd have to know about it, otherwise, who would vote for me?"

"I can answer that question for you," Jackson said. "Nobody would vote for you, because nobody is going to vote for a drunk."

"What do you want, Dempster?" Cummins asked. He picked up the glass of whiskey and drank it himself. The bantering was over.

"I just saw Cletus Odom coming into town," Dempster said.

"Cletus Odom, you say?" Cummins replied. "You saw him coming into town?"

"Yes. He was riding right down the middle of Central Street, just as big and bold as you please."

"What about that, Marshal?" Jackson said. "Cletus Odom is in town."

There was a matter-of-fact tone to Jackson's comment that Dempster found disturbing.

"Mr. Dempster, why did you feel you had to come tell me about Cletus Odom?" Cummins asked.

"Because you are the marshal."

"And?"

"And because Cletus Odom is a wanted outlaw."

"Not in Purgatory, he isn't," Cummins said.

"Of course he is. He's wanted all over the Arizona Territory," Dempster said.

Cummins shook his head and made a clucking sound with his tongue. "And you once defended him," he said. "What kind of lawyer are you, Dempster, that you would turn on a man you once defended?"

Dempster had never told anyone that he had once defended Odom, until he shared that information with Montgomery just a few minutes earlier.

"How—how did you know I once defended him?"

"Because Cletus told me you did," Cummins replied.

"Odom told you? I don't understand. When did you and Odom ever have a conversation? And why would he have told you that?"

"Because brothers share things," Cummins answered.

"Brothers? You and Cletus Odom are brothers?"

"Half brothers," Cummins said. "Cletus!" he called. "Get out here, I want you to meet an old friend of yours!"

A door at the back of the room opened, and Cletus Odom stepped out. Dempster noticed, in shock, that Odom was wearing a star pinned to his vest.

"Mr. Dempster, meet my newest deputy," Cummins said.

Chapter Twenty-one

It started raining about an hour before Matt reached Quigotoa. Although rainfall was scarce in the desert, when it did rain it was often a torrential downpour. This was just such a rain, and Matt had to be careful to avoid dry creek beds, arroyos, and low-lying areas for fear of a sudden flash flood.

Matt put on a rain slicker and hunkered down in the saddle, but nothing helped.

"Just a little farther, Spirit," he said to the horse, who, with frequent tossing of his head, showed his discomfort with the downpour. "I'll find a place to get you dry, I promise."

Finally, cresting a ridge, Matt saw the town of Quigotoa in the distance, low-lying and gray behind the diaphanous curtain of the rainstorm.

"There it is, boy," Matt said. "I told you it wouldn't be much farther."

It took another fifteen minutes or so after the little town was spotted before Matt reached it. The street was a slurry of mud mixed with horse apples, the droppings reconstituted by the water so that the stench was released. He saw a stable that was no more than a roof over a pen. It wasn't exactly a livery, but it would provide Spirit with some shelter from the rain, and from the sun after the rain passed.

He rode up to it, then dismounted. At first, he didn't see anyone; then, at second glance, he saw someone sitting in one corner of the stable where, in addition to the roof, there were half walls, thus providing a bit more shelter from the rain.

"Is this a public livery?" he called, having to raise his voice to be heard through the rain.

"*Sí, señor.* Ten cents, one night," the man responded without leaving the partial shelter.

"Here's fifty cents," Matt said, fishing the coin from his pocket. "Give him something to eat, and take care of my saddle."

The prospect of fifty cents was enough to bring the old Mexican away from the shelter, and he had a big smile on his face as he approached.

"*Gracias, señor. Cuidaré muy bien de su caballo.*"

"You hear that, Spirit? He is going to take very good care of you."

After turning his horse over to the stable hand, Matt found a board stretched across the street, and though it didn't keep the rain off him, it did keep him out of the muck and mud. Reaching the boardwalk on the other side of the street, he walked down to the Casa del Sol Cantina.

Inside the cantina, a long board of wooden pegs was nailed along one wall about six feet from the floor. Matt dumped the water from the crown of his hat, then hung his slicker on one of the pegs to let it drip dry. A careful scrutiny of the saloon disclosed a card game in progress near the back. At one of the front tables, there was some earnest conversation. Three men stood at the bar, each complete within themselves, concentrating only on their drinks and private thoughts. A soiled dove, near the end of her professional effectiveness, overweight, with bad teeth and wild, unkempt hair, stood at the far end. She smiled at Matt, but getting no encouragement, stayed put.

"What'll it be, mister? the bartender asked, making a swipe across the bar with a sour-smelling cloth.

"Whiskey, then a beer," Matt said. He figured to drink the whiskey to warm himself from the chill of the rain, then drink the beer for his thirst. The whiskey was set before him and he raised it to his lips, then tossed it down. He could feel its raw burn all the way to his stomach. When the beer was served, he picked it up, then turned his back to the bar for a more leisurely survey of the room.

Ascertaining that there was nothing here that represented an immediate threat, he turned back to the bartender.

"I'm looking for Moses Schuler," Matt said. "I'm told I might find him here."

"Why do you want Schuler?"

"That's between Schuler and me," Matt said.

"You the law?"

"Schuler," Matt said again without answering the question.

"We don't care much for the law around here," the bartender said.

Suddenly, Matt reached his left hand across the bar and grabbed the collar of the bartender's shirt. He twisted it into a knot that put pressure on the bartender's neck, making it hard for him to breathe.

"Mister, I've ridden half a day in a driving rainstorm," Matt said. "I'm in no mood for games. I'm going to ask you one more time where I can find Schuler. If you don't answer me, I am going to break your neck, then find someone who will answer me."

To illustrate his point, Matt twisted the collar even tighter, so tight now that when the bartender tried to talk, it came out as an unintelligible rattle.

Matt eased up just enough to allow the bartender to speak.

"I'll see if I can find him," the bartender said.

"I appreciate that," Matt replied.

"Juan," the bartender called.

A Mexican boy in his teens stepped out of the back room. He was wearing an apron and holding a broom.

"*Sí, señor?*" the boy replied.

"You seen Schuler around?"

"*Sí, señor.* He is sleeping in the back room," Juan answered.

"Get 'im out here. There's someone who wants talk to 'im."

"I will try, *señor.* Maybe I cannot wake him up," Juan said. "He is sleeping very hard."

"Sleeping, or passed out?" the bartender asked.

"I think maybe he is passed out," Juan replied.

The bartender poured a drink into a glass, then slid it down the bar toward Juan. "Give him this," he said.

"Tell 'im there's someone out here that wants to buy him another drink. That'll bring him out." The bartender looked at Matt. "You will buy him a drink, won't you?"

"Yes," Matt said. "Give me a bottle."

The bartender handed Matt a bottle, Matt took it, looked over at Juan, then pointed to an empty table. "I'll be over there, Juan," he said. "Bring him to me."

"*Sí.*"

Juan disappeared into the back room. After a long moment, a bent, white-haired man came out of the room. At first, Matt was about to say this wasn't the one he was looking for. This man looked nothing like the robber he had seen in the express car. But as he studied him more closely, he saw that this was, indeed, the same man. Dispirited, but the same man.

"Someone is going to buy me a drink?" Schuler asked.

"That man over there, *señor,*" Juan said. He pointed to the table where Matt was sitting, and Schuler shuffled over toward him, unabashedly scratching his crotch as he did so. Matt had rarely seen a man who had come down as far as Schuler had since the last time he saw him. Schuler needed a shave, and his clothes reeked of stale whiskey and sour vomit. How could this be? Didn't Schuler get his share from the robbery?

Schuler pointed at Matt with a shaking finger.

"Do I know you?" he asked. "Who are you?"

"I am a friend of Jennie Schuler," Matt said.

Schuler looked at Matt for a moment, as if trying to process what he had just heard.

"Anyone who has money is a friend of Jennie Schuler," he said. "She is a whore."

"I am also the man that's going to buy you a drink," Matt answered. He poured whiskey into a glass, then slid it across the table toward Schuler.

"What—what do I have to do for it?"

"Just give me a little information," Matt said. "That's all."

"Information? I don't know anything about anything," Schuler said quietly.

"Oh, you know something about what I want," Matt said. Matt reached out to pick up the glass, then began pouring it back in the bottle.

"Wait!" Schuler said. "What do you want to know?"

"First, let me ask you something. With all the money you got from the train robbery, why are you having to beg for drinks now? Have you already spent it all?"

"I don't have any money. Paco cheated me out of—" Schuler started to say, then he stopped in mid-sentence. "What money?" he asked.

"The money you got cheated out of," Matt said. "That is what you were about to say, isn't it? That Paco cheated out of your share of the money from the train robbery?"

"What train robbery?" Schuler said. "I don't know anything about any train robbery."

"Don't lie to me, Schuler," Matt said. "I don't like being lied to. I know you took part in the train robbery because I was there. I was on the train when it wrecked."

"That doesn't mean anything."

"Oh, but it does. It means that you, Odom, Paco, and Bates are guilty of murder."

"I didn't murder anyone," Schuler said.

"If you are talking about the deputy, I know you didn't shoot him. I know that he was shot by Cletus Odom."

Schuler's eyes opened wide in surprise. "How do you know that?" he asked.

"I told you," Matt said. "I was there. I saw it. I was in the express car when you and the others came in. I saw everything, Schuler. I'm talking about all the people who were killed when you and the others wrecked the train. I'm talking about a little four-year-old girl who was traveling with her mother and her brother. Do you know what happened to that little girl?"

Schuler was quiet for a long moment. "I ain't got any of the money," he said. "Like I said, Paco stole it."

"I don't care about the money," Matt said.

"You don't care about the money?"

"No."

"Then what do you want?"

"I want Odom," Matt said.

"There are three others," Schuler said.

"No, there is only one other."

"You are forgetting Paco and Bates."

"I'm not forgetting them," Matt said. "They are dead."

"Dead?"

"I killed them both," Matt said calmly.

Schuler made no response, but looked at the bottle and empty glass on the table. Matt waited for a long moment, then refilled the glass and slid it across the table toward Schuler.

Schuler reached out with a trembling hand— picked up the glass—spilled some, then, steadying it with his other hand, drank it down in one swallow.

"Where is Odom?" Kyle asked.

"I don't know."

"You're lying," Matt said matter-of-factly. "What are you afraid of, Schuler?"

"Nothin'," Schuler answered. "I don't know where he is, that's all."

"You do know, don't you, Schuler?"

Schuler held his empty glass out, and Matt refilled it.

"Don't be afraid," Matt said. "I'm here."

"You're here?" Schuler said. He tried to laugh, but it came out as a weak bark. "So, you're goin' to protect me if he comes for me? There's not one man in ten who wouldn't pee in his pants if he comes face-to-face with Cletus Odom."

"You think that's what I would do, Schuler? You think I would pee in my pants?"

"I don't know," Schuler said. "Who are you?"

"Doesn't matter who I am," Matt replied. "You know where he is, don't you?" he asked.

"What if I do?" Schuler asked. He tossed down the second drink.

"Tell me where to find him," Matt said.

"I can't," Schuler said.

Matt slid the bottle of whiskey toward him. "Forget about the glass. I'll give you the whole bottle."

"Not for a bottle, not even for a case of whiskey will I tell. What good is whiskey to a dead man?"

"Schuler, I want you to think about something," Matt said quietly.

"Think about what?"

"You are afraid of the wrong man. Odom isn't here."

"That doesn't matter. If I tell you how to find him, then he'll find me."

"I've already found you," Matt said.

"What?"

"Think about it," Matt said. "I found Bates, and I killed him. I found Paco, I killed him. When I find Odom, I will kill him." He paused for a long moment. "And like I said, I found you."

"I—I'm afraid," Schuler said, his voice so quiet that he could barely be heard.

"You should be afraid," Matt said.

"Yeah," a patron at a nearby table said, laughing. Ever since Schuler had come out of the back room, the patron had been watching and listening to the conversation. "Like the man said, he's scared of—" the laughter died in his throat when he saw the expression on Matt's face. It wasn't one of passion, or even cold fury. He wasn't sure what he saw—maybe something in Matt's eyes. But he felt the hackles stand up on the back of his neck as he realized he was looking into the face of death. "My God, Schuler, he means it," the patron said quietly.

The patron's words stopped everyone in the room as if there had been a gunshot. A nearby card game came to a halt, the three men at the bar turned around, the bartender stopped polishing glasses, and there was a deadly silence in the room.

The clock ticked loudly.

Schuler's bottom lip began trembling and a line of spittle ran down his chin.

"Now, I'm going to ask you again, Schuler. And I want you to think about it. And while you're thinking, I want you to know that I'm here and Odom isn't. Tell me what you know, or I will kill you where you sit."

Schuler drew a deep breath and held his hands up. "All right, all right, I was with them, just like you said. But I didn't know they was goin' to be a lot of people killed. I wouldn't of had nothin' to do with it if I had known there was goin' to be a lot of innocent people killed."

"I know. I was there, in the express car, remember? I heard you tell Odom that you didn't know that he planned to kill anyone. In fact, if I hadn't heard you talking to Odom, I would've already killed you by now."

"Just so's you know," Schuler said.

"Where can I find him?"

"Why you lookin' for him? Why are you doin this? You ain't the law, are you?"

"No. This is personal. One of the people killed was a little girl, about four years old. One minute she was riding on the train with her mother and brother, and the next minute the train wrecked and a large stake was driven through her heart."

"No!" Schuler said. He closed his eyes and began shaking. "I didn't know about the little girl," he said. "I didn't know about any of them."

"Where is Odom?" Matt asked again.

"You got any money?"

"Why?"

"If I give you any information, I'm going to need enough money to get out of here. My life won't be worth a plugged nickel if Odom finds out I told you where to find him."

"How can I find him?"

Schuler poured himself a glass of whiskey before he spoke again. He drank it, then wiped the back of his hand across his mouth.

"It's goin' to cost you fifty dollars."

Matt pulled fifty dollars from his pocket and handed it over. "All right. Here's you money. Now, start talking."

"Do you know Odom?" Schuler asked, taking the money and stuffing it down into his pocket. "I mean, do you really know him?"

"No."

"Well, he's real crazy," Schuler said. "I've never known anyone before who likes killing, but Odom actually likes it. They say he killed his first man when he was fifteen. They's been others that's killed for the first time when they was only fifteen, but the man Odom killed was his own pa."

"Where will I find him?"

Schuler took another drink of whiskey. The whiskey had a somewhat calming effect, and he put the bottle down, this time without the shakes.

"Did you hear what I said? The first man he killed was his own pa."

"I heard."

"You'll find him in Purgatory," Schuler said.

"What makes you think he's gone to Purgatory?"

"The marshal there is a fella by the name of Cummins," Schuler said. "Him 'n' Odom is brothers."

"Brothers?"

"They don't have the same name 'cause they got different papas, but they got the same mama. And after Odom killed his own pa, he moved in with his mama, Cummins, and Cummins's papa."

"Thank you," Matt said.

"Don't be thanking me," he said. "If you are going to Purgatory after Odom, you are going to have to deal with Cummins and all his deputies. And you might find out you've bitten off more than you can chew."

"I'll take my chances," Matt said. "I'm going."

"To face all of them?"

"Yes."

"That's bold talk, Matt Jensen," another voice said.

Jensen? Who knew that he was Matt Jensen?

Turning slowly, Matt saw a big man with gray hair and a sweeping mustache leaning against the wall. The man's arms were folded across his chest. He, like everyone else in the room, had been listening to the conversation. He let his arms drop by his side, with one hand hovering near his pistol. When he did so, it revealed that he was wearing the star of a U.S. marshal.

Matt moved his own hand into position to draw.

The tension in the room grew palpable, and everyone moved out of the way of what they were sure was an impending gunfight.

"You are Marshal Kyle, aren't you?" Matt asked. "We met at the train wreck."

"Yes, we met there," Kyle said. "But I believe you were telling people your name was Cavanaugh then."

"My name is Cavanaugh," Matt said.

Kyle shook his head. "No sense in lying about it now. I know that you are Matt Jensen."

Matt nodded. "Yes, I am Matt Jensen," he said. "But Cavanaugh is the name I was born with."

Kyle chuckled. "Well now, this can be a little confusing," he said.

"Marshal, I didn't cause that train wreck, I didn't kill Deputy Hayes, and I didn't steal any money," Matt said.

"Odom killed the deputy," Schuler said, speaking quickly.

"You say Odom killed the deputy?" Kyle asked.

"Yes."

Kyle nodded. "I suspected that," he said. "I appreciate the confirmation." He looked back at Matt. "You don't deny killing Deputy Gillis, do you?"

"I killed him," Matt said, without further clarification.

"Gillis drew first?"

"He tried to," Matt replied and, inexplicably, Kyle laughed.

"That's a good way of putting it," Kyle said. "Now, about your going to Purgatory . . ." He let the sentence hang.

"I'm going," Matt said resolutely.

"Oh, I'm sure you are going," Kyle said. "I'm going with you."

"Well, Marshal, I appreciate your interest, but I prefer to do this alone."

"Oh, don't misunderstand me, Matt Jensen," Kyle said. "I'm not asking for permission to come with you. On the contrary, I'm giving you permission to go with me."

"You are giving me permission?"

"Let's say, I'm asking you to come with me," Kyle corrected. "As a deputy U.S. marshal."

"Wait a minute. You are going to make me your deputy?"

"As a temporary thing," Kyle replied. "Just until we get Purgatory cleaned up."

"But I don't understand. What about the other thing?" Matt asked.

"What other thing?" Kyle replied. Then, suddenly, he smiled broadly and reached into his shirt pocket. "Oh, you must be talking about this." He walked over to hand the paper to Matt.

"What is this?"

"Read it," Kyle said. "If you have any questions, I'll explain it. Though, how difficult is it to understand a full governor's pardon?"

Chapter Twenty-two

"Damn," Kyle said.

"Yeah," Matt replied. "I see them."

The two were looking at vultures, wings outstretched as they rode the thermal waves.

"Coyote?" Kyle suggested.

"No. Too many for a coyote. It's bigger than that."

"Deer? Horse?"

"Look how they are staying away," Matt said. "If it was a deer or a horse, they'd be on it. No, whatever it is, they are afraid of it."

"There's only one thing they are afraid of," Kyle said.

"Yes," Matt replied. He didn't have to say it aloud. He knew, and he knew that Kyle knew, that what the buzzards were circling was a man.

It took at least half an hour before they reached the body. It was hanging from the branch of a cottonwood tree, twisting slowly at the end of the rope. Some of the vultures had gotten brave enough to descend to the upper branches of the tree, but none had actually reached the body yet, because it showed no signs of vulture feeding.

"It's Dempster," Kyle said.

"He was just a drunk. Who could a drunk make angry enough to do something like this?"

"He had stopped drinking," Kyle said. "And he is the biggest reason the governor granted you a pardon."

"I'll be damn," Matt said as he sat on his horse and looked at Dempster's body. "He tried to defend me in the trial. I guess he never gave up."

"And my guess is, that's what got him killed," Kyle said. "He made an enemy of Cummins and his deputies."

"We can't leave him just hanging like this," Matt said.

"Want to bury him?" Kyle asked.

"No. I have a better idea."

Matt and Kyle arrived in Purgatory at just about supper time, and along with the spicy aromas of Mexican cooking, they could smell coffee, pork chops, fried potatoes, and baking bread.

Matt was pulling a hastily constructed travois. Dempster's body was in plain sight, tied onto the travois.

"Frederica?" a woman called.

"*Sí, señora?*" a young Mexican girl answered.

"Take the clothes down from the line, will you?" the woman ordered.

"*Sí, señora,*" the servant girl replied.

The servant girl, startled by sight of the dead man

on the travois, gasped, and took a step backward. Matt touched the brim of his hat in greeting, then urged his horse on.

A game of checkers was being played by two gray-bearded men in front of the feed store, watched over by half-a-dozen spectators. A couple of them looked up at Matt and Kyle rode by, their horses' hooves clumping hollowly on the hard-packed earth of the street.

"Son of a bitch!" one of them said. "That's Demp-ster. That's Bob Dempster's body he's a'pullin."

Amon Goff came through the front door of his shop and began vigorously sweeping the wooden porch. His broom did little but raise the dust to swirl about, then fall back down again. He brushed a sleeping dog off the porch, but the dog quickly reclaimed his position, curled around comfortably, and within a minute was asleep again.

Goff watched the two men ride by, then, nervously, went back into his shop and started pulling down window shades.

"What are you doing that for, Amon?" he wife asked. "It ain't time to be a'closin' yet."

"Hush, woman, and get into the back," Goff said.

"What?"

"Do like I say, woman!" Goff said. "There's about to be some killin' and we'd best be out of the way."

Matt and Kyle stopped in front of the city mortuary, and Matt dismounted, then cut the travois loose. A tall, cadaverous-looking man, dressed all in black, stepped out of the building.

"You the undertaker?" Matt asked.

"Yes, sir, Prufrock is the name."

"Take care of him, Prufrock," Matt said.

"Well, I—uh, would be glad to," the undertaker replied. "Is the city going to pay for it?"

Matt handed the undertaker a fifty-dollar bill. "No," he said. "I'm paying for it. The city will be paying for the others."

"What others?" the undertaker asked, clearly not understanding what Matt was talking about.

"Marshal Cummins and his deputies," Matt said flatly.

"Wait," Kyle said. "Prufrock, my name is Ben Kyle. I'm a United States marshal. I'm going to ask you just one time and if you know what is good for you, you will tell the truth. Have you ever heard of a man named Jerome? Cornelius Jerome?"

Prufrock didn't answer.

"You have five seconds to answer," Kyle said. "Or when we have finished with Cummins and his crowd, we will be coming back for you."

"He's buried out here in Boot Hill," Prufrock said quickly. "Under the name Bill Smith."

"If you knew his name, why did you bury him as Bill Smith?"

"It was what Marshal Cummins ordered," Prufrock said. "He killed him."

"Cummins killed Jerome? Why?"

"He didn't mean to kill him. He was tryin' to shoot his hat off his head. It was an accident," Prufrock said.

"An accident?"

"Yes."

"This is what I want you to do, Prufrock. I want you to write that out for me and sign it," Kyle said.

"I can't do that," Prufrock said. "Cummins would—"

"Don't worry about Cummins. He'll be dead," Kyle said in a flat, matter-of-fact voice.

Leaving the startled undertaker with Dempster's body, Matt and Kyle rode slowly down to the far end of the street, then tied their horses off at the hitching post in front of the Pair O Dice Saloon. When they dismounted, Kyle drew his pistol, pointed it into the air, and pulled the trigger. The gunshot echoed through the quiet streets for a long time. Then it was silent.

The gunshot attracted several of the townspeople and they looked toward the saloon, at the two men who were standing in front, one with a smoking gun.

A curtain fluttered in one of the false fronts.

A cat yowled somewhere down the street.

A fly buzzed past Matt's ear, did a few circles, then flew away.

A face appeared over the top of the batwing doors, then looked out at Matt and Kyle.

"Are you one of Cummins's deputies?" Kyle asked.

The man shook his head no.

"Then get the hell out of the saloon."

"Why should I do that?"

"Get out or get killed," Kyle said.

Without another word, without even looking back into the saloon, the man left and walked hurriedly on down the street.

"Hear me!" Kyle shouted.

The two words echoed back down the street. "Hear me—hear me—hear me."

"Anyone in the saloon who isn't with Marshal Cummins, come out of there now!" Kyle called.

From inside the saloon, Matt could hear the sounds of chairs and tables being scooted across the floor as people hustled to leave. A few seconds later, almost a dozen men came through the front door, then hastened to get out of the way, though they didn't go so far as to not be able to see the show they were certain was about to take place.

Kyle looked over at Matt.

"Are you ready?" he asked.

Matt didn't answer. Instead, he stepped up onto the porch, then pushed through the batwing doors and went inside, backing up against the wall as he did so. At the bar, a glass of beer in front of him, his lips dripping with moisture, stood Cletus Odom. Also at the bar, but separated by the length of the bar from Odom, stood Marshal Cummins.

Matt's lips twisted into an evil smile. Part of him wanted to kill both men this very instant, while part of him wanted to delay the pleasure. He could imagine the fear Dempster had shown when about to be hanged, and he wanted these two men to know that same terror.

"Cummins," Kyle said. His words were cold, flat, menacing. "As a United States marshal, and acting upon the authority of Governor Fremont, I am here to inform you that your office of city marshal, and the offices of all deputies under you, have been vacated. You no longer have any legal standing. In addition, I am placing all of you under arrest."

Cummins didn't turn around, didn't even look up at the mirror. Instead, he just stared into his glass of beer.

"Now just what makes you think I'm going to let you do that?" Cummins asked.

"There's no *letting* to it, Cummins," Kyle said. "We're doing it."

"You and that murderer with you?"

"This man is a deputy U.S. marshal," Kyle said.

"A deputy U.S. marshal, is he? And what does that mean?"

"That means I can kill every damn one of you and it'll be legal," Matt said in a cold, deadly voice.

"I'm going to ask all of you now to unbuckle your gun belts and let them drop to the floor," Kyle said.

"No, thank you. I got no plans to go hang."

"You're going to die at the end of a rope, or you're going to die here today," Kyle said.

Cummins turned away from the bar and looked toward Odom. Odom and Cummins were at opposite ends of the bar. Jackson and Crack were also in the saloon, Jackson near the piano, Crack by the little pot-bellied stove. The four men were all spread out, which was going to make them more difficult targets than they would have been if they were closer together.

"Could be that you two are the ones that's goin' to do the dyin'," Cummins said. "You might'a noticed that there's four of us and only two of you."

"Marshal, you take Cummins," Matt said flatly. "I'll kill Odom."

Saying that he would "kill" rather than that he would "take" Odom was deliberate on Matt's part, and it had the desired effect. He saw Odom flinch slightly; then he saw Odom's tongue slide out to lick his dry lips.

Matt's comment was followed by a long pause, the

silence broken only by the ticking of the clock that stood against the back wall.

"Now!" Cummins suddenly shouted, and he, Odom, Crack, and Jackson all started for their guns.

Matt reacted to the sudden move quickly, drawing his own pistol faster than he had ever drawn it before. He had his own gun out in time to take quick but deliberate aim and shoot Odom in the gut. Odom, the barrel of his own pistol just topping the holster, pulled the trigger, shooting lead into the floor. A red stain began to spread just over his belt buckle.

Cummins had his gun out before Kyle and his pistol shot cracked an instant after Matt's. The bullet from Cummins's pistol hit Kyle in the left shoulder, even as Kyle was pulling the trigger of his own gun. Kyle's bullet hit Cummins in the chest and the outlaw marshal went down.

Even as Odom's gun was clattering to the floor and he was putting his hands over his belly wound, watching the blood spill through his fingers, Matt was turning his attention to Jackson and Crack. But, because they were some distance apart, he had to be very deliberate in selecting his target, so he went after Jackson first, getting what was his second shot off, even before Jackson could fire his first. Matt's bullet hit Jackson in the forehead, and he pitched back crashing into the piano, raising a cacophonous and discordant clang before bouncing off and landing on the floor.

An acrid, blue smoke from the discharge of the weapons formed a big cloud that was already beginning to drift toward the ceiling.

Knowing that Crack was behind him and had not yet fired, Matt threw himself down just as Crack did fire. Crack's bullet fried through the air exactly where Matt had been but an instant earlier.

Firing up from the floor, Matt's bullet hit Crack under the chin, then burst out through the top of his head, emitting a detritus of blood, skull bone fragments, and brain matter.

Getting up from the floor but still holding on to his smoking gun, Matt looked over at Marshal Kyle. Kyle was leaning against the bar, holding his hand over the bleeding wound.

"How bad is it?" Matt asked.

"It hurts like a son of a bitch, but I'll live," Kyle replied.

Hearing Odom groan, Matt walked over to look down at him.

"You know why I shot you in the gut instead of the head?" Matt asked.

"Because you couldn't hit me in the head," Odom answered. He tried to laugh, but it came out a barking cough. Little flecks of blood sprayed out on his lips and on his shirt.

"Oh, I could have," Matt said. He stood up and rammed his pistol back in his holster. "But I wanted you to die real slow."

"Why?" Odom asked. "Why did you take such a personal interest in killing me?"

"Even if I told you, you wouldn't understand," Matt said.

From outside, there came the sound of dozens of footfalls on the boardwalk. Both Matt and Kyle whirled toward the batwing doors, their pistols raised and ready.

"No, hold it, hold it! Don't shoot!" a man shouted, pausing just outside the batwing doors. He had both hands up to show that he wasn't armed.

"It's all right, Jensen, I know him," Kyle said. "Bascomb, what are you doing here?"

"We came to check up on you, Marshal," Bascomb said.

"Well, you'd better get out of here before the rest of Cummins's deputies get here."

Bascomb smiled. "You don't have to be worryin' none about them, Marshal."

"What do you mean?"

"I mean Duke, Warren, and Gates are in jail," Bascomb said. "Soon as the folks comin' out of the saloon told us what was goin' on, we figured them boys would probably be goin' down there to help out Cummins. So we just waited for 'em, and got the drop on them."

"You got a doctor in this town?" Jensen asked.

"Yeah, we do," Bascomb answered.

"Well, quit standing here palavering. Go get the doctor for the marshal."

"Oh," Bascomb said. "Oh, yes, I didn't think about that." Turning, he yelled up the street. "Get Dr. Urban up here! Get Dr. Urban up here to tend to the marshal."

"To hell with tendin' to the marshal, let the son of a bitch die!" someone called back.

"I'm talkin' about U.S. marshal Kyle," Bascomb replied. "Marshal Cummins is already dead."

Matt waited until Dr. Urban arrived, then stood by as the doctor examined the wound.

"How bad is it, Doc?" Matt asked.

"Not bad at all," the doctor said as he began cleaning the wound. "Looks like the bullet just left a little crease. If it doesn't putrefy, it should heal up quickly."

"That's good to know," Matt said. He took the badge off his shirt and handed it to the marshal.

"You are welcome to keep that deputy's badge," Kyle said. "I can always use a good man like you. The law can always use a good man like you."

"I appreciate it, Marshal," Matt said. "But I think I'll just be getting on."

"Where are you headed?"

Matt paused for a moment, then smiled. "You know—I haven't really given that any thought.

"What about me?" Odom asked.

"What about you?" Matt replied.

"Ain't you goin' to let the doctor look at me?"

"It wouldn't do any good for the doctor to see you. You're going to die no matter what he does," Matt said.

"But you can't just leave me here to die on the floor," Odom said.

Matt thought of Suzie Dobbs, and all the others, killed and injured in the train wreck caused by this man.

"You can't leave me like this!" Odom shouted again.

Matt started for the door. Then, just before he left, he looked back at Odom. "Yeah, I can."

"You son of a bitch! I'll see you in hell!" Odom shouted.

"Not likely," Matt replied. "I've done my time in Purgatory."

TURN THE PAGE FOR AN EXCITING PREVIEW OF

Sidewinders

**An Exciting New Western Series
by William W. Johnstone and J. A. Johnstone**

*In frontier literature, the name "Johnstone" means big,
hard-hitting Western adventure told at a breakneck pace.
Now, the bestselling authors kick off a rollicking, new
series—about a pair of not-quite-over-the-hill drifters.*

*Meet Scratch Morton and Bo Creel, two amiable drifters
and old pals. Veterans of cowboying, cattle drives, drunken
brawls, and a couple of shoot-outs, Scratch and Bo are
mostly honest and don't go looking for trouble—it's
usually there when they wake up in the morning.*

*Now, in remote Arizona Territory, they're caught up in
a battle between two stagecoach lines. The owner of one,
a beautiful widow, has gotten both Scratch and Bo hot
and bothered—each trying to impress her as they fend
off the opposing stage line aiming to destroy her. But
nothing is what it seems to be in this fight, and two
tough sidewinders are riding straight into a deadly trap.*

Sidewinders

by William W. Johnstone
with J. A. Johnstone

Coming in September 2008
Wherever Pinnacle Books are sold.

*Man that is born of woman
is of few days and full of trouble.*
—Job 14:1

We're peaceable men, I tell you.
—Scratch Morton

Chapter One

"All I'm sayin' is that a man who ain't prepared to lose hadn't ought to sit down at the table in the first place," Scratch Morton argued as he and his trail partner, Bo Creel, rode along a draw in a rugged stretch of Arizona Territory.

"You didn't have to rub his nose in it like that," Bo pointed out. "That cowboy probably wouldn't have gotten mad enough to reach for his gun if you'd just stayed out of it."

"Stay out of it, hell! He practically accused you of cheatin'. I couldn't let him get away with that, old-timer."

There was a certain irony in Scratch referring to Bo as "old-timer." The two men were of an age. Their birthdays were less than a month apart. It was true, though, that Bo *was* a few weeks older. And neither Bo nor Scratch was within shouting distance of youth anymore. Their deeply tanned, weathered faces, Scratch's thatch of silver hair, and the strands of gray in Bo's thick, dark brown hair testified to that.

The Arizona sun had prompted both men to remove

their jackets as they rode. Scratch normally sported a fringed buckskin jacket that went well with his tan whipcord trousers and creamy Stetson. He liked dressing well.

Bo, on the other hand, usually wore a long black coat that, along with his black trousers and dusty, flat-crowned black hat, made him look like a circuit-riding preacher. He didn't have a preacher's hands, though. His long, nimble fingers were made for playing cards—or handling a gun.

He had been engaged in the former at a saloon up in Prescott when the trouble broke out. One of the other players, a gangling cowboy with fiery red hair, had gotten upset at losing his stake to Bo. Scratch, who hadn't been in the game but had been nursing a beer at the bar instead, hadn't helped matters by wandering over to the felt-covered table and hoo-rawing the angry waddy. Accusations flew, and the cowboy had wound up making a grab for the gun on his hip.

"Anyway, it ain't like you had to kill him or anything like that," Scratch went on now. "He probably had a headache when he woke up from you bendin' your gun over his skull like that, but he could'a woke up dead just as easy."

"And what if that saloon had been full of other fellas who rode for the same brand?" Bo asked. "Then we'd have had a riot on our hands. We might have had to shoot our way out."

Scratch grinned. "Wouldn't be the first time, now would it?"

That was true enough. Bo sighed. Trouble had a

long-standing habit of following them around, despite their best intentions.

Friends ever since they had met as boys in Texas, during the Runaway Scrape when it looked like ol' General Santa Anna would wipe the place clean of the Texicans who were rebelling against his dictatorship, Bo and Scratch had been together through times of triumph and tragedy. They had been on the drift for nigh on to forty years, riding from one end of the frontier to the other and back again, always searching for an elusive something.

For Scratch, it was sheer restlessness, a natural urge to see what was on the other side of the next hill, to cross the next river, to kiss the next good-lookin' woman and have the next adventure. With Bo, it was a more melancholy quest, an attempt to escape the memories of the wife and children taken from him by a killer fever many years earlier. All the fiddle-footed years had dulled that pain, but Bo had come to realize that nothing could ever take it away completely.

After the ruckus with the redheaded cowboy, they had drifted northward from Prescott toward the Verde River, the low but rugged range of the Santa Marias to their left. Some taller, snowcapped mountains were visible in the far, far distance to the northeast. Flagstaff lay in that direction. Maybe they would circle around and go there next.

It didn't really matter. They had no plans except to keep riding and see where the trails took them.

Changing the subject from the earlier fracas, Scratch went on. "I think we ought to find us some shade and wait out the rest of the afternoon. It's gettin' on toward hot-as-hell o'clock."

Bo laughed and said, "You're right. Where do you suggest we find that shade?"

He waved a hand at the barren hills surrounding the sandy-bottomed draw where they rode. The only colors in sight were brown and tan and red. Not a bit of green. Not even a cactus.

Scratch rasped a thumbnail along his jawline and shrugged. "Yeah, that might be a little hard to do. Could be a cave or somethin' up in those hills, though. Even a little overhang would give us some shade."

Bo nodded and turned his horse to the left. "I guess it would be worth taking a look."

They had just reached the slope of a nearby hill when both men heard a familiar sound. A series of shots ripped through the hot, still air. The popping of revolvers was interspersed with the dull boom of a shotgun. Bo and Scratch reined in sharply and looked at each other.

"Sounds like trouble," Scratch said. "We gonna turn around and go the other way?"

"What do you think?" Bo asked, and for a second his sober demeanor was offset by the reckless gleam that appeared in his eyes.

The two drifters from Texas yelled to their horses, dug their boot heels into the animals' sides, and galloped up the hill. The shots were coming from somewhere on the other side.

Bo was riding a mouse-colored dun with a darker stripe down its back, an ugly horse with more speed and sand than was evident from its appearance.

Scratch was mounted on a big, handsome bay that was somewhat dandified like its rider. Both horses were strong and took the slope without much trouble. Within moments, as the shots continued to ring out, Bo and Scratch crested the top of the hill and saw what was on the other side.

The rocky slope led down to a broad flat crossed in the distance to the west by a meandering line of washed-out green that marked the course of a stream. A dusty road ran from the east toward that creek, and along that road, bouncing and careening from its excessive speed, rolled a stagecoach.

The driver had whipped his six-horse hitch to a hard gallop, and for good reason. Thundering along about fifty yards behind the stagecoach were eight or ten men on horseback, throwing lead at the coach. Even in the bright sunlight, Bo and Scratch could see spurts of flame from the gun muzzles. A cloud of powder smoke trailed after the pursuing riders.

As if the circumstances of the chase weren't enough to convince Bo and Scratch that the men on horseback were up to no good, the fact that they had bandannas tied across the lower halves of their faces to serve as crude masks confirmed that they were outlaws bent on holding up the stage. The two drifters brought their mounts to a halt at the top of the hill as their eyes instantly took in the scene.

Scratch reached for his Winchester, which stuck up from a sheath strapped to his saddle. "We takin' cards in this game?" he called to Bo.

"I reckon," Bo replied as he pulled his own rifle from its saddle boot. He levered a round into the Winchester's firing chamber and smoothly brought the weapon to his shoulder. As he nestled his cheek against the smooth wood of the stock, he added, "Since we don't know the details, might be better if we tried not to kill anybody."

"I figured you'd say that," Scratch grumbled as he lined up his own shot.

The two of them opened fire, cranking off several shots as fast as they could work the levers on the rifles. The bullets slammed into the road in front of the masked riders, kicking up gouts of dust. The men were moving so fast it was hard to keep the shots in front of them, and in fact one of the bullets fired by the Texans burned the shoulder of a man's mount and made the horse jump.

That got the attention of the outlaws. They reined in briefly as Bo and Scratch stopped shooting. It was their hope that the masked men would turn around and go the other way, but that wasn't what happened.

Instead, the gang of desperadoes split up. Three of them dismounted, dragging rifles from their horses as they did so, and bellied down behind some rocks. The other seven took off again after the stagecoach.

"Well, hell!" Scratch said. "That didn't work. We should'a killed a couple of 'em."

"Come on," Bo cried as he wheeled his horse. "They're going to try to pin us down here!"

Sure enough, the three men who had been left behind by the rest of the gang opened fire then. Bullets whined around the heads of the Texans like angry bees, one of them coming close enough so that Bo heard the wind-rip of its passage beside his ear.

They heeled their horses into a run again, following the crest of the hill as it curved to the west. The outlaws continued firing at them, but none of the bullets came close now.

The hill petered out after about three hundred yards. Bo and Scratch started downslope again, angling toward the wide flats and the road that ran through them. They glanced over their shoulders, and saw that the three men who had tried to neutralize the threat from them had mounted up again and were now fogging it after the rest of the gang, which had carried on with its pursuit of the stagecoach.

In fact, the outlaws had cut the gap to about twenty yards, and from the way one of the men on the driver's box was swaying back and forth and clutching his shoulder, he looked like he was wounded. The other man, who was handling the reins, looked back and appeared to be slowing the team.

"He's gonna stop and give up!" Scratch shouted over the pounding of hooves. "Those owlhoots got their blood up! They're liable to kill everybody on that coach!"

"They might at that!" Bo called in agreement. He had rammed his Winchester back in the saddle boot. Now he unleathered the walnut-butted Colt on his hip and said, "We won't hold back this time!"

Scratch whooped. "Now you're talkin'!" He drew one of the long-barreled, ivory-handled, .36 caliber Remington revolvers that he carried.

Both men opened fire as they veered toward the road. The hurricane deck of a galloping horse wasn't the best platform for accurate marksmanship, but Bo and Scratch had had plenty of experience in running gun battles like this. Their flank attack was effective. A couple of the outlaws were jolted by the impact of the drifters' slugs and had to grab for the horns to keep from tumbling out of their saddles.

Despite having a heavy advantage in numbers, the masked outlaws began to peel sharply away from the road. They threw a few shots at Bo and Scratch, but didn't put much effort into it. The Texans slowed their horses as the would-be robbers abandoned the chase, picked up the three stragglers, and galloped off to the east.

"We goin' after 'em?" Scratch asked.

Bo's forehead was creased in a frown. "Have you gone loco? With five-to-one odds against us, I plan on thanking my lucky stars that they decided it wasn't worth it to rob that stagecoach after all!"

"We winged at least a couple of 'em. I saw the varmints jump."

Bo nodded. "Yeah, I did, too." He inclined his head toward the coach, which had rocked to a halt by now, with thinning swirls of road dust rising around it. "Let's go see how bad that fella on the stage is hurt."

The wounded man was still conscious. They could tell that from the furious cussing they heard as they approached. The driver had climbed down and was helping the other man to the ground. As the hoof-beats of the Texans' horses rattled up, the driver turned and pulled a gun.

"Hold on there, son!" Bo called as he reined in. "We're friends."

Scratch brought his bay to a halt alongside Bo's dun. "Yeah," he said. "In case you didn't notice, we're the hombres who got those owlhoots off your tail." He jerked a thumb over his shoulder in the direction that the gang had fled.

The driver nodded and holstered his gun. "Yeah, I know that," he said. "Sorry. I'm just a little proddy right now."

"You've got reason to be," Bo said as he swung down from his saddle. "How bad is your friend hurt?"

The driver was a young man, probably in his mid-twenties. He wore a brown hat and a long, tan duster over denim trousers and a blue, bib-front shirt. A red bandanna was tied around his neck. His wounded companion was considerably older and sported a brush of bristly gray whiskers. He had lost his hat somewhere during the chase, revealing a mostly bald head.

He answered Bo's question by saying, "How bad does it look like I'm hurt, damn it? Them no-good buzzard-spawn busted my shoulder!"

The right shoulder of his flannel shirt was bloody, all right, and the stain had leaked down onto his cowhide vest. Crimson still oozed through the fingers of the left hand he used to clutch the injured shoulder.

"Take it easy, Ponderosa," the younger man told him. "Sit down here beside the wheel, and we'll take a look at it. It might not be as bad as you think it is."

"Oh, it's bad, all right," the old-timer said. "I been shot before. Reckon I'll bleed to death in another few minutes."

"I don't think it's quite that serious," Bo said with a faint smile as he tied his dun's reins to the back of the coach. Scratch had dismounted, too, and tied his horse likewise. Bo went on. "My partner and I have had some experience with gunshot wounds. We'd be glad to help."

"Much obliged," the young man said. "If you'll give me a hand with him . . ."

Bo helped the driver lower the old man called Ponderosa to the ground. Ponderosa leaned back against the front wheel while Bo pulled his vest and shirt to the side to expose the wound. Under Ponderosa's tan, the bearded, leathery face was pale from shock and loss of blood.

While Bo was tending to the injured man, Scratch glanced inside the coach and said to the driver, "No passengers, eh?"

"Not on this run," the young man said with a shake of his head. "And not much in the mail pouch either. If those outlaws *had* caught up to us, they would have been mighty disappointed." He held out his hand. "My name's Gil Sutherland, by the way."

"Scratch Morton." As Scratch shook Gil Sutherland's hand, he nodded toward Bo and added, "My pard there is Bo Creel."

"And I'm Ponderosa Pine," the old-timer said, introducing himself through gritted teeth as Bo probed the wound. "Given name's Clarence, but nobody calls me that 'less'n they want'a tangle with a wildcat."

"We wouldn't want that," Bo said with a dry chuckle. "Good news, Ponderosa. That bullet didn't break your shoulder. I think it missed the bone and just knocked out a chunk of meat on its way through."

"You sure? It hurts like blazes, and I can't lift my arm."

"That's just from the shock of being wounded. We'll

plug the holes to stop the bleeding, and I think you'll be all right." Bo looked up at Gil Sutherland. "How far is the nearest town?"

"Red Butte's about five miles west of here," Gil replied. "That's where we were headed when they jumped us. This is the regular run between Red Butte and Chino Valley."

"Let's get Ponderosa here on into town then. He needs to have a real doctor look at that wound, just to be on the safe side."

"That's assumin' there's a sawbones in this Red Butte place," Scratch added.

Gil nodded. "Yes, there's a doctor. Don't worry, Ponderosa. We'll take care of you."

"Ain't worried," Ponderosa muttered. "Just mad. Mad as hell. I'd like to see Judson and all o' his bunch strung up."

"Who's Judson?" Bo asked as he used a folding knife he took from his pocket to cut several strips of cloth from the bottom of Ponderosa's shirt. He wadded up some of the flannel into thick pads and used the other strips to bind them tightly into place over the entrance and exit wounds.

"Rance Judson is the leader of the gang that was chasing us," Gil explained.

"Him and those varmints who ride with him been raisin' hell in these parts for six months now," Ponderosa added.

Scratch asked, "If folks know who he is and that he's responsible for such deviltry, why don't the law come in and arrest him?"

Gil Sutherland shook his head. "We're a long way

from any real law out here, Mr. Morton. There's a marshal in Red Butte who does a pretty good job of keeping the peace there, but he's not going to go chasing off into the badlands after Judson's gang. That would be suicide, and he knows it. We all do."

Bo finished tying the makeshift bandages into place. He straightened from his crouch, grunting a little as he did so. "Old bones are stiffer than they used to be."

"Tell me about it," Ponderosa grumbled. "And I'm quite a bit older'n you, mister."

"Let's get you in the coach," Gil suggested. "It won't be all that comfortable, but it should be better than riding up on the box."

"Wait just a doggone minute! I signed on to be the shotgun guard, not a danged passenger!"

"I'll ride shotgun the rest of the way," Bo said. "Where's your Greener?"

"On the floorboard where I dropped it when them polecats ventilated me, I reckon."

Gil said, "I don't think Judson and his men will make another try for us. You don't have to come with us into town."

"We don't mind," Bo said.

"Truth to tell, all this dust has got me thirsty," Scratch added with a grin. "You got at least one saloon there, don't you?"

"Several," Gil admitted.

"Then what are we waitin' for? Let's go to Red Butte!"

Chapter Two

Once they had loaded the still-complaining Ponderosa Pine into the stagecoach, Bo climbed onto the driver's box next to Gil Sutherland, leaving his horse tied at the back of the coach. Scratch mounted up and rode alongside as Gil got the vehicle moving.

"Used to be a Butterfield coach, didn't it?" Bo asked as he swayed slightly on the seat from the rocking motion. He had Ponderosa's double-barreled scattergun across his knees.

"How did you know?" Gil said.

"You can still see some of the red and yellow paint on it in places."

Gil grunted. "We didn't strip the paint off on purpose. The sun and the dust and the wind in this godforsaken country took care of that for us."

"We?" Bo repeated.

"My father was the one who started the stage line. It runs from Cottonwood to Chino Valley and on over to Red Butte, where the headquarters are. There's another line that runs from Flagstaff down to Cottonwood and then on south, but there was no transportation from Cottonwood west to the Santa Marias until my father came along. Chino Valley and Red Butte were growing fast because of all the ranching and mining in the area, so he thought it would be a good gamble that they'd need a stage line. He figured some other settlements might spring up along the way, too."

"Sounds like a worthwhile gamble," Bo said with a nod. "How's it working out?"

Gil scowled and shook his head. "Not so good."

"Because of those outlaws? Folks are too scared of being held up to ride the stage?"

"Well, it didn't help when Judson and his bunch started raising hell, but that's not all of it. Those other settlements never sprang up. There's just Chino Valley and Red Butte. And the mines played out, for the most part. There's only one still operating at a good level."

"So there's not as much business as your pa thought there would be."

"That's right. It's been a struggle to make ends meet." Gil's voice caught a little. "It didn't help matters when my father got sick and died."

Bo looked over at the young man with a frown. "You're running the stage line now?"

Gil shook his head again. "My mother's in charge. I do what I can to help, just like when my father was still alive. I've got a younger brother, too, but he—" Gil stopped and drew in a breath. "Let's just say that he's not much for hard work and leave it at that."

Bo didn't say anything in response to that. Clearly, there were some hard feelings between Gil Sutherland and his little brother, and they might well be justified. But Bo knew it usually didn't pay for a fella to stick his nose into family squabbles.

Gil drove on in silence for a few minutes, then said, "Thanks for pitching in back there. Judson's bunch would have caught us in another minute or two, and there's no telling what they might have done, especially when they found out they weren't going to get much in the way of loot."

"It looked like you were about to stop and let them catch up," Bo said.

"That's right, I was. I knew we couldn't outrun them, and the way Ponderosa was only half-conscious and bouncing around on the seat, I was afraid he might get pitched off and break his neck. I was hoping they'd just take the mail pouch and let us go."

"Is Judson in the habit of doing things like that?"

Gil shrugged. "They've killed a few men during their holdups, but only when somebody tried to fight back. Like when they hit the bank over in Chino Valley last month."

"They're not just stagecoach robbers then."

"No, they've rustled cattle and run them south across the border into Mexico, they robbed the bank like I said, and they raided the Pitchfork Mine and stole an ore shipment that was about to go out. They've stopped the stage half-a-dozen times, I guess, even though they've never made a very big haul at it. Killed a driver and a guard, though, so nobody wants to work for us anymore. Ponderosa and I have been taking all the runs ourselves lately. Now he's going to be laid up for a while, more than likely." Gil sighed. "I don't know what we'll do. Shut down, I guess."

Bo didn't say anything to that either. He had some thoughts on the matter, but he kept them to himself for the time being.

The creek that Bo and Scratch had seen from the top of the hill turned out to be a narrow, shallow stream, not much more than a twisting thread of water in a gravelly bed. As Gil drove across it at a ford, he said, "This is Hell Creek. Not much to look at, but it's the only water this side of the Santa Marias and it never dries up, no matter how hot the weather gets."

"Spring-fed, I reckon," Bo said.

Gil nodded. "That's right. North of here, in the ranching country, it's bigger."

Bo sniffed the air. "Sulfur springs, too, unless I miss my guess."

"That's how it got its name," Gil said. "From the smell of brimstone. Not very pleasant, but the water doesn't taste too bad. You get used to it after a while, I suppose."

The terrain began to rise a little once they were on the other side of Hell Creek. The slope was very gradual at first, but became more pronounced. More tufts of grass appeared, and even some small bushes. Bo saw trees up ahead, where the foothills of the Santa Maria Mountains began.

A little over an hour after they left the site of the attempted holdup, the stagecoach arrived at Red Butte. Bo and Scratch saw why the settlement had gotten its name. A copper-colored sandstone mesa jutted up from the ground about half a mile north of the town, which had a main street, half-a-dozen cross streets, and a couple of streets paralleling the main drag. The buildings were a mixture of adobe, lumber from the trees growing in the foothills, and brick that must have been freighted in from Flagstaff or some other big town.

"Not a bad-lookin' place," Scratch commented. "Wouldn't exactly say that it's boomin', but it don't look like it's about to dry up and blow away either."

"There are enough ranches along the Santa Marias, both north and south of town, to support quite a few businesses," Gil said. "Throw in the Pitchfork, too, and folks do all right. They just don't have much need of a stage line except to deliver the mail." His mouth twisted. "And we probably won't have that contract much longer."

"What do you mean by that, son?" Bo asked, but Gil didn't answer. The young man was busy bringing the stagecoach to a halt at the edge of the settlement, in front of a neatly kept adobe building with a wooden barn and some corrals behind it. Someone had planted cactus roses on either side of the three steps that led up to the shaded porch attached to the front of the adobe building. The bright yellow roses were blooming, providing a welcome splash of color in an otherwise drab setting.

The front door of the building opened while the coach was still rocking back and forth on the broad leather thoroughbraces that supported it, after coming to a stop. A dark-haired woman wearing a long, blue dress with tiny yellow flowers on it came onto the porch. She pushed back her hair from her face, and relief showed in her eyes as she looked at Gil.

That relief was fleeting, lasting only a second before it was replaced by worry. She looked at Bo, a sober, almost grim stranger riding with Gil, and at Scratch, another stranger who had reined his horse to a halt alongside the team. Then she asked anxiously, "Where's Ponderosa?"

The old-timer swung the door of the coach open before Gil could answer, saying, "I'm right here, Miz Abigail—what's left of me anyway!"

The woman cried out in surprise and lifted a hand to her mouth. Then she hurried forward. "For God's sake, Ponderosa!" she exclaimed. "What happened to you?"

"Judson's men again, Mother," Gil said from the box. "They hit us about a mile the other side of Hell Creek."

The woman, who was obviously Abigail Sutherland, turned her head to look up at her son as she was helping the wounded man from the coach. "Did they get the mail pouch?" she asked, and the slight quaver in her voice was evidence of just how important that question was to her.

Gil shook his head. "Not this time. These two strangers came along and lit into Judson's bunch. They wounded a couple of the outlaws and ran them off."

"Not in time to keep me from gettin' plugged, though," Ponderosa grumbled.

Scratch had dismounted. He came around the back of the coach, leading his bay with the reins in one hand. He used the other hand to sweep the cream-colored Stetson off his head and gave Abigail Sutherland a big, toothy smile.

"Scratch Morton, at your service, ma'am," he said, introducing himself.

Abigail turned to him. "Thank you for your help, Mr. Morton," she said. "And your friend is . . . ?"

Scratch waved the hand holding the Stetson in Bo's general direction. "That's Bo Creel. Don't let that look on his face fool you, ma'am. He ain't as sour in disposition as he appears. Not quite."

Bo grunted and said from the driver's box, "I'm pleased to make your acquaintance, Mrs. Sutherland. Just wish it was under better circumstances."

"So do I," said Ponderosa. "In case anybody's forgotten, I got a dang bullet hole in my carcass!"

"Yes, and I'll take you down to Dr. Chambers' house right now," Abigail told him. "Can you walk all right?"

Ponderosa sniffed. "I reckon. Got hit in the shoulder, not the leg. I was a mite dizzy earlier, but I'm feelin' better now."

Abigail got an arm around his waist to help support him, and they started along the street toward the rest of the settlement. She glanced up at her son as they passed the front of the coach, and asked, "Can you take care of the team, Gil?"

"Sure. But where's Dave?"

"I don't know," Abigail said, and that worried look was back on her face, as well as the concern in her voice.

"We'll give you a hand with those horses, son," Scratch said as he put his hat back on. "Won't we, Bo?"

"Yeah." Bo placed the shotgun on the floorboard where he had found it.

Gil got the team moving again, and drove the stagecoach around the adobe office to the barn in the rear. He took the coach all the way into the barn before stopping. Scratch followed, leading his horse.

Bo and Gil climbed down from the box. Along with

Scratch, they went to work unhitching the horses. Watching the sure, practiced actions of the older men, Gil commented, "You fellas have worked around stagecoaches before, haven't you?"

"We ran a way station in Kansas for a while," Bo replied.

"And we hired on as jehus and shotgun guards in other places," Scratch added. "Fact is, you won't find many jobs on the frontier that we ain't done at one time or another. Ain't that right, Bo?"

"Except for donning aprons and clerking in a store," Bo said. "I don't think we've ever done that."

A shudder went through Scratch. "And we ain't gonna," he declared.

When the team had been unhitched and the horses turned out into the corral, Gil reached into the compartment under the driver's seat on the coach and pulled out a canvas pouch. "I'll take the mail down to the post office," he said. "If you're going to be staying around Red Butte for a while, feel free to unsaddle your horses, give them some grain, and put them in the corral with the others if you want to."

Scratch looked at Bo and asked, "What do you think? We gonna be stayin' in these parts for a while?"

"We don't have anywhere else we have to be," Bo replied. "And Red Butte looks like a pretty nice little town."

Scratch grinned. "That's what I was thinkin'." To Gil, he added, "Much obliged for the hospitality, son."

Gil lifted a hand in farewell and left the barn while Bo was untying his dun from the back of the stagecoach. Bo commented, "I notice you started calling that boy 'son' as soon as you got a look at his mother. Thinking about settling down with the Widow Sutherland, are you?"

"Me?" Scratch held his hand over his heart for a moment, then grinned. "You got to admit, Bo, she's a fine figure of a woman."

"It *was* a pretty picture," Bo mused, "her standing there on that porch with the wind in her hair and those cactus roses blooming at her feet. But we don't know a blasted thing about her, other than the fact that she's got a couple of sons and a stage line started by her late husband. We don't even know how long he's been gone. She may still be in mourning."

"Wasn't wearin' black," Scratch pointed out.

"No, she wasn't, that's true," Bo admitted as he undid one of his saddle cinches.

"And she's got a whole heap o' problems on her plate, from the sound of it. Might be we could give her a hand with 'em."

"Nobody's asked us for our help."

"Give it time. Anyway, ain't you curious about what's goin' on around here? You always did like to get to the bottom of any trouble we ran into."

"That's true," Bo said with a shrug. "I guess we could hang around for a while and see what happens. Like I said, it seems like a pretty nice little town."

Scratch grinned. "And a pretty nice little woman, too."

Bo just rolled his eyes and shook his head.

Chapter Three

There were a couple of rocking chairs on the porch of the adobe office. Bo and Scratch walked around the building after tending to their horses, and sat down in those chairs to wait. They weren't sure what they were waiting for, but that was a pretty common situation. Years of drifting had taught them to be patient.

They didn't have to wait long for something to happen. Three men came down the street, stopped in front of the headquarters of the Sutherland Stage Line, and dismounted. One of them was young, twenty or twenty-one more than likely, and his brown hair and the cast of his features resembled those of Gil Sutherland. Bo figured he and Scratch were looking at the heretofore-missing Dave Sutherland, Gil's younger brother.

The other two men were older, but still in their twenties. One was tall and scrawny, with a shock of straw-colored hair under a battered, pushed-back hat. The other was short and broad, built like a bull with an animal-like dullness in his eyes and on his face. He wore a derby over dark hair that grew down low on his forehead.

"You hombres looking for somebody?" asked the young man Bo and Scratch took to be Dave Sutherland. He swayed back and forth, and his speech was slurred enough to indicate that he'd been drinking.

The afternoon was well advanced, so it wasn't like he was drunk first thing in the morning or anything like that. Still, he was a mite young to be putting away enough liquor to get him in such a condition. His companions might have been drinking, too, but they didn't appear to be as drunk as young Dave.

"We're waiting for Mrs. Sutherland to get back," Bo said.

"If you wanna buy tickets on the st-stage, you might as well wait until morning. There's one due in this afternoon any time now, and there won't be another one leaving until tomorrow."

Dave was making a visible effort to stand up straight, and he was being more careful and precise when he talked now, two more signs that he'd guzzled too much rotgut.

"Today's stage is already in," Scratch said. "We came in with it."

"Then why are you hanging around here? Go on about your business!"

Bo frowned. "What did you say, mister?"

"You heard me! You look like saddle tramps to me. Probably want a handout or something. Well, you won't get it here!"

"You're makin' a mistake, son," Scratch said.

"You're the one who made the mistake, old-timer.

I'm Dave Sutherland. My ma owns this stage line, and I'm telling you to rattle your hocks!"

Dave had confirmed what Bo and Scratch already suspected, that he was Abigail's younger son, but his belligerence took them by surprise. Some people got proddy like that when they'd had too much to drink, though, and evidently Dave was one of them.

The tall, straw-haired man stepped forward. "You heard Dave. Vamoose, you two old pelicans!"

Scratch frowned, too, and looked over at Bo. "You hear what he called us?"

"Yeah," Bo said. "Looks like this town isn't as friendly as we thought it was."

"Hey! We're talkin' to you!" the straw-haired man said.

Scratch nodded. "Oh, we heard you. Either that or there's a donkey brayin' somewhere close by."

The man's hands closed into bony fists. "Why, you—"

"We'll just wait here for Mrs. Sutherland," Bo cut in. "We're not looking for trouble."

"You got it whether you're lookin' for it or not. Now drift or—"

"Or what?" Scratch said.

"Or Culley and me will make you wish you had!"

Scratch nodded toward the short, broad man and said to Bo, "You figure the baby bull there's Culley?"

"I reckon," Bo said.

"He looks strong enough to bend a railroad tie."

The straw-haired man sneered. "He is, and you're about to find out for yourself, old man."

"But dumb as dirt," Scratch went on as if the other man hadn't spoken.

Bo heaved a sigh. If a fight hadn't been inevitable

to start with, it sure as blazes was now. Culley's face darkened with slow anger, and he started toward the porch steps. He was so muscular that his walk had a peculiar rolling gait to it.

Bo made one final attempt to stave off a ruckus. He stood up, held out a hand, and said, "You boys don't want to do this." He looked at Dave. "I'm betting your mother won't like it if there's a brawl on her front porch."

"My mother doesn't tell me what to do," Dave shot back. "And you shouldn't have mouthed off to Angus and Culley."

"Hey!" Scratch said indignantly as he got to his feet. "I'm the one who mouthed off, and don't you forget it!"

Culley spoke for the first time, rumbling, "Gonna rip you apart, old man!" He charged up the steps, followed closely by the straw-haired man, whose name was Angus, evidently.

Scratch lifted his right leg, planted his boot heel in Culley's chest, and shoved. Culley went backward into Angus, knocking him over like a ball in a game of ninepins. Both men sprawled in the dirt in front of the porch, looking surprised. Scratch hadn't seemed like he was moving very fast. His movements had appeared almost casual.

Dave gaped. "You gonna let that old varmint do that?" he demanded, the slur slipping back into his voice.

"Not hardly," Angus vowed as he scrambled to his feet. He had to help Culley up, because the muscle-bound man was flailing his arms and legs like a turtle that's been flipped over onto its back.

Once they were both up, Angus said to his companion, "All right, we're gonna go at this different. I'll take the preacher, you handle the fancy Dan in the buckskin jacket."

Culley nodded. He didn't have much of a neck, just a thick column of muscle. "Yeah. Gonna bust him to pieces."

Scratch grinned and said, "Come on, baby bull. You try it."

Angus and Culley advanced up the steps side by side this time, moving more slowly and more carefully. The Texans split up, Bo going down the porch to the right, Scratch to the left.

"Try not to bust up those rockers," Bo called to his trail partner. "They're pretty comfortable. Be a shame if they got broken."

"Yeah," Scratch agreed. "Might upset Mrs. Sutherland, too."

Dave yelled, "You leave my mother out of this, saddle tramp!"

Angus charged, swinging a malletlike fist at Bo's head. At the same time, Culley barreled toward Scratch.

Bo blocked Angus's punch with the same sort of effortless ease that Scratch had demonstrated in kicking the two ruffians down the porch steps a few minutes earlier. In a continuation of the same movement, Bo's right fist shot forward in a short, sharp blow that landed flush on Angus's nose. Blood spurted under the impact. Angus staggered back with a howl of pain.

He retreated only a couple of steps, though, before he caught himself and attacked again, this time windmilling punches at the black-clad stranger. Bo blocked the first few blows, but then one of Angus's knobby fists clipped him on the jaw. Angus might be scrawny, but his punches packed plenty of power. Bo was knocked against the railing that ran along the front of the porch. With a shout of triumph, Angus crowded in on him, trying to seize and hold the advantage.

Meanwhile, at the other end of the porch, Scratch had his hands full with Culley. The pocket-sized titan was slow, but even though Scratch was able to land several sizzling punches, Culley just shrugged them off. He appeared to be able to absorb as much punishment as Scratch wanted to deal out.

At the same time, he swung his tree-trunklike arms in lumbering roundhouse blows that Scratch was able to avoid without much trouble. If one of those big fists ever landed, though, it would be like being hit with a piledriver. Scratch would go down hard.

He didn't intend to let that happen. He darted in and out, peppering Culley's face with punches in hopes that sooner or later the fella's brain would realize how badly he was being pummeled.

To his horror, Scratch suddenly felt Culley's arms snap closed around his torso like bands of steel, and he knew that he had made the mistake of getting too close. Scratch's arms were still loose, but Culley just ignored the blows and squeezed. As those brawny arms tightened more and more, Scratch grunted and felt his ribs begin to creak.

While Scratch was trying to deal with that bone-crushing threat, Bo thrust a foot between Angus's ankles as the straw-haired man tried to crowd him into the railing. Angus lost his balance long enough for Bo to hook a left to his jaw and stagger him. Bo reached out, grabbed the front of Angus's shirt, and heaved him around in a turn that sent Angus hard into the railing.

The wooden rail was sturdy enough so that it didn't break under the impact of Angus's body. Instead, Angus's momentum caused him to flip over the railing. With a startled cry at this unexpected turn of events, he fell to the ground in front of the porch.

And landed right in those cactus roses.

Bo winced at the sudden screeches of agony that came from Angus as his flesh was pierced by hundreds of the razor-sharp cactus needles. Angus tried to jump up, slipped and fell again, and just made his situation that much worse as he landed in the cactus again. He finally rolled clear of the spiny plants, but continued shrieking in pain.

Some of the roses had been crushed. Bo shook his head in regret at that. The blooms had been mighty pretty.

He turned to see how Scratch was doing, and was alarmed to see that Culley had Scratch trapped in a bear hug. Bo could see Scratch's face over Culley's shoulder. It was almost purple from the lack of air, and Scratch's eyes were open wide in pain and desperation.

Bo palmed out his Colt as his long legs carried him quickly to the other end of the porch. He raised the gun, reversing it as he did so, and brought the butt crashing down on Culley's skull. Bo didn't hold back, figuring that Culley was one hardheaded son of a gun. The blow landed with a heavy *thunk!*

Culley just shook his head and kept squeezing.

Bo hit him again, and this time Culley's grip relaxed a little. It took a third wallop, though, before the baby bull finally let go. Scratch slipped out of the bone-crushing, suffocating embrace and slumped against the adobe wall of the building, his chest rising and falling violently as he tried to drag air back into lungs that were starved for it.

Culley swung around ponderously toward Bo. His little piglike eyes still glittered with fury, but they glazed over as he took a step forward. The damage he had taken finally soaked all the way into his brain, and he pitched forward to land at Bo's feet, out cold.

Bo stepped over to Scratch and put a steadying hand on his friend's arm. "You all right?" he asked.

Scratch managed a shaky nod. "I . . . I will be . . . once I . . . catch my breath."

"Hey!" That was Dave Sutherland again. "You can't do that!"

Bo turned toward the young man and saw that Dave seemed more sober now. Seeing his two friends being defeated like that must have gotten to him. Culley was unconscious, and Angus was curled up in a ball on the ground. He had stopped screaming, but was still whimpering pathetically.

Furious, Dave reached for the gun holstered on his hip. Before he could even touch it, Bo's Colt had flipped around again so that his hand was curled around the walnut grips and he had a finger on the trigger. The barrel was centered on the young man's chest.

"Don't do it, Dave," Bo said in a quiet, solemn tone.

"I don't want to hurt you, but I won't stand here and let you shoot me or Scratch either."

Dave stared at him, taken by surprise yet again. Clearly he hadn't expected Bo to react so swiftly. His hand hovered over the butt of his gun as he visibly struggled with the decision of what to do next.

He was saved from having to make it by the sharp, angry voice that cut through the air. "Mr. Creel! What are you doing threatening my son?"

THE FIRST MOUNTAIN MAN SERIES BY
WILLIAM W. JOHNSTONE

THE MOUNTAIN MAN SERIES BY
WILLIAM W. JOHNSTONE

THE LAST GUNFIGHTER SERIES BY
WILLIAM W. JOHNSTONE